PRAISE FOR M. L. BUCHMAN

A fabulous soaring thriller.

— *TAKE OVER AT MIDNIGHT,* MIDWEST
BOOK REVIEW

Meticulously researched, hard-hitting, and suspenseful.

— *PURE HEAT,* PUBLISHERS WEEKLY,
STARRED REVIEW

Expert technical details abound, as do realistic military missions with superb imagery that will have readers feeling as if they are right there in the midst and on the edges of their seats.

— *LIGHT UP THE NIGHT,* RT REVIEWS, 4 1/2
STARS

Buchman has catapulted his way to the top tier of my favorite authors.

— FRESH FICTION

Nonstop action that will keep readers on the edge of their seats.

M L. Buchman's ability to keep the reader right in the middle of the action is amazing.

The only thing you'll ask yourself is, "When does the next one come out?"

The first...of (a) stellar, long-running (military) romantic suspense series.

I knew the books would be good, but I didn't realize how good.

Buchman mixes adrenalin-spiking battles and brusque military jargon with a sensitive approach.

13 times "Top Pick of the Month"

Tom Clancy fans open to a strong female lead will clamor for more.

Superb! Miranda is utterly compelling!

Miranda Chase continues to astound and charm.

Escape Rating: A. Five Stars! OMG just start with *Drone* and be prepared for a fantastic binge-read!

The best military thriller I've read in a very long time. Love the female characters.

SKIBIRD

A MIRANDA CHASE TECHNOTHRILLER

M. L. BUCHMAN

SIGN UP FOR M. L. BUCHMAN'S NEWSLETTER TODAY

and receive:
Release News
Free Short Stories
a Free Book

Get your free book today. Do it now.
free-book.mlbuchman.com

Other works by M. L. Buchman: (* - also in audio)

Action-Adventure Thrillers

Dead Chef
One Chef!
Two Chef!

Miranda Chase
Drone*
Thunderbolt*
Condor*
Ghostrider*
Raider*
Chinook*
Havoc*
White Top*
Start the Chase*
Lightning*

Science Fiction / Fantasy

Deities Anonymous
Cookbook from Hell: Reheated
Saviors 101

Contemporary Romance

Eagle Cove
Return to Eagle Cove
Recipe for Eagle Cove
Longing for Eagle Cove
Keepsake for Eagle Cove

Love Abroad
Heart of the Cotswolds: England
Path of Love: Cinque Terre, Italy

Where Dreams
Where Dreams are Born
Where Dreams Reside
Where Dreams Are of Christmas*
Where Dreams Unfold
Where Dreams Are Written
Where Dreams Continue

Non-Fiction

Strategies for Success
Managing Your Inner Artist/Writer
Estate Planning for Authors*
Character Voice
Narrate and Record Your Own
Audiobook*

Short Story Series by M. L. Buchman:

Action-Adventure Thrillers

Dead Chef

Miranda Chase Origin Stories

Romantic Suspense

Antarctic Ice Fliers

US Coast Guard

Contemporary Romance

Eagle Cove

Other

Deities Anonymous (fantasy)

Single Titles

The Emily Beale Universe
(military romantic suspense)

The Night Stalkers
MAIN FLIGHT
The Night Is Mine
I Own the Dawn
Wait Until Dark
Take Over at Midnight
Light Up the Night
Bring On the Dusk
By Break of Day
Target of the Heart
Target Lock on Love
Target of Mine
Target of One's Own
NIGHT STALKERS HOLIDAYS
*Daniel's Christmas**
*Frank's Independence Day**
*Peter's Christmas**
Christmas at Steel Beach
*Zachary's Christmas**
*Roy's Independence Day**
*Damien's Christmas**
Christmas at Peleliu Cove

Henderson's Ranch
*Nathan's Big Sky**
*Big Sky, Loyal Heart**
*Big Sky Dog Whisperer**
*Tales of Henderson's Ranch**

Shadow Force: Psi
*At the Slightest Sound**
*At the Quietest Word**
*At the Merest Glance**
*At the Clearest Sensation**

White House Protection Force
*Off the Leash**
*On Your Mark**
*In the Weeds**

Firehawks
Pure Heat
Full Blaze
*Hot Point**
*Flash of Fire**
Wild Fire
SMOKEJUMPERS
*Wildfire at Dawn**
*Wildfire at Larch Creek**
*Wildfire on the Skagit**

Delta Force
*Target Engaged**
*Heart Strike**
*Wild Justice**
*Midnight Trust**

Emily Beale Universe Short Story Series
The Night Stalkers
The Night Stalkers Stories
The Night Stalkers CSAR
The Night Stalkers Wedding Stories
The Future Night Stalkers

Delta Force
Th Delta Force Shooters
The Delta Force Warriors

Firehawks
The Firehawks Lookouts
The Firehawks Hotshots
The Firebirds

White House Protection Force
Stories

Future Night Stalkers
Stories (Science Fiction)

ABOUT THIS BOOK

WHEN THE POLITICAL BATTLEFIELD SPREADS TO ANTARCTICA, CAN the team survive the deep freeze?

Those who work there call Antarctica "The Ice." A secret Russian cargo jet crashes into a crevasse near an Australian Station. The Aussies call in the top air-crash investigators on the planet.

The best of them all, Miranda Chase, must face the Russians, Chinese, and use her own autistic abilities to keep her team alive. As the battle spreads across The Ice, are even her incredible skills enough?

Or will they all be buried in the frozen wasteland?

PROLOGUE

Altitude: 43,000 feet
Off the coast of Antarctica
69°22'25" S 76°22'18" E
approximately

"Kolya, I am going to rip out your eyes and crap in your skull!"

"This is not my doing, Captain."

Captain Fyodor Novikov knew it wasn't his navigator's fault, but he needed someone to vent at and Kolya would know that. They'd started as young men together in flight school and knew each other's ways.

The Ilyushin Il-76's airframe creaked worse than his *deda's* knees in a Moscow winter—a topic his grandfather loved to discuss in excruciating detail. Like Deda, his plane had earned the right to creak. Of the more than a thousand 76s built, it wouldn't surprise him if his was the oldest remaining in service for the Russian military.

The storm slammed the big cargo jet one way and then

another across the Antarctic sky. Nothing to see out the windshield except a world of white—snow and cloud. At least it was daylight as it was high summer and they were below the Antarctic Circle. Below, he knew though he couldn't see it, lay a world of death. Nothing but a storm-tossed ocean thick with ice floes down there.

When he and his four crewmates had departed Cape Town International Airport seven hours ago, the report called for clear weather all the way to Progress Station in Antarctica. And it had been...for the first four thousand kilometers of the flight.

But then Antarctica had decided to have a fit worse than his mother had when he'd brought home Aloysha the first time. The shouts, the pounding of fists on the armchair. In his bedroom that night they'd lain together listening to Mama's vicious mutterings through the thin wall.

He wished Kolya was sitting beside him in the cockpit instead of the party-hack copilot. He flew well enough, but couldn't speak without spouting off some brainwashed nausea.

Kolya, however, sat alone in the lower navigator's cockpit. Though they were mere meters apart, their compartments connected back in the cargo bay. The party hack sat to Fyodor's right and the engineer and loadmaster sat close behind him. No privacy this side of a good bar.

The chaotic headwind flipped to a tailwind in a sharp, sixty-knot gust. The plane plummeted two hundred meters in the next three seconds as if the bottom had fallen out of the sky. He heard a grunt from the copilot who hadn't known to tighten down his harness in a storm and had now bruised himself on the overhead. The engineer and loadmaster were old hands and had long since strapped down and were trying to sleep. Their work mostly happened on the ground.

Fyodor waited five seconds. Six. Seven...they were down another four hundred meters before the gust dissipated and the plane began climbing again. Patience.

This storm was as angry and foul as Mama had been— where patience had *not* worked.

Flying headlong into that first storm, he had married the gorgeous Tatar blonde from Kazan—and regretted it ever since.

Within the next year, she'd entered into an extended affair with his commander, which had caused one type of problem. Major Turgenev had assigned Fyodor to the most remote and long-lasting assignments, keeping him far from Moscow.

Then she'd moved on to *his* commander in turn, which had caused Fyodor an entirely different type of problem. In retribution, Major Turgenev now assigned him the oldest aircraft on the worst routes.

It wasn't his navigator, it was *Aloysha* who should have her eyes ripped out. Little status-climbing *sterva!* Whose bed would the bitch find next, the Russian President's? The Lord knew that enough others had. Rumors of his numerous unclaimed children and lovers who were quietly disappeared abounded like Russian ghost stories.

At least that's what he'd expected of her, but he'd checked his messages shortly before takeoff from Cape Town. Aloysha's low voice had left a long, rambling apology of how he'd been the only man to ever treat her properly and how could she make it up to him?

Not a chance, woman.

He'd rather spend the rest of his days battling the

physical storms, the ones he could fly into and fly back out of like this one. Storm above, sea-torn ice below, he'd fly right down its throat and land at Progress Station like he had fifty times before. Then he'd get good and drunk because tonight's ride was a beast—the next gust sent his big sweetheart of a jet skittering sideways in a sharp crosswind.

Aloysha had then turned fortune teller, as so many Russian women did who plunged into that Christmas tradition each December. She spoke of salvaging his career using everything she had learned while sleeping with his superiors and promised he could replace them with a few easy tactics.

With her aid—of course.

There would be a catch—of course.

He knew her well enough now to know her supposed change of heart must be wholly self-serving. Aloysha might elevate his career but would use it as a launching point to strike yet higher for herself. Better than flying an ancient aircraft into a spawned-in-hell Antarctic storm?

That was the problem. He'd proven he was too tactless to climb the ranks on his own. Turgenev had once been a fellow pilot but was now his unit commander.

For once, he was thankful for this long flight. It placed him out of reach for several days while he, by a miracle please, convinced himself to say *Nyet!* Sadly, he knew full well his answer would be *Da!*

Perhaps he'd find a way to use Aloysha this time. Or at the very least break even out of the deal.

The control yoke bucked against his palms as a fresh gust slapped at them from straight ahead. Please let that be momentary. If it stayed sustained at that level, he might not reach the continent at all.

The forty-year-old Ilyushin Il-76 cargo jet had been modified for long range and could fly over nine thousand kilometers when traveling empty. With a full load of forty-eight tonnes, his range should be six thousand. It would have left him sufficient fuel reserve to return to South Africa when the storm notice had reached them as they crossed the sixtieth latitude south.

However, the damned administrators of the Arctic and Antarctic Research Institute were cutting corners. In fact, the ARRI were cutting off whole sides—they'd increased his payload by cutting his fuel load. It was hard to blame them as they were trying to keep Russia's five Antarctic stations operational, down from the Soviet Union's twenty-three. And frankly, those five were hanging by the thinnest of threads.

Another of Deda's favorite topics, while consuming an excess of vodka, was discussing the collapse of the Motherland in a far too loud voice.

*When we built the Pole of Inaccessibility Station in 1958...*so many of his diatribes began with that. Fyodor knew it was the high point of the old man's life, but each repetition stretched Fyodor's patience thinner than his chances of a blissful marriage with the faithless Aloysha. He'd rather wrestle with a storm than yet another of her games any day.

Deda's expedition had occupied the station for twelve days, the farthest point in Antarctica from the ocean in all directions. The last time it was visited—which happened about once a decade—all that remained of the original two-story hut was the bust of Lenin that had perched at the top, the lone tip of a radio antenna, and an anemometer that no longer spun. The rest had been buried beneath the drifting snow.

The Geographic South Pole, where the Americans

squatted in their deluxe super-station, lay eight hundred kilometers from the center of the continent.

To build at the Pole of Inaccessibility? That had taken Russian know-how! Then Deda would pound the table with the bottom of his empty glass, making his point as well as fresh dents in the old wood.

It was Russian *stupidity* as far as Fyodor was concerned. The traverse across the ice in each direction had taken longer than the occupation of the station itself. In that same year, the Americans had moved to the South Pole—and been there for all of the sixty-plus years since.

The question now was, how much longer would the few remaining Russian stations last?

The freak, mid-December storm—currently offering such marginal visibility through the thick clouds and blowing snow that he could barely see his own wings when he looked back—was worthy of the dead of winter, not the height of the Antarctic summer. However, with too much cargo and not enough fuel to turn back, the only answer was to continue through and land in Antarctica.

This cargo is top priority, Captain Novikov. Highest security, Major Turgenev had told him. *Straight from Colonel Romanoff.* The head of the entire Antarctic program.

There were a couple tons of foodstuffs, and all the rest was need-to-know and it had been deemed that he didn't need to know. *Fine!* He didn't care what he was carrying. Let them play their games. Let Aloysha flaunt her fine ass elsewhere. He was a damn fine pilot and for now, that would be plenty.

The four-engine Il-76 Candid was one of the largest cargo planes in the world. This old bird was his to command and he loved it for that. It was big enough that while the storm battered it, it was also tough enough to fly through it.

Though it *did* rattle like a tin can of old bolts being shaken by the ogress Baba Yaga herself as she strove to raise the demons of the wind. He muttered an old prayer of Grandmother's asking Baba Yaga to wander back to her usual occupation of kidnapping misbehaving children to cook for her dinner.

She didn't depart.

"Sustained winds at ninety kmph, gusts to one-twenty." Kolya sounded as dour as ever, like he was singing the closing dirge of a Mussorgsky opera. The man could make a wedding toast seem funereal.

"The heading, Kolya. You had better keep me on the heading." As if he wouldn't.

"You keep us in the air and I'll make sure we don't die until we get there."

"Good! I'll try to make sure we don't die after that."

The copilot looked at him aghast, but Fyodor knew his navigator's skills were unmatched and it was his attitude that had him assigned to these remote flights. Any sane commander who feared death would want Navigator Kolya and his dire pronouncements flying as far from them as possible. Any pilot with half a brain wouldn't care because no one was better at finding a safe landing despite storm, broken equipment, and archaic machinery.

The Il-76 was so ancient, thanks to Aloysha dumping Major Turgenev, that it had never been upgraded to a digital cockpit. Fyodor had to fly using all dial instruments. His lone screened instrument, the GLONASS global-positioning system, had been mounted on a spindly arm, which had snapped two months ago during a rough landing and been completely destroyed. Maintenance was *waiting for parts,* which either meant the repair order was stalled in Major Turgenev's inbox or that Deda was right about modern Russia's failures. Or, more likely, both.

To carry a backup GPS receiver to position himself by using the American satellite system was forbidden, though any American could access it by looking at their phone.

So it was up to Kolya, seated in the Il-76's navigation station directly below their feet, to keep them on course. He always managed, and Fyodor was careful not to ask how. Kolya probably used his personal phone and an illegal app for GPS positioning, as the GLONASS satellite system— when it was working—always seemed to have a gap at the most awkward moments.

They had to take care though. With party fanatic copilot aboard—who Major Turgenev wisely also wanted kept as far away as possible—they couldn't use American technology in his presence. Fyodor always warned Kolya when the copilot left his seat in case he decided to visit the navigator's station below.

There wasn't much chatter, they were all at dead ends in their careers and only Lieutenant Ultranationalist Copilot didn't know it. Below them, seated before the curve of the down-and-forward-looking windows and surrounded by his instruments, Kolya flew alone with the best view from the plane. It was these windows on the underside of the nose that gave the Il-76 the appearance of an evil toothed grin to all who approached.

Somehow, out in the blinding whiteness, Kolya would find their landing strip. In mid-December the ice runway on the sea by Progress Station would be marginal. The summer heat would melt out the ice shelf shortly. This was the last possible delivery of the season until the sea refroze.

Fyodor hoped that the ice crew had that right and he didn't simply sink through the ice upon landing. Also that they'd done a better job of grooming the ice since his last landing. He'd thought that it would be his last one—ever. How the landing gear remained attached that time was both a miracle and a testament of old Soviet engineering. Another point favoring Deda's tirades.

The runway had better be perfect now or he might pass on a dose of Major Turgenev's revenge. Of course, the days of threatening underlings with a trip to the Gulag were gone, again much to Deda's disappointment.

However, Fyodor had offered the men responsible for the runway maintenance an assignment to the Navy's *pride and joy* if they didn't take better care of the landing surface. The country's sole aircraft carrier, the *Admiral Kuznetsov,* was no better than a prison ship. And every person in the Russian military knew it.

It had to be towed to sea and anchored there for flight operations, when it was operational at all. Numerous pilots and planes died in horrific crashes during supposedly simple fair-weather daylight operations. They never attempted night or foul weather flights like the Americans. It definitely offered crew members a shortened lifespan from hazardous materials, fires, accidents, and poisonously bad food and air. One day it would simply sink, the way its dry dock had before the latest round of repairs could be started.

With a gut-churning plunge and a raucous protest from the wings' joints, he began his descent while still a hundred and fifty kilometers away from the coast.

Because of Major Turgenev's various assignments,

Fyodor was exceptionally practiced at flying old equipment through horrid weather. Flying down into the maelstrom was nothing new to him. With his trusty old Ilyushin-76, he'd make a safe landing and simply have another bad-weather-flight story to tell.

But his descent into the maelstrom of the sultry Aloysha when he next reached Moscow? If he decided to fly that particular route again, he didn't need one of Kolya's dire predictions to know how *that* storm would end.

At least Mama would be happy. When Aloysha had moved on, it had taken Mama months to find a new topic to rail at him about, along with her son's boundless stupidity.

Storm system Aloysha? No question that would be a disaster of epic proportions.

Was she worth the risk?

Almost certainly not.

Almost.

But he could never be sure.

———

THE INCOMING PROJECTILE DESCENDED AT THIRTY-FOUR kilometers per second—five times the reentry speed of a manned space capsule. It entered the mesosphere eighty kilometers above the ground, ten times the height of Everest, the first layer of the atmosphere with enough density to affect its motion to any measurable extent.

Upon striking the thin traces of the upper atmosphere, its hypersonic speed compressed the air like a battering ram until the air glowed white-hot around it.

It bore no wide heat shield designed to slow its passage. The common misunderstanding—that heat shields existed to slow down spacecraft—was backward. Reentry vehicles intended to reach the surface intact presented broad surfaces in order to dump orbital speed through atmospheric aero-braking. The friction with the air generates immense heat and the heat shield is designed to slowly burn away during reentry.

Narrow projectiles have different aerodynamic considerations. Not designed to reach near-zero velocity on landing, they didn't require large heat shields.

But that didn't mean they passed into the thick soup of Earth's atmosphere unscathed.

As the superheated air wrapped around the projectile, it protected the object. Between the rammed air and the main body itself, a thin envelope of trapped gas formed, which insulated it from the worst of the heat. What minor quantity of heat radiated through this barrier, scorched only the outermost molecules of the space-cold object before they were sloughed off, taking any accumulated heat with them.

The core remained a bare nine degrees above absolute zero.

Point-nine seconds later it entered the stratosphere. Crossing the thin, uppermost layers of atmosphere cost it a bare few percent of its velocity. Now, in thicker air, the object dumped kinetic energy and turned into a compact superheated inferno. The complex iron-nickel-cobalt alloy had sufficient density and mass that it didn't shatter against the massive pressure wave created by its own descent.

It slowed to a bare two kilometers a second as it traversed the twenty-five kilometers of the denser stratosphere.

At an altitude of twenty-one kilometers, the projectile calved into a swarm of multiple objects all moving at hypersonic speeds. Over the next twenty-two seconds, the swarm expanded to encompass an area a kilometer across.

Had they plunged unhindered through the lowest and thickest level of the atmosphere, the heat and pressure would have shattered most of them before they reached the surface.

But before that happened, at twelve-point-three kilometers above the ground—forty thousand, three hundred and nineteen feet—an Ilyushin Il-76 Candid cargo jet in a slow descent as it approached the coast of Antarctica flew into their path. The two most massive objects at the center of the swarm struck the plane, though it wouldn't have been spared anywhere within the kilometer-wide spread.

The main strike, a shaft as big around as Aloysha's trim waist and matching her Amazonian height, struck on the starboard side of the cockpit at an angle twenty-point-three degrees from vertical. This five-hundred-and-twenty-seven-kilo mass struck end on.

The shockwave of air that enveloped it was so intensely compressed that it burned at twenty-four hundred degrees centigrade—half the temperature of the surface of the sun.

His party loyalty didn't save the copilot as the object lanced into the cockpit, then through him from his right shoulder to his left hip. Next, it drove through the floor and vaporized a thirty-centimeter-long section of Navigator Kolya's thigh before blasting out the bottom of the airplane and continuing on its way. It also destroyed Kolya's phone, which he had resting on his thigh to monitor the Americans' GPS system.

The second piece hit at effectively the same instant and speed, but ten meters aft.

Though it was significantly smaller, it was this piece that ultimately sealed the Il-76's fate. A perturbation during the calving action flipped it into a fast tumble. A half-meter cube, it hit the jet and punched through the outer skin. Like a buzz saw, it sliced through a major structural crossmember of the cross-fuselage wing-box assembly—the strongest part of any airplane—vaporizing the aluminum frame.

The impact broke the second object in two.

The larger piece punched through the central fuel tank, sliced through a pallet-load of food supplies, flash searing a hundred kilos of bananas and three hundred half-kilo cubes of beef bouillon. Then it punched out the bottom of the aircraft.

The last of the jet's fuel began to dump down through the heat-formed tube to spill out below the plane and be safely scattered by the howling storm. All four engines would flame-out from fuel-starvation long before the Ilyushin-76 reached the ground, turning it into the world's largest glider for the duration of its final flight.

The larger piece of the aft strike that had slashed through the fuel tank and cargo area burned up on the final descent, leaving nothing bigger than dust on the roaring wind.

The smaller section of the aft strike, shattered by the collision with the heavy crossmember, sent tiny slivers streaming in all directions through the airplane's structure but caused no damage that affected the final outcome in any quantifiable way.

The main strike, which had blasted through the Il-76's cockpit, was slowed another point-seven kilometers per second by the impact. Slowed to subsonic speeds, it struck an iceberg that was drifting in Antarctica's Circumpolar

Current. It embedded less than five centimeters into the hard ice. Thirty-four days later and a third of the way around the continent, the iceberg would melt sufficiently to drop it unnoticed to the ocean floor on the tectonic ridge near Australia's Macquarie Island.

The fragments of the swarm that didn't impact the aircraft rapidly vaporized during the last of their descent through the breathably thick troposphere. Several failed catastrophically from the extreme heat and pressure, but the explosive force and spewed shrapnel of each was lost in the whirling Antarctic storm.

———

THE HORRENDOUS IMPACT RIPPLED THROUGHOUT THE PLANE.

Fyodor was first aware of it as a searing pain in his ears. The sonic boom of the object crashing through the cabin less than two meters away permanently deafened him and made his ears bleed.

He couldn't hear Kolya's screams as the navigator's femoral artery pumped out his life's blood, spraying red throughout the navigator's cabin below. The last thing Kolya saw was the red-colored hell he had always known awaited him. Even if his phone had survived to track the GPS, he could no longer guide the plane to its final destination.

The copilot had no respiratory system with which to scream. He could only stare in wide-eyed astonishment. For the rest of his life, which lasted only eleven more seconds but felt like an eternity, he tried to understand how this had happened. The party always promised to protect him if he did his duty.

He had.

It hadn't.

The incandescent blast of the object's hypersonic passage had only blinded Fyodor's right eye, covering his right side in second- and third-degree burns from the heat of its passage. The copilot's hot blood spraying over him felt cool in comparison.

The double holes through the cockpit, above and below, emptied the cockpit of pressurized air. Within seconds the air pressure had dropped to one-fifth of sea level. Fyodor had less than fifteen seconds of useful consciousness remaining.

When the shock wave slammed the yoke against the palms of his hands, it fired off deep-trained instincts despite the agony he was suffering.

With only one eye working and his right hand trapped by the melted plastic of the control yoke, it took him thirteen of those fifteen seconds to pull on an emergency air mask.

Once he could breath, he needed another twenty-nine seconds to think through the pain and take the next action— initiate an emergency descent.

He nosed the big plane down toward more breathable air, not knowing the last of his crew had died seventeen seconds earlier.

The engines flamed twenty-four seconds after Fyodor started breathing effectively and five seconds before he began the twelve-kilometer descent.

Captain Fyodor Novikov focused on the only thing not adding to his agony.

With his still-functioning left eye, he saw that one instrument had picked up a directional beacon. Throughout the long descent, he fought the controls to center the needle as it was all he could see through the splatter of the copilot's remains across the instrument panel.

Fyodor fought the thrashing winds and kept gliding toward the beacon.

He had no idea of his altitude until the "*Too low terrain. Pull up.*" radar alarm began blaring—which he couldn't hear but he could see the flashing red through the remains of the copilot's spleen.

He couldn't lower the wheels because his right hand was fused to the yoke. Fyodor had sufficient mental faculties remaining to decide that a belly landing was probably the safer option anyway.

Had he had engine power to control his final approach— and the ability to remove his right hand from the yoke to work the controls—he might have landed mostly intact.

But he couldn't.

And he didn't.

The landing did spare him from deciding what to do about Aloysha and his mother—forever.

1

———

Spieden Island, Washington State
8:30 a.m. Pacific Standard Time

"CERTAINLY DIDN'T SEE MUCH OF THIS STUFF GROWING UP."
Holly Harper studiously ignored Mike Munroe's suggestion
that she leave her cozy nest to go out in it.

Hit by a rare snowstorm, Miranda's personal, private
island lay coated with a foot-deep layer of the fluffy white
stuff. The snowfall had been heavy enough that the Douglas
firs towering beyond the big picture window of the second-
story sitting room were emerging from the pre-dawn
darkness brilliantly white instead of forest green. Only
rarely did snow stick in Washington State's San Juan Islands.
Even rarer, it had happened mere days before Christmas and
it was predicted to be cold all week.

A white Christmas. Being from Australia, she'd never
had one of those and was looking forward to it—from inside
the cozy confines of Miranda's lovely timber home.

Three years ago, her first Christmas at Miranda's had

promised a storm, but that had fizzled in the night of Christmas Eve and barely dusted the brown grass. The second Christmas here had been warm enough that the grass had been mostly green.

This time, it looked as if a white Christmas was a done deal. Holly was feeling so mellow that she would probably only offer minimal protest when the other three members of the team put on one of those sappy old Christmas movies with singing, dancing, and happy-ever-after nonsense.

Indoors, the world had been muffled by the snow, not that it was particularly noisy on Miranda's island. But it was like one of those postcards, all quiet beneath the breaking dawn.

"You do understand that white stuff is snow, right, Mike? Frozen water. As in cold."

"Brisk! Besides, compared with where I used to live—"

"Blah. Blah. Denver. Blah. Blah. Skiing in Aspen. Blah. Blah. Blah. I remain one unconvinced Aussie. Where I grew up, a cold winter's day was thirteen degrees—"

"Then you're fine, it's only down to twenty-seven this morning." He waved out the second-story window to where a thin streak of ruddy sunrise cut through the scattered clouds to glint off the brilliant snow.

"Centigrade, you Yank. That's fifty-five degrees to you, and only fools went out and about in such bitter weather. I'm staying here. Besides, my toes are all warm and snoozy. Never tick off your toes, Mike, they'll find ways to get back at you."

Mike began making chicken noises. Thankfully, he wised up before she had to hurt him. Also, being a wise man, he succumbed and was soon tucked under the big quilt with her. Shoulder to shoulder they semi-lay on the big couch, their feet tangled on the coffee table.

Beyond the window, the trees only filled part of the view. Farther on, past the long roll of the island, were the deep blue streaks of the Spieden and San Juan Channels. Not a single boat on them this wintry morning. Beyond those, San Juan Island likewise pushed its snow-capped head up against the slate-gray skies. Wandering snowflakes suggested that the blizzard wasn't through with them yet. Definitely a day to remain inside.

Miranda and Andi came in. They'd clearly been out in it already this morning. Holly hadn't made it downstairs for breakfast yet.

"If you loved me, you'd have brought up tea."

Mike slipped out from under the quilt and headed for the stairs.

"I was joking..." But her words trailed off. She hadn't meant it the way she'd said it, had she? No! Utterly daft. She ignored Mike's unquestioning response because then she'd have to think about her own and that was *not* going to happen.

Focus on Miranda and Andi instead.

The two women looked so happy and healthy, with the bright red glow of the outdoors on their cheeks, that Holly felt yet more of a slug. She managed to shrug it off when they curled up side by side on the other couch and drew another quilt over themselves. Andi's fluffy slippers, made to look like a pair of Shih Tzu dogs complete with soulful plastic eye buttons, stuck out past the edge alongside Miranda's practical sheepskin ones.

"All the walks shoveled and the airfield plowed?"

"Nope!" Andi said happily. "But we took a snowcat out to

spread around hay, feed, and dried apple rings for the deer and sheep."

"You have a snowcat?" Holly didn't know why she bothered asking. It might snow only once in a great while here, but Miranda...

Holly echoed Miranda's words as she said them, "I like to be prepared."

Andi laughed and they all traded smiles. Snug as three dingo puppies in their den. Mike returned with a massive mug of tea and a scone. "I could—" No way had she almost said she'd marry him for that. He set it close by on a side table, then slid back in beside her. "Uh...thanks."

"Too bad Taz and Jeremy are stuck in Georgia," Mike settled against her side once more, acknowledging her thanks with a simple nod. "It would be nice to have the old team together for Christmas."

"I miss them," Miranda agreed. "But solving commuter plane crashes can be trickier than commercial airliners. They are far less well monitored. Instead of three tiers of backup flight computers, they rarely have more than an autopilot."

"Well, there's one bit of good news about them flailing around in Georgia's Okefenokee Swamp in midwinter." Mike wrapped a leg over Holly's. She sipped her tea to distract herself. One sugar, no milk. He *was* a good man.

"What's that?" She leaned against him until he raised an arm and she slid against his warmth. This was far too familiar but she didn't pull away because it was also far too comfortable.

"It isn't *us* slogging among the gators and snakes!"

"*That* we can agree on." The Georgia swamp would be warmer than here, but far wetter too.

A bald eagle soared into view from high over the house. It hung there, riding the air currents beyond the big picture window and perhaps considering the pair of black cormorants winging swiftly across the island, before soaring onward.

Holly couldn't think of the last time she'd been so comfortable. Willing to simply sit and be. Andi and Miranda looked equally content. With their mismatched slippers and Miranda leaning against Andi's shoulder.

"How long have you two been together?" she asked.

"Coming up on eight months on New Year's Eve." Andi's smile lit her face.

She thought about her own question. She and Mike had been...

"Whoa!"

"What?" Mike asked from so close that it tickled her ear.

"Nothing. Random thought." *Three years?* She'd known Mike for three years now on Miranda's team. And they'd been sleeping together for at least two of that. Maybe two and a half? It made this her longest relationship by...

Don't think about it!

Like that was going to ever happen.

Revel in the comfortable. That'll block thoughts about anything as daft as a long-term relationship.

Except the complacency worked no better than the internal command.

She was no wanton or good-time girl. But in the past, when it had stopped being fun or deployment orders had sent her off in a new direction, that had been...*that*. Done. Moving on.

The only place she'd ever worked as long as she had with Miranda's team had been Australia's Special Air Service

Regiment. And Special Operations had meant she was constantly on the move. She hadn't been this stable since before she'd run away from home at sixteen.

"Hey." Mike nudged his hip against hers and spoke louder, "Hey! Your phone's ringing."

She fished out her phone but didn't recognize the number. For three years, if anyone called her, it was a member of this team. She'd thoroughly burned every bridge behind her and studiously ignored the few survivors until they faded into the past where they belonged. Her friends were all here. Not exactly a wide circle.

She did recognize the country code: 61, Australia.

"Harper," she answered.

"Are you available for a launch?"

"Barty! How are you, mate?" Her old boss hated being called that, but she'd created the nickname and it had stuck. Actually, he maybe technically still *was* her boss. He headed up the ATSB, the Aussie version of the National Transportation Safety Board that she'd been seconded to for six months to join Miranda's team—three years ago. Barty had long since backfilled his team and she'd managed to dodge his increasingly rare attempts to drag her back to Oz. Far too many memories there and few of them any good.

"Fine, Harper. Are you available for a launch?" As humorless as ever.

Mike lay close enough to overhear easily, as her head might have been resting on his shoulder, and looked at her wide-eyed.

"I'm, uh, snowed in at the moment. What's going on?"

Barty grunted heavily, never content unless he was ordering someone about. "Is your phone encryption capable?"

Holly offered a confirming grunt of her own.

"I've got your file here. Punch in your birthday." Then his phone squealed painfully as he encrypted his end of the conversation.

Holly punched it in, then for good measure selected speakerphone before raising her finger to her lips for the others.

"You there?" Barty sounded less gruff, which was far more likely to be the compression of the encryption algorithm than any actual change in her boss. He was a fixture at the ATSB the same way that the big red rock of Uluru anchored the middle of Australia's Red Centre.

"Aye."

"Look, you've been training with that genius woman at the NTSB, right?"

"More like working my ass off, Barty. You've got no idea the kind of stuff she gets into." She smiled across at Miranda so that Miranda would understand it was all good. Holly liked the hard work and the tough challenges. Miranda's autism made it hard for her to read emotions, so making them clear was always a good idea.

Despite her attempt, it wasn't until Andi whispered the double meaning to her that Miranda returned the smile. They were a seriously cute couple: the five-four brunette air-crash genius and the five-two San Francisco Chinese heiress turned wizard military helicopter pilot turned crash investigator.

Under the cover of the quilt, Mike squeezed Holly's butt to show quite how hard she *wasn't* working at the moment. She offered him an elbow to the ribs, but not hard enough to bruise. *Mellowing with age, Holly.* She'd left her thirtieth behind a few years ago but at least was closer to thirty than forty—barely.

"Yeah, I know what she gets into," Barty continued. "Saw the job you two did on that Qantas crash out on Johnston Atoll in the South Pacific last year."

"Like I said, Barty, you've got no idea." Nor was she about to give him one. The crash had been sabotage of an entire airliner to target her personally—though only the folks in this room knew that. That crash, the initial move in a series of events, had ultimately cost far more lives than had been lost in that first wreck. But Barty wouldn't know that part because it was all highly classified.

"We need that level of expertise, internationally recognized expertise on this one," Barty was saying. "Probably with a dose of your old SASR operator skills thrown in for good measure. How soon can you be in Hobart?"

"Tassie? I don't know, I don't keep airline timetables in my head. *What* is going on, mate?"

Barty offered another heavy grunt before condescending to sound at least half human. "We've got a Russian cargo jet down on our soil. One of their big ones. Down ugly. Russians are going to be blaming us."

"What were the Russians doing flying big cargo to Tasmania?"

"They weren't. They crashed at Davis Station. I want to solve this before they send one of their big-ass Backfire bombers winging over to destroy their wreck and Davis along with it. The way they're running that country these days, I'm surprised they haven't done it already."

"Davis Station? Like in Antarctica? *That* Davis Station?" She couldn't have heard that right.

"I'm not talking about Harry's digs." Harry Davis had a big cattle station outside Perth in West Oz that he often let SASR use for training. It's where she'd met Barty long before either of them joined the ATSB. Harry always threw a righteous party round his big barbie after a training, making it a regiment favorite.

"No, that isn't right," Miranda spoke up, then slapped a hand over her mouth when Andi shushed her. Miranda's eyes shot wide with worry.

Barty snapped out, "Who was that?"

"*That* was the genius woman you mentioned. I've got you on speakerphone."

"Aw for Christ sakes, Harper. You think I went secure for you to broadcast this to everyone?"

"This entire team is cleared Top Secret or better, Barty. Same as you and me." Actually, well above Barty's pay grade but it wouldn't do to rub that in. Holly turned to Miranda. "What's not right?"

Miranda shook her head vigorously, but didn't dislodge her hand.

Experience had taught Holly the problem. Logical conflict always threw Miranda off course because, Lord knew, she was one seriously logical gal. "It's okay, Miranda. You can ignore my earlier request to keep quiet."

"Okay," she mumbled, then removed her hand. "The Russians service their Antarctic stations from Cape Town, South Africa, including the Progress Station, which lies a hundred and ten kilometers from Davis Station. A Tupolev Tu-22M Backfire bomber doesn't have the range to fly from Cape Town to Davis Station and return safely. It is also incapable of landing in Antarctica for refueling. It's simply too far. In order to bomb Davis Station and safely make the round trip from Cape Town, they would most likely use the older Tu-95 Bear bomber or the newer Tu-160 White Swan. They both have more than sufficient range to make the return trip safely with a full load of ordnance as well as provide sufficient loiter time to assure the task was complete. That's all."

"There. Feel better, Barty?"

"I wasn't being literal."

"Oh," Miranda winced.

"Thanks, Miranda. Good to know," and Miranda's frown cleared. "Besides, Barty, with the Russian president right now? Anything is possible."

"Don't I know it. How fast can you get to Hobart?"

"Twenty hours flying commercial out of Vancouver," Mike waved his phone at her.

"Christ sakes, Harper, you got a marching band there?"

"Absolutely, we're working the next Super Bowl halftime show. We're performing a round of musical numbers starting with 'Waltzing Matilda' and ending with 'Down Under'." She began singing, "*I come from a land down und—*"

"Well, waltz your damn butt to Hobart as fast as you can. I'm holding a flight there for you, which is pissing off the scheduled scientists. Nothing in the world more annoying than a bunch of squawking egghead dags."

"Except maybe a Russian cargo jet crashed at your station?"

Barty offered his favorite commentary, another grunt.

Holly looked around the room. Everyone was quiet, watching her closely.

"Well, mates of mine, have any plans for Christmas?"

Miranda opened her mouth and Holly knew that a list would be forthcoming. She tended to over-plan for team visits to her private island, offering multiple-choice activities at the least provocation. A combination of nerves about visitors and whatever rules she'd memorized about part of being a good hostess.

"Let me amend that. Any plans more important than investigating a Russian Ilyushin-76 crash in Antarctica?"

Miranda closed her mouth.

"Barty? Make that seats for four. I'll let you be the chap to notify the NTSB that you're calling our team for help." And she hung up before he could protest.

Mike was grinning.

"What?"

"You do understand that they have snow, ice, and freezing temperatures in Antarctica, right? Year-round."

Crap! She hadn't thought about that.

2

Miranda's snowcat was no bigger than the golf cart she usually used to get around the island in nicer weather. It could carry two people, a bale of hay, and not much more. In lieu of making multiple trips, they tromped out into the freezing morning of Spieden Island wearing their go-bags and crash investigation kits.

Holly considered it to be neither crisp nor bracing, it was bloody cold. Cold enough for the occasional giant snowflakes to stick on her face like frozen mosquito feet, no matter how often she brushed at them.

She'd worked in deep snow before, but only for SASR training or when investigating a winter crash with particularly bad timing—like any time it wasn't a warmer season. Tramping through a foot of powder this quiet morning was a new experience in silence. It was as if the entire world had been frozen into stillness. Even the words they spoke were swallowed by the snow.

Other than the path Miranda and Andi had roughly packed down earlier with the mini-snowcat, the only marks on the smooth surface were the crisscrossing tracks of the island's four-footed residents.

Walking the half-mile from the house to the hangar was eerie. The squeak of the snow as it compacted beneath their boots crunched overloud, jerking all of her spec ops training to the fore. Telling herself it didn't matter did nothing to calm her nerves. She'd been trained to move in silence— neither the other three team members nor the snow cooperated.

Miranda's grass runway was deeply covered, but once they reached the hangar, the snow was so lightweight that it took the four of them only a few minutes to shovel clear a space for Miranda's helicopter to be tugged into the open. Several of the island's curly horned mouflon sheep watched them with curiosity from the verge of the trees across the field.

They scattered into the Douglas fir woods when Andi spun up the dual turboshaft engines of the MD 902 Explorer to a painful whine. As they took off, the downward blast of the main rotor created a complete whiteout of turbulated snow that made Holly glad they had a former US Army Night Stalker pilot at the controls. Andi was an amazing flyer. The flurry outside and the heater inside also made Holly glad that she was now watching the show from inside the helo.

The fifteen-minute crossing from Miranda's island in northern Washington to Vancouver International Airport in southern British Columbia was a busy passage of air traffic control spaces and tightly controlled approach corridors. Holly could fly a helicopter but wouldn't have liked to try this flight. Andi made it look like a beginner's route.

Nineteen hours in flight from Vancouver to Sydney aboard a 787.

Last year when she'd crossed this ocean, her flight had crash-landed on a tiny atoll in the middle of it. She did her best not to think about that, or that she'd have been dead if the atoll hadn't been there. Then she'd flown on to Australia to visit her childhood home and deal with the bits and bobs that remained of her parents' estate—after not having spoken to them for most of two decades. The only way it could have been worse would have been if her parents had been above the ground and not under it.

She'd crossed the Pacific twice since then and hadn't been bothered. Why this time? No reason that she could think of. She considered asking Mike if he had any idea. Thankfully, he was asleep by the time she thought of her question so he didn't offer a ridiculously solicitous and kind question about was she okay. *No!* But she didn't know why.

Barty had sent them no new information, but Miranda had downloaded everything the US military had on the Ilyushin-76 cargo jet—which was quite a bit, as they'd done a bit of horse trading with the Indian Air Force to try one out and snag copies of all of the documentation. Miranda and Andi began studying it intently, but Holly simply couldn't focus. In between naps, Mike read the basics, but he wasn't a technical guy—he specialized in the people. Their subtext, not an airplane's.

She herself had briefly studied the plane back in her SASR days, mostly how to blow them up using minimum explosives for maximum destruction, or how to board one if a hostile takedown was called for. That would have to do, as all she could focus on was the eleven thousand miles of nothing but ocean that was passing by seven miles below them.

They had a brief layover in Sydney, long enough for a better than half-decent meat pie but not long enough for a proper sit down with a cold one.

No chance of a beer at all in Hobart as their feet barely touched the ground there. Folks from the AAD, the Australian Antarctic Division, hustled the entire team out of the terminal and onto the waiting C-17 Globemaster III. The monster jet was painted with the RAAF colors—blah-gray with *Royal Australian Air Force* in big letters and a small Australian flag. The American-built jet was one of the few cargo planes larger than the Russian Il-76.

The cargo bay was packed with pallets of building supplies and fuel drums. A snowcat, full-sized, had been crammed aboard as well with more gear strapped into its pickup-style bed. Pallets of scientific gear filled the rest of the space, leaving people as an afterthought. The fold-down benches along either side were crammed with folks and their gear. Every one of which offered looks that could have frozen Hell or boiled off the Antarctic icecap.

She wondered how long they'd been camped in the plane. Surely Barty hadn't kept them all waiting aboard for the entire twenty-three hours it had taken to transit from Miranda's island to Tasmania.

Four hours later Holly wondered if she'd been ruined for life. One thing a Spec Ops soldier could always do was sleep on a plane or helicopter. Once they hit the ground, who knew when the next rest would be? Even that would be interrupted by pulling night watch, alerts, and any intruders larger than a mouse into a secured zone.

Miranda's putative area of coverage for the NTSB was the

Western Region of the US. That included Alaska and Hawaii, but neither of those were that far from Seattle. Investigating crashes farther afield happened, but were not *that* common. It had been months since their last one.

The skill had eroded without her even noticing. By the time they'd entered their final descent toward Antarctica, she hadn't managed to sleep once—until the last fifteen minutes. She fell asleep during the final descent and woke with a start when the big piston for the C-17's rear cargo doors that she'd been sleeping against hissed to life.

"Welcome to The Ice," a handler called to them the moment the rear ramp had lowered to the runway—the runway made of hard-frozen ice. "It's what we locals call Antarctica."

"Crap!" Holly tried to scrabble a parka out of the cold kit that Barty had left for each of them. She was the only one aboard who wasn't already wearing a Big Red as the heavy parkas were known for eye-blindingly obvious reasons— petite Andi and Miranda were nearly invisible inside their bulk.

But being last aboard, they were the ones closest to the end of the ramp. The scientists and other personnel pressed from behind, without *quite* pushing and shoving. She was forced to stumble out into the cold while seriously underdressed. Not a one of the other passengers had spoken a word to them during the entire flight—which was nigh impossible over the engine noise and the required ear plugs, but it might have been nice if they'd at least tried.

The ramp attendant grimaced at her frantic efforts. "You caught a warm one, only five below today."

"Perfect, mate. I'll slather up in sunscreen and be catching a few rays." She eyed the sun once she'd struggled into the parka, which Barty had thoughtfully placed at the bottom of the cold kit. The sun was skimming low along the horizon. "What time is it anyway? I'm set to Seattle time, I think."

"That's the first rule, by the way." He turned to the deplaned scientists who'd gathered around and announced loudly. "Down here you live in sunscreen. No going out of doors without it until sunset...and that's about a month off, mates."

Holly found it in a side pocket of the cold kit, waved it at the others in her group, but the ramp guy stopped her. "Nothing but a warning for you lot. Don't bother with it now; your next flight is waiting. It's 0330 hours."

Which probably explained why everyone else on the flight had been so grumpy. She hadn't been paying attention to the time in Hobart, but it had been dark. Barty holding up their flight had turned the trip to Antarctica into a red eye and every soul on board knew it was their team's fault. Perfect.

"We're in three weeks of continuous sunshine here at Casey, so no need to run you the sixty kilometers to the Station and back for the night." He managed to complete the sentence without too much ire. He waved them toward a red-and-white Basler BT-67. "Have a good flight."

"So pretty!" Andi cooed the same way young girls did at kittens, like she wanted to adopt the seventy-foot-long plane.

"Su-weet! Always wanted to fly on a DC-3." Mike hadn't bothered to zip his parka.

Holly had her hood raised and was debating if it was worth the pain to lower it to wrap a scarf around her neck. She lowered the zipper from her chin to half down her neck. Nope! She re-zipped it until the fur hood made a small tunnel that completely blocked her peripheral vision. Which was unacceptable, but the moment she unzipped it a single inch, she changed her mind and battened down the hatches once more.

"Technically," Miranda turned to Mike, "it's no longer a McDonnell Douglas DC-3. It has had a large number of conversions made to it for improved operation in Arctic and Antarctic conditions. Long-range fuel tanks, a fuselage extension, retractable skis, and improved avionics. It is quite a different plane now."

"It's a DC-3 at heart," Mike sighed happily. "That's all I care about. The clean lines. It's a two-engine taildragger. That's a classic no matter what they do to it."

"You're a romantic, Mike." The instant Holly said it, she prayed that her parka's muffling was sufficient to bury her voice.

"Only about certain things, Holly." He bumped his shoulder against hers.

She opened her mouth to protest, but that would lead the discussion to places she didn't want to go. On one side of the wall big enough to humble the Great Wall of China was all of that romantic crap, and on the other side, *way* on the other side, was her. She didn't live anywhere near places that had enjoyed snuggling up against Mike on the couch this morning. Yesterday morning...*two* yesterday mornings ago because they'd also crossed the International Date Line.

Luxury was not one of the upgrades made to convert a DC-3 into a Basler BT-67. A large cargo door had replaced the passenger door. It was big enough that passenger seats could be quickly removed and replaced with cargo. This trip was about half and half. As passengers, they were crammed into the forward portion of the cargo bay. Because it was a taildragger with a low wing, it meant that the big plane rested at a steep tilt to the surface during ground operations—it would level off the moment she was airborne.

They threaded their way through the cargo, which included a brand-new snowmobile. It was like climbing *up* a playground slide to reach their seats. Seats were four across, two on a side in the seven-foot-wide cabin, which meant that she was once again crammed hip to hip with Mike.

Normally that didn't bother her, but his raised arm offering to let her slid in closer was seriously annoying. She batted it aside.

Maybe there was a parachute so that she could throw herself off the plane—safely. None were in sight. While she'd been looking around, the plane taxied and took off. Too late she realized that she could have simply not climbed onto the plane in the first place.

They'd been together for thirty-odd months, so why was their relationship bugging her so much today? Returning to Australia? They'd been on the ground there under two hours total and airports never really counted as visiting a place.

She looked out the window at nothing but white ice, which didn't even have the decency to *look* like it could be Oz so that she could be pissed about being dragged back.

No, it was this aura of relationship that suffused from Mike's pores until it created a fog for her to stumble about in like a lost puppy.

On this final four-hour leg, she slept so fitfully that she'd have been better off staying awake. The landing jolted her head from Mike's shoulder. He kissed her temple, as if thanking her for every minute of slumber she'd found there.

"Are you okay with this?" she whispered so that the

others wouldn't hear as the plane revved its engines to taxi to wherever they were going.

"This, meaning us?" Mike never did miss much. "I'm enjoying it plenty." Then he shrugged. "Comfortable with it?"

He didn't answer his own question. He was as much of a loner as she was in many ways. An ex-conman, playboy, and FBI stooge, Mike's past relationships had been far more frequent than hers. But by the few stories he'd told, they hadn't lasted even as long as her brief encounters.

They'd come down on a smooth expanse of ice. Less than a kilometer away—she had to blink because it looked so odd—a massive ship was parked atop the same ice. The hull was bright orange and looked as if it had been sliced off at the waterline and plopped onto the frozen white sea.

Mike twisted to follow her gaze as the plane slowed. "Cool! I've never seen an icebreaker before."

The perspective shifted. Now it made her uneasy in a different way. The big ship had broken through the ice and floated in water deep enough to be safe. *They,* on the other hand, had landed a heavy plane on ice thin enough for the icebreaker to punch through.

Then she saw a boxy Hagglund snowcat pulling a skied trailer and a heavy snow groomer pulling another as they drove across the ice from the ship. They were heavily laden, yet looked as if this was all perfectly normal. She supposed, as long as she didn't see quite how thin the ice was, it was time to calm down and focus.

"Is everyone all caught up on their sleep?" Andi asked as they deplaned, in a chipper tone that said she absolutely had.

Mike nodded.

Holly looked around for a snowbank to shove him into. None handy.

Miranda glanced at her watch. "It's six-thirty in the morning. We might as well stay awake until bedtime and get started."

Holly checked her own watch that she'd reset at Wilkins Aerodrome. "No, Miranda, it's seven-thirty."

"We flew west," Mike told her. "Which means—"

"—that we fell back yet another time zone." Holly reset her watch again and felt the extra hour further she was from nabbing a bit of sack time.

3

HER FIRST STEP OUT ONTO THE ICE WASN'T AS SHOCKING AS Miranda expected. The ice itself felt harder underfoot than a concrete runway. The surface wasn't slick, instead it was slightly crunchy.

The air was so dry that it didn't have the penetrating bite of Spieden Island when they'd left. Of course at night it would...except the next night was over a month away. She could get used to this.

Through the soles of her boots, she could feel the heavy rumble of the two big tractors as they dragged their loads from the ship, past the iceway—a landing strip built on a floating ice shelf—and headed for the station. At least she assumed that the cluster of brightly colored buildings was Davis Station.

Not far from the plane, bare ground rose several meters.

Andi looked around, as much a gawker as the rest of them. "I wasn't expecting bare ground. I thought the continent was all covered in ice."

"This is one of the few places on the continent that isn't,"

Miranda pointed out. "That's why the station is here in the Vestfold Hills. See the white line in the distance? It looks like clouds." She pointed south, away from the sea.

"Sure."

"That thin stripe along the horizon?" Holly asked.

"Yes. That's the beginning of the East Antarctic Ice Sheet. Once you reach that, I think the next time you can find exposed ground is at the American McMurdo Station on the far side of the continent. From California to Florida. The South Pole Station would be roughly where Chicago is. Off to the side a bit."

Holly looked at Miranda. "How did you do that?"

Miranda paused, then shrugged enough to briefly raise the Big Red coat that enveloped her slight frame. "I don't know. I juxtaposed one continent over another as an analogy without stopping to consider it."

Holly held up a hand and Miranda high-fived it.

"What was that for?"

Andi held up her hand as well. "Your autism doesn't typically allow you to do things like that."

An accurate assessment. But why was this time different? That was—

"Oi! Who are you lot?" A woman came striding toward them across the sea ice from the direction of the station.

"Ah, the voice of home," Holly answered back. "Well, not the Outback or the Red Centre, but definitely of the NT."

The woman's parka was unzipped. Under the big red coat she wore a thick-knit sweater. Miranda couldn't make out the pattern, but the colors were Christmassy—a Christmas sweater. A mustard-yellow hat with ear flaps and an orange pompom pulled low, and dark wraparound sunglasses more akin to goggles than glasses, including a nose piece for keeping off the sun. A thin strip of dark skin from the goggles to the sweater's high collar was all that showed.

"Oi, yourself. I be Holly Harper. The ATSB—"

"Aye, Barty warned me. You're messing the hell out of my schedule. You were supposed to be two climatologists, a new mechanic—who I need in the worst way—and a spanking new fire pump. Be glad the ship had the gear to patch our old one or I'd toss you down an ice crack. Better yet, I'll tell my crew that you cost us a load of freshies. You won't be able to survive that lot." She hooked a gloved thumb toward the station.

"Well pardon us for living."

"Nah, that's your own problem," the woman flashed a smile. "Now you're going to want a helo. The crash is forty kilometers inland from here," she pointed toward the distant ice shelf. "It came down in a short, hard blow that's cleared off since. A ruddy mess by the photos, haven't had time to take a mosey out there myself. Got a station to run and the yearly supply ship being in and all. God, the ice team is going to string me up when you snag the helo."

"Maybe we could take one of your Hagglund snowcats?" Miranda could see a second one trundling out toward the ship along a well-marked ice road.

"They're far more precious. Besides, we don't have a path surveyed to the skiway in summer—have to wait for the winter freeze before we can do that. You drop my Hagglund into a crevasse and we'll have serious words that you won't enjoy a bit."

"That's assuming we're alive after falling into one."

"I could always hope. Maybe I *will* send you in the cat..."

Miranda could only sputter. "But didn't you say how dangerous it was to—"

"Easy, Miranda," Holly rested a hand on her arm. "You're in a bit of Australia now. She's having us on." Holly turned back to the woman and introduced the team.

"Bridgette Cane," she replied. "Bridg for short. Davis Station Manager. Let's get you settled. The helo is—"

Holly held up a hand.

The distinct thwock-thwock-thwock of a helo slipped in and out of hearing as a morning sea breeze swirled around the Basler plane they'd gathered by. It sounded as if it was reflected off the hard blue arch of sky that had replaced the storm.

Bridg looked at her watch. "Kev isn't supposed to be back for another hour. I hope nothing's gone wrong." She pulled out a radio and popped the squelch, which answered with a sharp burst of static, proving that her radio was working.

"What model is your helo?" Holly shoved back her hood and cocked her head.

Miranda looked about the breaking overcast, now showing rips of aching blue; she didn't spot it, but she didn't need to.

To the trained ear, it was more like a high-speed whisk rubbing the sides of a steel bowl than any beating rotor. The counter-rotating blades of a Kamov Ka-32S Helix were utterly distinctive.

Not a chance Australia would be flying that bird—it was Russian.

4

———————

THE BIG RUSSIAN HELICOPTER LANDED CLOSE BESIDE THE Basler that had delivered them. It stirred up a huge cloud of icy poniards as it landed, stinging Holly's face and the backs of her hands before she thought to turn away.

Once the cloud settled, it was possible to see the big bird. Most helos working in Antarctica were small because fuel was precious. Ones that could hold a few scientists, their gear, and a lot of cold-weather modifications, including extended-range tanks for operating far from rescue over the ice fields.

There was nothing small about the Helix. It had twin main rotors atop the cabin. Because of the counter-rotating main blades, it needed no tail rotor, instead sporting two large flat-panel wind vanes at the stern. The bird looked like nothing so much as a ticked-off puffer fish painted with the white-blue-red of the Russian flag.

Holly glanced around, but no one here was armed. She had a couple of weapons, but other than her knife, they were broken down and stowed in the bottom of her travel pack.

The Helix was big enough to carry a full squad and all of their gear; it would be capable of overwhelming the entire station in minutes. However, no stream of Spetsnaz operators streamed off the bird once it ceased rocking on its four skis.

Instead, a single person stepped off the Helix, and Holly could read that he was trouble from that alone. His stiff-necked strut, which no one below Russian-senior-officer grade would dare to use, didn't bode well either. In fact...

She brushed the idea aside. It was simply her paranoia from her last encounter with a Russian agent that this man might be another of the same. Besides, he didn't walk like a trained operator as Elayne Kasprak had. He moved as much like a martinet as any Pentagon lacky impressed with his own self-importance. A total mongrel.

Paranoia. It wasn't like her. She'd write this off to sleep deprivation and the hyper reactivity that her training had instilled under those conditions.

"Hello, can you be guiding me to your station manager?" His English was more British accented than Russian. He had a low voice that was smooth like a singer's—or from coaxing confessions out of purported criminals?

"Bridgette Cane," Bridg's voice was far stiffer than it had been on greeting them.

"Excellent. I'm Nikolas Romanoff, that o-f-f not o-v like the tsar. I find it helps if I make that clear at the beginning."

"Whatever you say, mate." Bridgette sounded as if she'd been as unlikely as Holly to pick up on that distinction.

A hundred years on and it continued to matter to them. Holly reminded herself that Russian history was taken personally back to when years were counted with only three digits.

"What can we do for you?"

"Where is my crash? I have word that you have found one of our planes? I have been come to secure it as property of the Russian Federation." He looked around the white ice shelf as if he expected the wreckage to emerge magically from the flat ice sheet floating on the bay like a breaching whale.

Holly glanced around at Miranda and the others. Well, if the crash was taken from their jurisdiction, then maybe she could go straight to bed. If they hurried, they could be back on Miranda's island in time for Christmas. Of course, that would mean MGM musicals, oversweet eggnog, and who knew what other horrors. Miranda might not be the most Christmassy person, but Holly would wager that Andi was already as bad an influence on Miranda as Mike would be on her—if she let him.

Yeah and, if she scooted, Barty would have her guarding a termite mound for the rest of her days for abandoning her post.

"Well, mate," Holly let her accent roll out thick. "Your pilot may have parked the bird, but he parked it on Aussie turf. So, I wouldn't go making a lot of claims to it unless you think that spending a few centuries down a handy crevasse is your idea of fun."

"You are not being of seriousness." He said it as if she was joking. When she kept her expression bland, his smile slowly faded.

"Good, glad we got that squared away," Holly turned her back on him. "Bridg, we've had a bushman's brekkie. Got a fix for that?"

"The Basler pilots must've been properly annoyed with you to not offer anything. Sure, head up to the station. Dark green building, first on the left. I have a ship to deal with." And she waved at the next passing Hagglund trundling empty out to sea. It was a cubicle vehicle in two parts, head and caboose, which looked like a snowcat with its nose bashed in. Their big tracks made them look undersized, but the Swedish Army had known what it was doing when it designed them—they were dog tough.

It slowed enough for Bridgette to jump onto a running board and hold on for the ride out to the icebreaker.

Ashore, half a kilometer across the ice, the buildings were color-coded. Green, blue, yellow, red...that told her more about the winter environment than she wanted to know. In winter, they'd be the only colors other than ice-and-snow white. In summer there was the added glory of bare gray rock and a black sand beach.

"Join us," Holly told the Russian. "Maybe over breakfast you can sweet talk me out of finding a handy seal's air hole to slide you down, *tovarisch*."

He rose on his toes as if ready to attack but must have thought better of it. In this day and age, she'd insinuated he was the worst kind of party hack. Only the military used the word without irony. His smile remained in place but his cheeks suffused with red hot anger to replace the pink of cold. Good. Angry people made mistakes.

To cover his annoyance, he offered a mock bow for her to lead the way. Then he turned to the waiting Russian pilots and spat out a quick command. Despite the clue she'd given him, he was self-centered enough to assume she didn't speak Russian, which again pointed to bureaucrat and not soldier.

"*Stay here! No one, and I mean no one, goes to the crash without me,*" he instructed the pilots.

Old Romanoff's politeness didn't even run skin deep,

though his smile was back in place by the time he turned from the helo. "I was telling them that I would bring them breakfast, but to keep the helicopter ready."

"Good onya."

Miranda opened her mouth as she also spoke fluent Russian but stopped herself at Holly's headshake. She was getting better about not adhering to the perfect truth in every situation.

5

AFTER LOCKING THEIR GEAR IN A SERVICE SHED RESTING ON the ice—not a chance was she going to trust the Russians with it—Holly shifted to walk beside Miranda to explain. It was physically impossible for her to hold her tongue for long without a reason.

Mike and Andi picked up the cues to walk to either side of the Russian and ask him questions about the Ka-32S helo —S was the snow-and-ice variant—that he'd never be able to answer.

"He's up to something, Miranda," Holly kept her voice quieter than the scrape and scuff of their boots over the ice. "To lie about something so simple as what he told the pilots, it's best if we pretend we don't speak Russian until we can learn what he's about."

"Okay." Miranda seemed content with that. "I've been considering timelines. We were remarkably efficient in our traverse from Spieden Island to this location. While he most likely departed from Moscow, which is nineteen percent closer than Spieden Island, to arrive at the same time we did means that he was also logistically efficient."

Holly should rub her face in the snow to wake up but they walked on solid ice swept clean by the wind. It's the first thing she should have thought of. "Perhaps he launched when their aircraft was reported late."

Miranda nodded uncertainly as a Hagglund ground by, dragging a heavily loaded sled.

Holly had never thought about Antarctica much. She'd always figured it would be quiet and dark, with the Aurora firing off overhead.

But the temperature was not fifty or a hundred below zero, on anyone's scale. The sun was actually warm on her face.

And the place was noisy. Everyone was hustling about on the ice, and machinery was humming along everywhere. Pumps were refueling the Basler from a long hose that reached all of the way back to the station. A far longer hose ran the couple of kilometers from the ship to the station, refilling the big storage tanks with a million liters of fuel to see them through the next year. The Basler's few hundred would barely be missed.

A bristle-brush street sweeper was running up and down the runway, shooshing a cloud of ice chips to the side. She could hear the thrum of the icebreaker's engines surfing over the ice.

Once the cat had passed landward and a treaded tractor had gone the other way towing a trailer piled high with blocks of used cardboard bound up for recycling, Miranda spoke again. The roar of their engines said they were hustling hard.

"And how many people were informed of the location of the crash?"

Holly knew that nobody on the flight down had heard a thing, not even the Basler pilots who'd brought them over from Casey Station.

Barty would have told Bridgette to keep it under wraps as well. But it was an easy guess that everyone here at Davis Station knew, there would be no secrets in so small a community. At the peak of summer, the staff rose from winter's twenty to a hundred. But news wouldn't move fast between stations.

Miranda continued, "I'll be interested to see if the wreck has an emergency beacon for the Russian COSPAS satellite-tracking system. Over the last decade they have been removing them."

"They have?" How had Holly missed that?

"Yes. The number of crashes picked up by the international COSPAS-SARSAT satellite system was providing detailed information about the severe aging and unreliability of the Russian Air Force, so the government began removing the emergency transmitters."

"Which makes it stupid hard to locate a crash."

"Yes," Miranda agreed. "But with the equipment removed, each incident is *not* automatically reported to the West. We need to call and see if a signal was reported by our system."

Holly dug out her cell phone, then snorted in surprise when she saw she had full bars. Twisting around, she spotted the cell tower atop the tall radio mast. She nodded a thanks to whoever their comm tech was and dialed Barty.

"You there yet?" His voice crackled with the slice-and-dice of a marginal connection. "The cell tower must link through a satellite connection for its next stage. Well, at least they *had* the connection, worth the nod.

"Good morning to you too, mate. Getting brekkie. We've got uninvited company."

Barty grunted at that.

"We're wondering if their bird sent up a squawk?"

"Not a peep on the search-and-rescue satellite system. No radio that we intercepted. If it hadn't splattered at Whoop Whoop, we wouldn't know about it either."

"Whoop Whoop?" *Dingo-woop-woop* meant hell-and-gone past everything.

"Formally the Davis Plateau Skiway. The frozen-sea iceway you must have come in on is only good for spring and early summer. It will be breaking up soon or they wouldn't have sent the annual supply ship in. The nearest stable landing strip stays far colder year-round, it's forty kilometers away—five hundred meters high, up on the ice sheet. Much chillier. That's where you're headed."

Holly stared at the thin white horizon. "I utterly despise you, mate," and hung up on him.

6

"HAVE YOU EVER BEEN HERE BEFORE?" ANDI'S QUESTION surprised Miranda as they walked across the ice toward the station. She kept forgetting how new Andi was to the team and in her life. Andi didn't know everything about her—or she about Andi. Instead of being disconcerting to her autistic need for the familiar, there was an added interest of discovering more about each other.

"No, though I've certainly read every crash report. The agglomeration of which prove that Antarctica is an incredibly hazardous place to operate aircraft. The crash and burning of an LC-130 Hercules in 1987, while attempting to supply a remote camp. The camp was there to rebuild an LC-130 that had crashed in 1971, making it perhaps the most ironic crash on the continent. Though the fact that the freezing cold had so well preserved the older plane for sixteen years is of significant note. The air here is sufficiently dry that it proves as effective as the Arizona desert for preserving equipment."

"I suppose that's useful."

"In that particular case, perhaps it would have been better if the older craft had been unrecoverable. It was also interesting that most Antarctic transport is driven by smaller aircraft like the Basler BT-67, the DC-3 that it was derived from, and DHC-6 Twin Otters. This is evidenced by the lower percentage of them that appear in accident reports."

"How dangerous is this place? Maybe we should be hiking to the crash site."

Miranda looked at Andi.

Before she could speak to remind her of the forty-kilometer distance and the crevasses, Andi put a hand on her arm. "I'm joking. I'll take a helo any day. And I never have flown in a Kamov Helix. That'll be a first if we go that way. I'd love to talk to the pilots."

Miranda looked around, then lowered her voice though no one else was near them. "Don't let them know you speak Russian."

"I don't. So that's easy. Mandarin or Cantonese? Then I'm your girl."

And there was her hypothesis proved: there remained things to learn about Andi, too.

They reached the lumpy transition where ice met black sand. The heavy machinery had crushed the ice against the beach, which made it uncertain afoot. The pieces ground together awkwardly, offering sharp complaints that popped like muted gunfire. Yet it was hard to imagine that ice thick enough to stop an icebreaker, and safely land a ten-ton plane on, would be melted out in a matter of weeks.

If the San Juans ever froze that deep...well, it was strange enough when a puddle froze over on her island, never mind miles of sea ice.

Recognizing that her thoughts were going astray, she refocused on the air-crash incident history of the continent.

"However, the crash that was seminal to Antarctic flight safety has to be the New Zealand Air tourist flight of 1979. Two hundred and fifty-seven people died when a DC-10 flew straight into the side of the twelve-thousand-foot Mt. Erebus volcano at fifteen hundred feet. It was merciful that their deaths were instantaneous."

Andi shuddered strongly enough to shake her Big Red coat.

"My parents were most likely conscious for the eighty-three to ninety-seven seconds of the fall to their deaths during the crash of TWA 800. Instantaneous is, by comparison, a kindness I would think."

"Uh, right. I never had to think of it that way."

"Now you have," she was glad she was able to offer new experiences to Andi as well. "Until the New Zealand Air crash, no one had truly understood the aviation hazard of a sector whiteout. High clouds, the ice of the mountain, and that of the Ross Ice Shelf behind it—all scattered the low sunlight. It made the landscape utterly shadowless. Bad navigation information had been provided to the flight crew as well. The confusion of the settings routed them directly into the gigantic mountain temporarily rendered invisible by the sector whiteout. By the time the automatic ground proximity warnings of that era blared out, it was far too late."

"I'd rather be in a helicopter any day," Andi shuddered again.

Miranda decided that perhaps telling her about that category of crashes would *not* be comforting. Several helo pilots had died here as well, including one who had landed safely, stepped out of his craft, and plunged down a hundred-foot-deep crevasse. He was ultimately rescued but died of hypothermia shortly afterward as he hadn't been heavily dressed when he fell.

The Ilyushin-76 would be an interesting challenge. The station manager had stated it occurred during a *short, hard blow.* She hoped there was more accurate information available, as that was a decidedly general term at best. But she didn't like to get ahead of herself

To distract herself she studied the base as they climbed the long drive that reached from the beach to the station placed ten meters above sea level.

The tallest structure was a black radome that dominated this end of the camp. She knew that the sphere enclosed a large radio communications antenna. Inside the dome, it would be aimed a few degrees above horizontal to direct it at a geosynchronous satellite circling high above the equator. The ten major buildings were two-story rectangular structures all oriented the same way but not laid out on a grid. They had their short ends aligned like resting seagulls in a wind.

It seemed counterintuitive when she turned to look behind her. They neither faced the sea or the land directly. They were skewed at a curious angle that...ah.

"Look at the dirt," she told Andi who was walking beside her.

"It's black."

It was, but Miranda didn't understand how that was relevant. "Notice how it fills in around the back of boulders."

Andi scanned about and then turned unerringly to look southeast toward the continent. Davis Station perched on a peninsula on the eastern edge of a wide bay but every building was oriented to present its short face to the head of the vast bay. "The wind."

Miranda nodded. "The katabatic winds coming down off the high plateau of the Antarctic Ice Sheet, literally a flow of cold, heavy air falling off the high plateau, must be so severe that they oriented their buildings to offer the least resistance."

"*And* the best wind scouring. I'll bet that in the winter it sweeps the snow from between the buildings like magic."

"Yes," Miranda always appreciated Andi's insights. She saw the next steps so clearly. She didn't initiate lines of inquiry often but, once identified, she could follow them far more swiftly than anyone else on the team.

They'd come to a stop halfway up the long slope of the beach.

"Are those..." Andi's voice trailed off.

Miranda noted the direction of her gaze. "Adélie penguins." The thigh-high birds were scattered along the rocky beachfront, though none were near the busy road. They were poking along the shore doing penguin things, she supposed.

She could see that Andi wished to investigate, walk among the small birds, but it was one thing too many.

They were in Antarctica, which was alarmingly new.

The input of cold, no flora of any kind beyond a few mosses and lichens, the station, the icebreaker, the sharp stench of penguin guano and fish guts on the chill air, being on a new continent, legally standing in Australia though she was technically due south of India and roughly equidistant from Africa and Australia—and of course the plane crash. It was too much. She couldn't manage to also think about penguins.

She continued toward the station in the wake of Mike and Holly who were distracting the Russian. Andi soon followed.

Food. Transport. Crash.

That was the proper order of business.

The fact that it was a crash of a plane type she'd never investigated before was both a plus and a minus. It would be interesting to study an example of Soviet engineering, yet she'd never before studied that *in person*. What extrapolations would she have to make from known experience to the unknown that she'd never encountered before?

The crash of a Boeing 737 shared many fundamental similarities with the crash of a 747 despite the difference of scale—a commonality of manufacturer's design. A distinctly different yet similar aircraft like an Airbus A330 had a European elegance compared to an American hardiness, but was not notably different at its core.

Military aircraft only *seemed* to vary widely. Whether built by Boeing, McDonnell Douglas, Bell, Sikorsky, Lockheed Martin, or any of the others, there was a common stamp of the American military complex.

How different was a Soviet aircraft? What unique methods of construction would she encounter?

Or, like the Chinese Chengdu J-20 Mighty Dragon, was the Ilyushin-76 based on stolen American plans? The J-20 was almost a direct copy of the F-22 Raptor and the J-31 of the F-35 Lightning II. Had the Il-76 been copied from the C-17 Globemaster III?

That was a comforting thought as they went through the double portal that trapped the heat inside and the cold outside. They peeled out of their cold-weather gear and hung it along the hallway.

The smell of food on the warm air guided them to a large dining hall that was mostly empty except for a few bleary-eyed people who looked as if they'd worked through the night. Except there was no night right now.

"What's this? More stragglers?" The chef called out when he spotted them. "Bad enough having to serve this lot—who worked the swing shift unloading the boat—keeps us busy twenty-four hours a day for as long as it's here. You folks from the crash team they've been squawking about so fierce?"

"Aye, that be us." Miranda did her best to sound like Holly, which earned her surprised looks from the rest of the team. Maybe she'd simply keep her mouth shut in the future.

"Ah well, what's to be is to be. You'll take what I feed ya and like it too."

"Yes sir."

"Dan's the name. Been cooking for these folks onto five seasons. Know egg-xactly what folks new to The Ice need. A taste of home." He poured most of a pitcher of whipped eggs onto a big griddle. After chasing the edges together a couple times with big spatulas that he used like an extension of his arms, he tossed on a fistful of smoked salmon and another of dried chives until it was more buff and green than yellow. He set five plates on the warmer and waved a hand toward a large coffee urn. "Load yourselves up. Be done here quicker'n you can dance on a dime."

As the others were filling their mugs with coffee, she turned to inspect the room. Though it was the height of summer, Christmas decorations abounded.

Construction paper chains, intricately cut snowflakes taped to the big windows, twinkle lights, and other cheerful paraphernalia decorated the space. A banner had been hung that said, *Christmas at "The Ice" Beach.*

She'd traveled south of the equator only a few times and never at Christmastime. At least there was snow and cold. Christmas at the beach was a disorienting concept. It reminded her that, on Spieden Island, one of the tasks she'd planned to be done as a group activity had been decorating the house.

Should she have done it herself before their arrival? She'd been tempted, but been worried that if they spent the whole week there, she'd run out of things for people to do. So, not wanting her guests to become bored, she hadn't. But what if she was still here in Antarctica when Christmas arrived? Then would the house ever be decorated? It should be each year. It was one of the few disruptions of routine to the house that her younger, less-tolerant autistic self had always looked forward to.

Worrying wasn't going to change anything. She pulled out her notebook.

"What are you noting down?" Andi asked as she dumped hot chocolate packets into two mugs and filled them with boiling water from another urn.

"Reorganizing." She moved *Decorate House* up to the B-list of possible activities ahead of, no, after baking pumpkin pies—decorating could be done while the pies were cooling. She'd already completed the A-list before anyone's arrival, including: wrap presents, fresh sheets and towels in the guest bedroom, and the like.

Andi read over her shoulder, then leaned in to kiss her quickly. She kept doing things like that for unexplained reasons, but Miranda had never found cause to complain. She put away her notebook and thanked Andi for filling her mug.

True to Cook Dan's word, by the time they returned to the line, he'd folded together the massive omelet, slashed it in to five pieces with his spatula, then added sausage patties she hadn't noticed grilling, and a big hunk of fresh sourdough bread.

"That'll help ya grow."

"I seem to have passed by that option years ago," Miranda patted the top of her head.

He guffawed. "Have to see what we can do about that. Strange things happen out here on The Ice."

Miranda didn't see how that was possible. Besides, she was rather used to being five-four and her wardrobe had been chosen with that in mind. When she saw that the others were taking their plates away, she selected her own and thanked the chef.

The big table down the center of the bright dining room could easily seat twenty. The vinyl plank flooring was in a light pine and the large windows had a good view of the sea in the fine weather. Mr. Romanoff was sitting in a reading corner filled with a cluster of armchairs. He had a coffee mug and no plate.

"I already have eaten good Russian breakfast."

Holly selected a chair that put her back to the window.

7

"WELL, MR. NOT-THE-TSAR, ANYTHING SPECIAL ABOUT THE bird we're going to look at?" Holly then put a big piece of omelette on her slice of bread and took a huge bite.

Miranda didn't like mixing her foods like that and approached her own with more care. The butter was good on the bread. Then she set that aside, sipped her hot chocolate, and swallowed before cutting off a piece of the omelette. How could Holly possibly focus on each taste and texture, eating it all clumped together like that? Did it create a uniquely textural combination? Miranda inspected her own plate again but decided against changing what already worked.

"Yes," Nikolas Romanoff said heavily. "It is the property of the Russian Federation and I deny your right to—"

"Yada. Yada. Yada. If you can't be more useful than that, we'll kidnap your helicopter and leave you here to be all broody and Russian."

"Try that and you will be shot by my pilots."

Holly laughed aloud, added a sausage patty to the top of

her bread and omelette, took another large bite, then spoke around it without mangling a single word. "You think they could stop me. Oh, that's so naive of you." Then she swallowed and her tone and face became absolutely serious.

Miranda slid out her personal notebook and flipped to the emoji page Mike had given her. She'd long since memorized it, but she liked the confirmation that Holly's expression was now dangerously threatening.

"You do *not* want to fuck with me, *tovarisch*. We clear?"

"Nor you with me."

She wondered if Nikolas Romanoff was aware that his expression was a better match for *worried* than *threatening*.

They continued sparring through breakfast, much to Holly's apparent pleasure and the Russian's unease.

"How many planes have you lost this month, *comrade?*"

And before Romanoff could form a proper denial, she would attack again.

"And I'm not talking about the scores, or is it hundreds now, that you lost in your idiotic *Special Military Operation* in Eastern Europe. How many have simply fallen out of the sky already this year?"

"We lose no—"

"An Ilyushin-76 cost fifty-million US. Three billion rubles! That's gotta hurt."

He never finished his coffee or managed to deflect one of Holly's attacks for more than a few seconds. Miranda finally decided that it wasn't because he had nothing to say but rather that Holly never eased up long enough for him to get a word in.

By the time they were once more outside and trooping back down to the helicopter, he was as tongue-tied as Miranda frequently became.

It was Andi who had remembered to ask for breakfast for the two pilots. And they were thankful when she delivered the pair of egg-sausage sandwiches. They didn't mind that all of the foods were together in one.

In the time they'd eaten, the Basler plane had departed back the way it had come. The icebreaker hadn't moved though. For the moment only the Russian Helix sat on the near ice.

Bridgette the station manager hopped off a tractor that continued toward the station. She handed a radio to Miranda, who passed it off to Andi. They always made her uncomfortable when speaking to someone she hadn't met. The current paradigm that you had *met* after an e-mail, a text message, or a phone or radio conversation revealed an awkward inability of modern language to keep up with the times. The Merriam-Webster dictionary was quite clear on this—*To meet: to come into the presence of for the first time*—and therefore radio contact with strangers risked awkward conversational pitfalls she preferred to avoid.

"I'm guessing the Russians will be giving you a lift," Bridgette continued, "but I told Kev to be on the listen for you if they abandon you somewhere. He's got our AS350 Squirrel helo and will be working ship-to-shore the rest of the day." Sure enough, a bright-orange helicopter separated from the icebreaker with a large sling load dangling underneath. It swooped low overhead, far quieter than the big twin-engines of the Helix. Of course the Helix could lift five tons to the Squirrel's twelve-hundred pounds.

The Squirrel continued to the camp, where it eased down the sling close by the building they'd eaten in. Food supplies. Of course they'd get priority carriage from the ship's freezers to the station's.

When it lifted aloft once more, there was a strange tone to it. She was about to suggest that they needed to service the helo immediately as it definitely didn't sound right, when the noise separated into two source directions.

She turned to scan the horizon.

The Russian Helix helicopter had approached earlier from the southeast, the direction of their Progress Station. Now a plane was coming from that same direction.

Holly followed the direction of her gaze and then slid into action.

"What is this, Romanoff? Did you call for troops?" Holly had a knife up against his throat in one of those moves that Miranda could never follow.

The Helix's pilots, who'd been eating breakfast while sitting on the edge of the cargo bay in the open side door, twisted to reach into the shadows of the cargo bay behind them.

Andi had a sidearm aimed at the pilot's face before he could set down his sandwich. "Keep eating. Slowly. You know that it's bad to eat your food too quickly." Her voice was pleasant but her gun didn't waver for an instant.

"*Nyet*. I did no such thing. It is me coming here. Only me." Romanoff spoke quickly.

Bridgette was the last to react with a quick, "What the hell, mate?"

Miranda unzipped her parka enough to select a high-power monocular from her crash-site investigation vest. The black dot on the horizon resolved into, "It's a Basler BT-67, but painted red above and white below."

"Chinese," Romanoff spoke in a high thin voice. "They call it a Snow Eagle 601. They must come from Zhongshan Station. It is but a few kilometers from Progress."

"If you're so close, why didn't they tagalong with you?" Holly slid her knife back into its wrist sheath and yanked Romanoff's parka closed over his throat, which might be her form of an apology.

"We tell no one. It is our plane that is missing and our business alone."

"Until it crashed on Australian turf. But why is everyone so interested?"

Miranda was the only one facing Romanoff as Holly asked this, everyone else was facing the approaching plane. Many expressions crossed his features faster than she could catalog them. The way he looked from one person to the next reminded her of when one of the island's deer had slipped into her fenced vegetable garden after she'd accidentally left the gate open.

She hadn't spotted it until it had eaten its way well down a line of spinach plants. When she'd shouted *Hey!* it had looked at her in surprise. Then the deer searched all around as if helping her find whoever had eaten half her spinach crop, while its teeth continued to quietly grind up the most recent mouthful. She'd been laughing by the time she'd managed to shoo it out. The deer gave her a look as if she was being unfair.

Romanoff's wandering attention had fixed on her and she looked away quickly. Human faces were far more uncomfortable to look at than a deer's. But his last look had included the narrowed eyes, grimly straight mouth, and furrowed brow of the *suspicion* emoji.

She joined the others in watching the Chinese plane circle and come in for a landing. During breakfast, the Australian Basler had departed to return to Casey, so the airfield was no more than a stretch of ice, a tool shed, and the eight people clustered around the helicopter.

The Hagglunds and helo were all out at the icebreaker and their sounds were drowned out by the steady roar of the Chinese Basler's five-bladed Hartzell propellers. It lined up on the runway marked by a line of empty steel fuel drums, blackened from the rare times they'd had to have fires lit in them for nighttime operations. The pilot was good and settled neatly on the front wheels, keeping the snow skis retracted on the hard ice runway, letting the speed drop before lowering the tail. The small rear wheel contacted the surface.

They taxied over and shut down close by the group at the helicopter.

8

It was only then that Miranda noticed Holly was missing from their group.

Miranda finally spotted her as she climbed into the Helix helicopter's cargo bay from the far side behind the pilots. Moving in the shadows, she'd acquired a pair of AK-47 rifles and had squatted to watch and wait. The Russian pilots didn't notice her in the cargo bay, armed with their own weapons.

Holly was focused on the Chinese Basler, which had been clearly painted in English characters *CHINARE* for the China Arctic and Antarctic Administration. Once its engine cycled down, the rear stairs folded out and a lone individual descended.

Miranda could see no other heads in the windows down the side of the plane except for the pilots in the cockpit.

Miranda checked on Holly, who quietly set the AK-47s down on the deck before she slipped out the far side of the cargo bay with no one the wiser. She circled around the tail of the Helix helicopter and came up on the lone figure from behind.

"Greetings. I have come to offer the People's Republic of China's assistance in the loss of an aircraft." The woman was several inches taller than herself or Andi and spoke unaccented English. Her hood was back, revealing her Asian features and her black hair cut in a neat bob.

"Fly back where you came from," Romanoff spoke quickly. "You are not wanted here either. And take away these Americans and Australians with you. It is Russian plane. Ours. No one else."

Miranda had attempted to correlate rapidity of speech with emotion but had minimal luck with that avenue of research. Excitement, fear, and anger all prompted faster delivery. Perhaps it was the intensity of the emotion that altered the speed of speech? But that didn't work either. She'd observed that when Holly was most dangerous was when she spoke slowly. Miranda pulled out her personal notebook and crossed out the pages of data she'd collected on this hypothesis, then made a note at the bottom: *Insufficient consistency to postulate reliable correlations.*

"Well, it's a regular bash here, isn't it? Should I fire up the barbie and break out a slab of tinnys?" Bridgette looked from the fast-spoken Russian to the Chinese woman who showed no signs of going back to where she'd come from. "We've already got the Americans and Russians. I should have sent invitations. France and Italy are only a quick fifteen hundred kilometers away. Oh, and what about the Japanese? No ride-sharing though as they're fifteen hundred in the opposite direction. Even under the normal Antarctic cooperation this is quite the gathering."

"The Americans?" The Chinese woman turned to look

at Miranda, Andi, and Mike. She hadn't spotted Holly standing close behind her. But then she noticed where Miranda was looking and turned to look over her shoulder.

Holly rolled her eyes and Miranda mouthed a *Sorry*.

"A plane crash. And four Americans," she turned away from Holly as if she was no threat. "Does that make you Miranda Chase?"

Several things happened at once. Mike shifted to stand partly in front of Miranda. Andi, who had earlier pocketed her sidearm, withdrew it once more. Holly's knife reappeared in her hand.

"Technically, no. I've always been Miranda Chase. I wasn't made so at this moment."

"Ah, a real pleasure. I have heard so much about you. It was you who finally, ah, *incapacitated* my husband, Zhang Ru. I am Wang Daiyu. I am deeply in your debt." She offered a deep bow of respect.

"I didn't do that. Andi did," Miranda rested a hand on Andi's sleeve.

"You are married to...*that?*" Andi's tone was purest disgust.

Daiyu bowed deeply to Andi as well. "I *was* married to that. He suffered a further, shall we say, accident after his encounter with you and did not survive. The marriage was a purely tactical choice as we needed someone embedded in his household and I was best positioned at the time. It was only for a year but it is not an experience I would care to repeat."

"He was a very bad man," Miranda had said so before. While she didn't like to repeat herself, it felt appropriate under the circumstances. He had sabotaged numerous aircraft and killed numerous people in his climb to power within China's Central Military Commission.

"He was," Daiyu agreed. "The world is a safer place without him in it. I was told that there was a significant crash here at Davis, an assessment reinforced by your presence, yet I don't see an aircraft."

"It's at Whoop Whoop," Holly had moved up so close behind the woman before speaking that Daiyu should have jumped—Miranda would have—but she didn't.

"Ah, the skiway," and she turned unerringly to look up at the plateau. "Are we waiting for something before proceeding?"

Andi indicated the Helix pilots who hadn't finished their breakfast as they'd watched the goings on.

"No! No! No!" Romanoff protested. "Russians only. It is our plane and only we may—"

Mike rested a hand on his shoulder. "Romanoff, old buddy. You should have listened more carefully when Holly was warning you. This is an Australian crash investigation, which we were called in to investigate. You are our guest. Don't become confused on that point or my lovely Holly will remind you in ways that you'll find to be exceedingly unpleasant."

Romanoff yelled at the pilots in Russian, "*Strelyat'! Shoot them! Now!*"

Several things happened at once.

The pilots grabbed the AK-47s that Holly had set back on the cargo deck earlier.

Bridgette the station manager dropped to the ice.

Mike pulled Romanoff backward a stumbling step so that the man was directly between the two pilots on one side with Mike and herself on the other.

Andi and Daiyu both pulled out handguns and aimed them at Romanoff's head.

Everyone froze and was so silent that Bridgette shifting to look up from where she sprawled was the loudest noise.

Holly strolled up to Romanoff, completely ignoring the pair of rifles tracking her every step.

"You are not a smart man, *comrade*. There is only one person in charge here and it isn't you or me. It's her," Holly nodded toward Miranda.

Miranda smiled back. She'd forgotten that in the flurry of harsh words and emotions that had been going on since the moment they'd landed. She also noted that Holly had been speaking very slowly.

Holly returned the smile before facing Romanoff once more. "You might want to remember that, *comrade*." Then she reached into the pocket of her big parka and pulled out two curved AK-47 magazines.

Miranda looked at the pilots. In the momentary fray, neither had noticed there were no magazines in their rifles.

Holly tapped them lightly on Romanoff's chest, then offered a hand to help Bridgette back to her feet. She handed over the two magazines. "Next time your find a nice hole in the ice, feel free to drop these in it."

"With pleasure," Bridgette took them and walked away— she didn't look very steady on her feet to Miranda.

Mike patted Romanoff's shoulder again as if nothing had happened. "I did mention that you were *our* guest, didn't I, Romanoff?"

Wang Daiyu and Andi were the last ones to lower and pocket their weapons.

The pilots put away their empty rifles and began preflighting the helo. Holly waved the rest of them aboard as if she was the hostess before she and Mike trotted over to the storage shed to retrieve their packs.

After speaking with Bridgette, Daiyu told her own plane's pilots that they could wait in the station. Then she climbed aboard the Russian helicopter as if it was the most normal event of the day.

9

MIRANDA WASN'T SURE WHAT SHE EXPECTED AS SHE WATCHED out the window of the Helix helicopter as it climbed from Davis Station up to the Whoop Whoop Skiway, but it wasn't what she saw.

The first twenty kilometers they passed above were rugged rocky terrain. The bedrock of Antarctica hadn't been scraped smooth by millions of years of ice, instead it looked as if it had been broken. It was mostly devoid of snow or ice. The patches of white were few and scattered at this time of the summer. There were also several lakes—some frozen over, some not.

When they reached the edge of the ice sheet, it was as abrupt as a slap. A wall of jumbled white, the shattered leading edge, climbed five hundred meters in the space of ten kilometers. The top of the ice sheet wasn't a smooth surface either. It was an undulating plain of stark white that climbed forever, empty, into the distance.

She knew this wasn't true. Fourteen hundred kilometers away lay the Russian Vostok Station at an altitude of thirty-five hundred meters, above eleven thousand feet.

And it was all ice.

Often dubbed The Pole of Cold, it was the consistently coldest place on Earth. The ice there was thicker than most mountains. The land itself was thousands of feet below sea level, covered with miles-thick ice.

She felt a shiver from thinking about it. If Antarctica and Greenland melted, practically nothing of her island home would remain except for her house. The lower two hundred and thirty feet would disappear below the waters of Puget Sound. The runway would be too short to land her planes. Also, the island would no longer be able to support all of the animals that now lived there. That would be very sad.

The Davis Plateau Skiway was marked by three small sheds, in colors as bright as the station buildings they'd left behind. The compacted and groomed skiway itself was nearly invisible, a white line that looked little different from the rest of the ice plateau. It was a shade closer to pure white than the blue-white of the surrounding ice and snow. If not for dark markers along each side of the runway, she might not have seen it at all.

The east-west surface of the runway was bisected by an intermittent white line running roughly southeast to northwest. It looked as if someone had skipped a giant stone over the surface, creating shadowed divots in the snow. Then the perspective shifted. Something large *had* been bounced several times across the surface—a Russian cargo jet.

Beyond the skiway, the intermittent line continued. The helicopter followed the line of dots and dashes—for some were short and others much longer—in the snow for well over a kilometer.

To memorize the pattern, she translated it into Morse Code. She was disappointed when all she was able to spell was THA—*dah dit-dit-dit-dit dit-dah*—a big hit before the runway, four small skips on the far side, then a slight bounce and a final *dah* slam down.

THA? Thai Airways short code. An unlikely code to be spelled by a Russian aircraft.

Based on momentum, it should end with a much longer drawn-out final *dah* as the plane skidded to a stop—and then the wreck itself.

But that final *dah* was almost short enough to be considered a *dit*.

The final mark was framed by a single wing and the tail section.

But there was no fuselage or second wing. It was only when the helo had flown over the final truncated *dah* that she saw what had happened to it. The fuselage, after shedding a wing and its tail, had tumbled into a crevasse two kilometers from the skiway.

She saw the Helix helicopter was settling in to land.

"No! No! Do not land!"

The pilots fed in heavy power and she could see the ice and snow blast against the plane's wing and tail until it had created a whiteout. The helicopter slowly heaved aloft.

"Why do you say not to land?" Romanoff shouted at her.

"What if we landed in another crevasse, a hidden one?"

He turned pale white, then ordered the pilots to turn back to the skiway and land by the sheds.

It was only as they were landing that Miranda realized she'd shouted her warning in Russian. So much for Holly's secret. She hoped Holly wouldn't be too angry about that.

10

"OI! WHO ARE YOU LOT?"

Holly grinned and looked eager for a replay of this morning at Davis Station.

Miranda didn't have time for any of that, not with the crash in sight. She stepped forward to address the man and woman who had come out of one of the huts.

"My name is Miranda Chase. I'm the Investigator-in-Charge for the NTSB. I'm here to investigate the crash."

"Arriving in a Russian helicopter, with a," the man inspected the emblem on Wang Daiyu's jacket, "Chinese observer?"

"Yes. This is Wang Daiyu. The Russian is Nikolas Romanoff."

She spotted him opening his mouth.

"That's Romanoff like off, not o-v like the czar," she said quickly to stop him from diverting their attention.

The look that the Australian exchanged with the woman reminded her of Holly preparing for one of her *humorous* attacks.

Miranda continued her...preemptive strike, barely pausing long enough to acknowledge the metaphor, albeit strictly internally, as highly appropriate.

"First, do you have weather data from before and during the crash? Second, I need a safe passage surveyed to each element of the wreckage."

"Marla here has the weather data."

Her tactic had worked. She'd have to remember the power of a preemptive strike. She waved for Holly to accompany Marla to fetch the information, then addressed the man, "Have you mapped a safe route to the crash yet?"

"Aye. It came down quiet, no engine noise, at least not that we heard above the storm. Spotted that broken-off tail section the next morning, and the wing, with no plane attached. Went out there on a snowmobile with ground-penetrating radar to make sure the path was safe."

"And around to the initial impact point?"

"Aye. If you stay inside the loop of snowmobile tracks we made, you should be safe as houses."

"How safe are houses in Antarctica? I have no knowledge of such specifics."

The man looked at her a bit strangely. "Well, a normal house wouldn't survive a single real storm here. Last night was a baby one, barely crossing sixty knots, summer blizzard. That might strain your council houses more than they'd like."

"I would therefore prefer to be safer than houses."

He shook his head as if trying to clear it. "Stay inside the snowmobile tracks. The only crevasse we found is the one the plane fell into. Never had any reason to test the ice sheet so far outside the skiway before. We'll get ropes and ice gear out to you as quick as we can. You'll need them to go after the fuselage. We did go down ourselves...well, I did. Better at climbing than Marla. No survivors. I left them in place because, well, shit man. Besides, there's only the two of us up here prepping the skiway for when the ice runway by the station melts out. No way to retrieve anyone safely with naught but two people."

"Mike, find out what they saw and heard." Then she stopped thinking about them and turned to walk up the skiway. Romanoff and Daiyu fell in behind her and Andi.

When Romanoff asked why they were walking rather than commandeering the few snow machines, she simply ignored him. She knew it was impolite, but he didn't appear to be content unless he was complaining about something.

Daiyu asked Andi for the specifics of how she'd taken down Zhang Ru. Miranda had witnessed the event, so she stopped listening and focused on the skiway. The surface was surprisingly hard and impressively even.

A Twin Otter aircraft was agile enough that it or a helicopter had probably landed first on the ungroomed surface. Then a pair of snowmobiles running over the surface to lightly compact it, and dragging a chain between them would form the initial surface so that the larger Basler BT-67 aircraft could come in. Whoop Whoop had been improved beyond that. She could see the signs that this skiway had been compacted with heavy rollers and scraped smooth by plows. A big LC-130H Skibird could safely land on this surface if needed.

When she reached the point where the crashing plane had crossed the skiway, she saw that there was another *dit* in the middle of the hard-packed surface.

Did that make it TEHA—*dah dit dit-dit-dit-dit dit-dah*? Or perhaps NHA—*dah-dit dit-dit-dit-dit dit-dah*? There was no consistent pause to determine proper character grouping. She presumed that the Naval Helicopter Association had more relevance than the nonsense sequence of TEHA.

"Andi, have you joined the NHA? You are a military rotorcraft pilot."

"Um, no, why do you ask?"

"Their initials are spelled out here in the snow."

"They're...what?"

"Well, the snow *and* ice. I'll show you." She turned to the right.

"Ms. Chase, the crash is in the other direction," Romanoff pointed across the runway to where the tail section and one of the wings lay on the snow's surface. Nothing else was visible.

"No, it started over here." She found the snowmobile track the Australian people had made and followed it to the far point of the first impact, the lone mark on this side of the skiway.

Turning on the GPS feed on her tablet computer, Miranda walked the perimeter of the first long *dah*. "Andi, could you take packing density measurements of the undisturbed area and at the center of the deformed area?"

Holly or Mike would have asked how. If Jeremy was still on her team, he would have pulled out a snow saw, shovel, and Rutschblock line from his huge field pack, then spent hours excavating and testing each section with deep-dug holes and quantified measurements.

She was about to tell Andi that she didn't need that level of detail.

Before she could, Andi slipped a foldable ski pole out of her pack, removed the basket, and placed it point-down on the snow. She cupped her hands over the top and pushed down until she hung on it with all of her weight. She measured and recorded how much of the pole had sunk into the surface. Then she moved to the center of the big divot compacted by the airplane's hull and repeated the test. Her ski pole probe sank mere inches. Again she measured it.

It was a fast and elegant solution. Relative density could be obtained immediately. Once they calibrated Andi's weight and the penetrability of the ski pole, more than sufficient accuracy could be obtained.

Back on the skiway, Romanoff and Daiyu had waited and watched them without speaking. In fact, they were standing far enough apart that it would be difficult to converse without raised voices. A steady wind of, she pulled out a handheld anemometer, seventeen knots (thirty-one kmph) headed for the ocean, blowing off the heights of the ice plateau that blanketed most of the continent. She noted that the temperature was eleven degrees colder than down at Davis Station, before any wind chill factor.

Daiyu had ended up standing in the exact center of the *dit* in the middle of the skiway. She slowly spun on her heel to follow Miranda's progress as she mapped the perimeter. Andi did her probe test after moving Daiyu aside. Her test stopped after three inches in the packed skiway surface and less than an inch in the center of the *dit* where it had been compressed by the bounce of the plane.

She couldn't spot any sign of the wreck other than the tail and wing.

Miranda stared back along the line. Something was missing. It was always harder to see what wasn't there.

"What's missing?"

"The plane," Romanoff snapped out. "That is what is

missing. Because it is over there and you are wasting time looking over here."

Daiyu turned another full circle, then silently shook her head. She didn't see what was missing either.

"Andi?"

"What? Sorry, I was calculating the snowpack density. It's only a rough estimate."

"What's missing?"

Andi looked at her, then followed her gesture toward the initial impact point.

"No gouges from landing gear. He or she did a belly landing. A better bet than a wheels-down landing on an unknown surface."

Miranda hadn't thought about that, but Andi was absolutely right. If the gear had been down, they would have seen deep gouges in the plateau's frozen surface, which would have probably caused snapped-off landing gear and a much more violent end.

"Or maybe he didn't know he was landing. That first dent in the snow is surprisingly deep and well packed. You said it spelled NHA, the divots. That means after the initial heavy impact, he attempted to regain flight and skipped more lightly across the surface *dit-dit-dit,* losing speed until he hit that crevasse."

And that was exactly what they found as they measured and outlined each successive impact. The tail hitting first, making a narrow trough at the head of each *dit* in turn, indicating a nose-up attitude. Each tail hit was succeeded by a belly bounce as the nose slammed down. Each successive one grew slightly longer as the speed bled off and the wings lost lift.

"Look," Andi appeared remarkably sad. "The pilot was conscious and in relative control at the landing."

Miranda had reached the same conclusion.

But by the time the landing was done, and the plane lay in the bottom of a crevasse...

11

Eight o'clock at night already? He needed to get a life.

Drake knew he was like an addict, incapable of leaving an unread report in his inbox. Thank God his wife was of a similar mind or who knows what friction that might have caused. She was ensconced in her office as the director of the National Reconnaissance Office twenty-five miles away, and he was stuck in his office as the Chairman of the Joint Chiefs of Staff at the Pentagon.

Thankfully, the last item, which had dropped in at the same moment he'd reached out to shut down his computer, was short.

Miranda Chase and team launched by request of ATSB to NTSB. Sent to investigate Russian Il-76 Candid crash at Australia's Davis Station.

He had asked to be kept apprised of where she was daily. It rarely mattered. Her team were the best of the National Transportation Safety Board's air-crash investigation arm. Commuter planes and airliners were their normal fare. But she was also the leading specialist on military air crashes, far outstripping even the Air Force's Accident Investigation Board's skills.

And every now and then, that latter ability landed her in the midst of a disaster that rippled through governments and threatened the balance of global power—with minimal awareness on her part. Her autism kept her from seeing anything beyond the context of the aircraft crash itself. Keeping track of where her team mobilized had put him ahead of a crisis several times, or at least aware that one was on the verge of smashing onto his desk or the President's.

Why would a Russian cargo jet crashing in Australia be so unusual? Odd, yes. Worthy of an interagency call out for Miranda's team across international boundaries when there was no US hardware involved? Not so much. That he didn't understand why did not sit comfortably. Was it worth following up at this hour?

His private phone rang, and the Star Trek ringtone Lizzy had programmed into it for herself made him smile.

"Hey, beautiful."

"Hey, yourself," he could hear her smile. "Are you done for the night? I was thinking dinner out."

"I was thinking delivery dinner eaten in bed, General Gray."

"I like the way you think, General Nason."

The report remained on his screen. "Hey Lizzy, does Davis Station in Australia mean anything to you? Part of the Deep Space Network in the Outback or something?"

"The only Davis I know is in Antarctica. They're part of our satellite tracking network. Why?"

"Miranda is chasing a crashed Russian cargo jet there."

There was a long silence that he'd learned to respect. General Lizzy Gray had a suspicious mind—one coupled with a high rate of accuracy. She claimed it was women's intuition, he assumed mostly to tease him. He figured it was simply that she was as sharp as hell, which was only one of the many reasons he'd fallen for her three years ago.

When she didn't speak, he tried. "Given the current global mayhem that Russia is creating in NATO and the former Eastern Bloc, it seems unlikely that they are up to anything good."

"The Antarctic Treaty prohibits any military action, testing, or exercises anywhere below sixty degrees south latitude. If they've stepped back from the treaty…"

Drake swallowed hard. "Or were *planning* to step back from the treaty, they'd take action now to get a jump on whatever strategic target they'd selected before they announced it."

Again Lizzy answered him with silence.

"Shit! Did the Russians crash on their way to grab an Australian station?" There went any chance of a quiet dinner tonight in bed with his wife.

12

MARLA AND FREDDY, THE WHOOP WHOOP SKIWAY PREP TEAM, arrived with Mike and Holly in a lumbering Hagglund transporter. Holly could see that Miranda and Andi had worked all of the way along the track of the crash to the broken tail section. No one had approached the crevasse without the safety gear.

"What did you find out, boss?" Holly swung down before the snow machine had fully stopped, hopping clear of the wide rubber tracks.

"As I had surmised, the emergency transmitter *isn't* in the tail section." She turned to face Romanoff. "Removing the COSPAS satellite linkage was bad. You must get Russia to reinstall them."

"I will suggest it, but it is outside my purview. I'm only here to secure the aircraft. I deny your right to inspect or board Russian sovereign terr—"

Holly clamped a hand on his shoulder, squeezing down hard enough through the parka and her heavy gloves to focus his attention wholly on her. "Let me enlighten you, mate. You keep repeating yourself and you're going to simply annoy me. I'm not the sort of person you want to annoy. And if you don't get the COSPAS restandardized, you'll risk being labeled a *bad man* by Miranda there. You don't want to know what happened to the last person she said that about."

"I do not scare so easy," Romanoff attempted to shake off her grip, which, of course, didn't work but must have hurt quite a bit by the expression on his face.

Daiyu leaned in close enough for her whisper to take on a dangerous edge, "Crushed larynx, broken ribs, lost an eye, and two burst testes...before he was burned to death from the inside. He was a *very* bad man."

Romanoff's complexion matched the snow.

Holly decided that she could get to like this Daiyu. Then she thought about the implications of that last bit and wondered quite who Daiyu was. Far more than Zhang Ru's widow, especially considering that she'd been sent here.

Her own brain was being far too slow today.

Why Wang Daiyu and why here were the first questions she should have asked, and the first she would, as soon as they could get a moment alone.

Miranda hadn't heard Daiyu's whisper, but Andi had and she looked distinctly relieved. Hard to blame her, as Zhang Ru could no longer come seeking revenge upon any team member for the thrashing she'd given him.

"The black box," Miranda picked up where she'd left off when Romanoff had interrupted, "is a primitive design, tape-based instead of digital, probably not updated since the plane was built in the 1970s. But it survived intact as there was no fire or severe impact. I don't want to risk opening it out here in the weather. There's no fuel leakage that we can see from the remaining wing, though several of the wing tanks were fractured."

"Zero fuel." Holly looked at the seventy-five-foot-long wing. "The engines are still attached."

"The primary intake fan is plugged with packed snow, but there doesn't look to be any snow deeper inside the engine except for a thin accumulation," Freddy spoke up. "I'm Davis' head mechanic. I took a look. They weren't spinning when it landed."

Holly turned to him, "You got it in one, mate. Engine flameout, so you wouldn't have heard it coming down. Even without the storm, you might have missed it anyway."

His relief showed clear on his face.

"Time to look down the hole, mates."

"Righto!" Freddy and Marla began pulling out ropes and climbing harnesses from the rear of the Hagglund.

"Well, Miranda's done the groundwork. How do you feel about climbing down with me, Mikey?"

"C'mon, Holly, you have to stop calling me that. We—"

"Do not pretend that merely because I sleep with you on occasion—"

"I rented out your room at the team house twelve months ago and you never noticed," Mike was quick. And he was right—though some of her gear was in that bedroom, her clothes and bath stuff weren't anymore. Maybe she'd keep her mouth shut for a change.

Holly stepped into the leg loops of the full-body climbing harness. It was awkward over the heavy padding of snowpants and big red parka. Marla and Freddy moved in and helped her and Mike position and then cinch them down.

"How deep is the hole?" Holly asked as she snapped on a 9mm safety line.

Marla shrugged. "The fuselage is wedged around twenty meters down. The other wing fell edge-on and is more like a hundred."

"Feet?"

"Meters," Marla offered her a proper *gotcha* Aussie grin, which didn't cheer her up at all.

Holly swallowed hard. An entire football pitch on end. She'd done plenty of rock climbing and a bit of ice training. But that had been mountain search-and-rescue scenarios, not climbing down into an unstable cleft in the ice. "Chances of it closing up on us?"

"Pretty low," Freddy answered. "The ice up here is stable, or so we thought until the jet found this hole."

"Perfect," Mike rolled his eyes at her, but didn't hesitate as he snapped a line to the belay ring on his harness. The other end was tied to a winch cable mounted on the Hagglund.

"No one," Freddy raised his voice enough to have everyone's attention, "goes closer to the crevasse than where the Hagglund is parked without a safety harness and a line. This isn't a cakewalk. Antarctica never is. You fall into that cleft, we'll probably never find you. At the rate of glacial flow here, your corpse should reach the ocean in about a decade."

"That isn't quite accurate." Miranda was looking southward as if she could see into the ice itself. "This section of the East Antarctic Ice Sheet is partially stabilized by the Vestfold Hills, thus creating the mostly bare-ground oasis that includes the site of Davis Station. The likelihood of a corpse reaching the ocean in a decade is quite low. It is more likely to be released onto dry ground or into one of the summer lakes of the region after a somewhat longer period."

Freddy couldn't find a neat answer to that. He wisely began issuing lighter weight safety harnesses and tying off leads. Holly wanted to tell him to keep Miranda's too short to wander to the edge of the crevasse but was then afraid that she might unrope herself to see the wreckage.

When she spotted Miranda staring at Holly's full harness, she shook her head. "I know you want to see it in person, Miranda, but this kind of climb isn't in your skill set." She didn't point out that it was barely in hers.

"Here, this should help." Andi attached small cameras to her and Mike's helmets, then gave the viewing screen to Miranda.

"Rockin' it, girl." Holly gave her a high-five. "We'll be in constant radio contact, so you can tell us to look at whatever you need."

Miranda clutched the screen tightly in her thick-gloved hands and nodded as if trying to reassure herself. Romanoff and Daiyu, finally in their own harnesses, moved up to look over Miranda's shoulders, though the only thing to see at the moment would be themselves.

With the Hagglund winch keeping herself and Mike safe, Holly figured they needed one more line. She had Freddy hook it up to the back of a snowmobile and Holly took the other end with her. Marla moved to sit on the Hagglund's bumper with the winch control in her hands.

With Freddy and Marla staying with the equipment, the rest of them edged forward to the lip of the crevasse. She had to remind Romanoff twice not to cross his own line over Mike's or her own. Daiyu moved awkwardly with her rope, showing a lack of climbing skills, but had far more common sense.

Now close enough to see more of the structure, Holly swore the crevasse was ready to swallow her whole. It wasn't a neat rocky canyon with steep banks. The blue-white ice had shattered here, like a block of stringy mozzarella cheese ripped in two. The sides were vertical but that was too simple a statement. Fractures, undercuts, overhangs, it was a vertical mess.

When she'd edged close enough to see down into the wound gaping across the landscape, she could see the plane's fuselage. Except for the missing tail, it was surprisingly intact. It hadn't rolled or shattered. It had been parked lengthwise along the crack with about a twenty-degree nose-down attitude and a roll to the right as if it was ready to fly deeper at the slightest opportunity.

That's when Mike swore, vehemently, "Jesus, Mary, and Joseph!"

"Your Catholic is showing, Mike."

Instead of his usual protest of not being offered a choice of orphanages, he waved a glove downward. He was looking past the nose of the plane to where the crevasse plunged deep into the ice sheet. The ice seemed to be colored a deeper and deeper blue with depth, yet the bottom remained out of sight. There was only one vaguely darker blotch that must be the other wing, lost forever below in the murk.

"Yeah, you got that about right, Mikey. You ready to do this?"

"Not a chance."

Holly made sure her descent rope was tight and kicked at the edge of the crevasse. Small chunks broke off and rained down on the metal fuselage. With nowhere else to go, the bangs of ice against metal hull were massively amplified as all of the sound was directed upward.

Romanoff took her arm.

"I should be the one to descend and inspect the plane." But before Holly could knock him on his ass and gag him, he continued, "Regrettably, I have no mountaineering experience. You will report to me everything you see."

"That's the reason we're going down there, mate."

He nodded reluctantly and let her go.

She kicked her crampons into the ice, then leaned back against the belay to test her harness. She and Mike traded nods before signaling Freddy to ease the winch line.

Together, they walked backward over the lip of the crevasse and headed down to the plane.

13

When Colonel Nikolas Romanoff saw who had called his satellite phone, he felt ill. This would be worse than looking down into that gaping wound in the ice that had swallowed his plane.

Army General Mikhail Murov, the highest ranked officer in the entire Russian Federation. Murov was also the President's right hand, hatchet man, most likely successor, and head of the Federal Security Service. Known as the FSB, it had taken over the role of the Soviet KGB *before* it had become the hard-core *punishing sword* that now protected and fed the oligarchy.

None of the money had flowed to Nikolas personally—at least not on the scale it had flowed to that inner circle of the President's. Of course, he didn't make a habit of assassination and blackmail as they did.

He stepped well clear of the others before answering, "Colonel Nikolas Romanoff here."

"Have you taken possession of the plane yet?"

"No. It has fallen into a crevasse."

"Reachable?"

"A team is descending now."

The silence from the far end of the connection was colder than the Antarctic Ice Sheet. "What team?"

"American. Crash investigators."

Again the chill freeze of the Moscow winter reached up to space and down the line to make him as immobile as a continent-sized glacier.

"The Australians called them in. The plane landed in their territory."

"Are they on the plane now?"

He glanced over at the payout on the Hagglund's winch cable. It had gone slack to lay flat on the snow. That meant Mike and Holly's weight was off the line.

Murov read his non-response. "Destroy it."

"With them on it?"

"Yes. If they have boarded a Russian Federation aircraft, they are on our soil and must be disposed of."

Nikolas looked around and decided that wouldn't be terribly hard to do. Put the Hagglund in gear and let it roll into the crevasse. Everyone was tied to it, including the Australian airport workers who had secured their personal safety lines to it. He could undo his own line and it would take everyone else down. If he was lucky, it would drive the fuselage down into the depths past recovery.

"Okay." Everyone was at the edge of the crevasse now except Marla, who sat on the Hagglund's front bumper with the winch control in her hand. Then he spotted Daiyu in her Chinese red-and-white parka.

Relations with the Chinese were...interesting. They were buying Russian commodities—especially oil and wheat—at steep discounts as the West was no longer buying them. The

Chinese capital was the only real money flowing into the country with all of the sanctions and blockades the West had put in place. If he killed one of their nationals, how might they react?

"The Chinese woman as well?"

"What woman?"

"A Wang Daiyu. She flew in from Zhongshan Station."

"Wang Daiyu? *Colonel* Wang Daiyu?"

Nikolas wasn't sure. She hadn't mentioned a rank. Of course, neither had he.

"What is she doing there?"

"I don't know. Maybe she monitored my flight from Progress Station and decided to follow me to Davis."

"Don't be such a *dubina*. Colonel Wang would have come from Beijing, straight from the CMC. If you touch her, it could cause immense trouble. But why is she there?"

Nikolas was *not* as dumb as a block of wood. But he also didn't study Chinese politics. He was a troubleshooter who had started in the Air Force until they'd been merged into the Russian Aerospace Forces. In the ensuing battle for status and position he had survived, framing three of his Aerospace counterparts in a fabricated plan to overthrow the Commander-in-Chief of the Aerospace Forces. He had been promoted to replace their leader who was summarily shamed and executed despite his innocence.

Maybe Nikolas would try being honest.

"I have not followed Chinese politics closely enough to know of Colonel Wang, General Murov."

"The plane is a lower priority. Our records show Colonel Wang is closely associated with the senior vice-chairman of the CMC, the Number Two in the People's Republic. But we know nothing of how that connection works. Find out what she is doing there. If you destroy the plane, she will slip away. Find out quickly. Then the plane and anyone who has been aboard it must be removed."

Murov was gone before Nikolas could acknowledge the command.

He studied the Chinese woman standing at the edge of the crevasse, looking down into the depths. What was on the plane that had Murov rousting him in the middle of the night to scramble south to this icy hell?

And why *himself*? Had he simply been handy or was there a reason he'd come to Murov's attention? He was the head of the entire Antarctica mission, yet this seemed a proper job for a minion. Or it had until this moment.

Like Wang Daiyu's boss, General Murov was the second most powerful man in the country and Nikolas, like Daiyu, was a mere colonel. Men like himself were a ruble apiece to men like Murov.

If that was true of Daiyu, why was Murov worried about her? That was a question he'd probably never know the answer to.

As for himself, now that he asked the question, he knew why he'd been chosen.

That *babnik* Major Turgenev, who couldn't seem to keep his dick out of other men's wives, had notified him about a lost plane—seven *hours* after it was overdue. Romanoff had immediately called his own commander. Within minutes, he'd been sent to Antarctica with barely enough time to call his wife.

On the flight down, he'd read what limited background Turgenev had sent him. He recognized the woman in the pilot's file right away. The lush Tatar who had slipped out of Turgenev's bed, then Lieutenant Colonel Kurchenko's (before Nikolas had managed to rub out that thorn in his ass), and next tried to slip into his. Nikolas didn't doubt what his Inessa would do if he'd bedded the woman—she'd chop off his dick and serve it to him mashed into a solyanka stew. It had made him a cautious man.

But if Turgenev had been openly sleeping with the pilot's wife, it was no wonder the poor cuckold had ended up as captain on a forty-year-old plane flying cargo to Antarctica.

Cargo.

Turgenev's files had not a single mention of what cargo was on the plane. That was most unusual. The manifest was the key to every mission to Antarctica, not that he ever bothered to read them. But this flight didn't have one—the mandatory form was missing.

Cargo that Murov wanted destroyed.

Until...he had found out that the Chinese woman was here. That meant the Chinese were interested in the plane. In the cargo!

He had to deliver on both the woman and the plane.

The old guard KGB must start dying off soon. Murov and the President had come up through the ranks together and were both pushing seventy.

Maybe if he played this correctly, he could finally cross over and become the first of a new guard to replace the dwindling ranks of the prior generation. Inessa would like that status very much—as well as a cut of the money that flowed into the Kremlin but never came back out.

To finally become untouchable, protected by money and connections from even the worst scandals. Yes, he too would like that.

14

Up on the ice sheet, Daiyu helped the two Australian workers with the bodies. Five times, Holly or Mike radioed up from below to pull on the line with the snowmobile. Five times, body bags were dragged clear of the plane, raised the six stories, and laid out on the ice.

After opening the first one, Freddy and Marla had each taken a turn puking out their breakfast and several meals before that off to the side. They scrubbed their faces with snow, then lowered the line back down for the next one. They didn't look at any of the others, or even each other.

She herself was wholly unfazed. She'd seen worse any number of times. Her years as a star Army athlete had inured her to any hardship. Her time with General Zhang Ru —two years as his most trusted aide and another as his wife —had cured her of any mere physical horror.

Miranda Chase unzipped each body bag and inspected the corpses.

Curiously, not a bit frail despite her timid personality. She was as calm as a war-zone coroner. They began discussing the pattern of injury and burn variations preserved on each corpse.

Romanoff had seen the two Australians' reactions, then walked away without looking down. He'd closed himself in the warm cabin of the idling Hagglund like the weak Russian he was.

Andi moved aside, taking the tablet computer with her, maintaining communication with Holly and Mike.

That left only Miranda and Daiyu herself kneeling by the body bags.

"You do not trust the Russians, do you?" Many of Daiyu's ancestors had been murdered by them. If Romanoff fell into the crevasse today, she would not grieve, she would celebrate one less Russian in the world.

Miranda looked down at the body bags. "They're dead. Trust does not strike me as a relevant concern."

"I meant Romanoff," she kept her voice down though they were alone on the ice.

"Trust is an emotion. I'm not very good with emotions. I trust facts. You'd have to ask Mike if I should trust Romanoff. He's very good at things like that."

Daiyu didn't know what to say to that. Mike was down in the crevasse at the moment and therefore out of reach.

Miranda turned to inspect the corpses, so Daiyu did the same.

The bodies looked curiously artificial. Each Russian crew member remained in the seated position, frozen solidly into their final form over the last thirty hours.

The navigator and loadmaster had been burned from the front past recognition. Yet it hadn't burned through their clothes.

"The heat was intense but brief. This wasn't a fire,"

Miranda spoke as if discussing whether or not to add a log to a campfire. "An explosion, but not in any form I recognize."

Daiyu decided that was astute. She remembered General Liú Zuocheng's instructions before he'd sent her south. *They have called upon the American Miranda Chase, which tells us how important this is. She is a strange woman but she is the one you must listen to most carefully.*

Strange was the least of it. She hadn't once looked Daiyu in the face, or anyone else other than her girlfriend, as far as Daiyu could tell. She rarely spoke. Yet when she did, the team treated her every word as it was purest truth. Holly's threat to Nikolas Romanoff had been couched as the danger of being labeled *Bad*—by this Miranda Chase. It had been half in jest, or so Daiyu had assumed at the time. She was less sure now.

After a brief inspection, Miranda resealed the first two body bags and opened the next two.

"These two were directly in the damage path. That gives us the trajectory."

"The trajectory? Of what?" Daiyu's training and rank were in internal security. It had been a natural follow-on to her athletic endeavors—everyone underestimated a woman, until it was too late. They only saw the athlete, not the mind that had graduated at the top of every class, whether mathematics or hand-to-hand combat training.

Infiltrating Zhang Ru's household and extracting information to be passed on to the head of the Central Military Commission had been her first assignment after General Liú Zuocheng had discovered her. Analyzing aspects of an air crash were not in her skill-set, yet the general had selected her for this assignment. Her first-ever trip out of Asia and he'd sent her to Antarctica. She'd contemplated this on the long flight down, but gained no new insights for that effort.

"Didn't you see the hole in the top of the cockpit?" Miranda asked.

Daiyu had, but thought it was merely part of the general battering the plane had suffered during its impact and plunge into the crevasse.

"An object, hot enough to cause all of these burns, yet small enough to create a hole a bare half-meter across passed through the copilot," Miranda drew a gloved hand at an angle from her right shoulder to her left hip.

Daiyu looked at the mess in the first body bag once again. With Miranda's explanation, she could finally make sense of the copilot's corpse. Except for a thin line of skin and his spine, he was cut diagonally in half, with the whole center of the slice missing.

Miranda then pointed to the navigator's corpse. "And as the navigator's seat is centered in the lower cabin, two-point-three meters below the copilot's starboard-side seat, we have a seventeen-to-eighteen-degree angle of impact. Also, the missing section of his thigh indicates that the object was twenty-seven to thirty-two centimeters wide, slightly over one foot. Projecting the object's actual angle of descent assumes that the plane was flying straight and level at the time."

"Does that seem likely? It was flying through a storm."

Miranda shifted her gaze to study something off Daiyu's right shoulder, except there was nothing there other than brilliance of the Antarctic-blue sky. The low angle of the morning sun in Antarctica had their shadows stretching long across the ice in that direction.

"It is only a temporary placeholder on a meta-sphere of

conjecture until we can confirm it another way. However, it is not unreasonable. A highly injured pilot managed to land an Ilyushin-76 with no engines during a storm with minimal damage. That implies a high degree of skill and dedication. Therefore, in a storm, I would expect his flight to be well controlled."

"Him?" Daiyu pointed to the final body bag.

"The sole survivor."

"Of the initial impact," Daiyu said it as a comment on Miranda's extreme specificity. If she noticed, she didn't react.

"Yes. Badly burned on the side facing the copilot, including the loss of his right eye. Blood stains below both of his ears tells us that the impact was loud enough to burst his eardrums, which must have been excruciating." She frowned deeply for a moment. "No. Any mere impact should *not* have been more than painfully loud."

Daiyu tried to picture it.

What was loud enough to make the pilot's ears bleed?

Then she remembered how she'd arranged to come to Zhang Ru's attention. She'd replaced his usual escort driver for an early flight test of the fifth-generation J-31 Gyrfalcon fighter jet. During the flight test at Qionglai Air Base outside of Chengdu, she'd stood close behind him. A half step too close, so as to snag his notorious attention to the female form—any female form.

She should have known then to walk away from the assignment, but it had come from General Liú Zuocheng and she hadn't dared. He had long been a patron of her family, ever since grandfather had died in the Sino-Vietnam War.

It was the jet's first supersonic test flight, though she hadn't known this at the time. When everyone had looked to the left, she'd shifted to make sure that Ru couldn't see the jet without also seeing her profile. The small black dot had taken mere seconds to resolve, and then the jet flashed by over the field fast enough to hurt her neck trying to follow it.

The surprise of the crashing sonic boom was a body blow that knocked all of the air from her lungs. It would have knocked her over if she hadn't grabbed Ru's shoulder to steady herself.

Yes, he'd said with a deceptively charming smile, after scanning her body as if noticing her for the first time, *the sound can be most surprising the first time.* He'd said the last words with the perfect balance of fact and innuendo. Charm had always been one of his greatest skills—until he had someone irretrievably trapped in his vile clutches.

She'd managed to move into his entourage, though she'd kept his hands off her until last year. Her instructions were to avoid a dalliance, but to rather become a fixture in his life. Much to her chagrin, it had worked all too well. She'd traveled safely from secretary to most-trusted aide. Then General Liú Zuocheng's *suggestion*—that wasn't an order but in truth was—to become his wife.

"Sonic boom," Daiyu whispered at the memory.

Miranda's gaze shifted to her face for the first time, well, at least to her chin. "Yes! Of course!"

It was also the first time Daiyu heard actual emotion in Miranda's voice.

"A projectile, traveling through the cabin at supersonic speeds, would result in a sonic boom being trapped and reinforced in a small space. Look at his hands."

Daiyu did, but didn't see what about them was relevant to a sonic boom.

Then Daiyu understood that Miranda, with the sonic

boom explaining the bloody ears, had moved on to a different topic. No *Thank you*. No acknowledgement for Daiyu's contribution. Observation, explanation, moving on. Annoyance and amusement warred briefly inside her. *Strange woman* indeed.

Daiyu shifted her attention to the implications of the battered, burned, and bloody pilot's hands.

They'd been hard frozen out in front of him. Both fists were closed about the wheel that Miranda's team had removed from the plane. It took a second look to understand why they'd done that—his right hand wasn't holding the wheel—it had become a part of it. He'd fought the wheel until the last moment. Beyond that. Not even in death had his other hand let go.

Ultimately, Zhang Ru had been as badly burned, by her, as this man was. And though Ru's larynx had been crushed past usage, he'd given voice to his agony as she'd executed him as slowly as she'd seen him kill many others. Ru had never been averse to performing his own dirty work and on that one occasion she'd agreed with his methods. His final screams had let her sleep at night; the world was a far better place without him in it.

But to be in that level of pain and fly a plane? That was an amazing feat.

"They should make him a Hero of the Russian Federation."

"Why? He's already dead. What advantage would that have?" Miranda had stopped her inspection, looked at Daiyu's left knee where it rested on the snow as they knelt to either side of the pilot's corpse, and asked it in a perfectly matter-of-fact voice as if that was suddenly the only topic of conversation.

"Because he did something incredibly brave."

"I have never understood posthumous awards. My parents are still spoken of twenty-nine years after their deaths by others than me—or they were until Clark was murdered." Miranda pulled the zipper on the final body bag closed.

At its sound, Daiyu could see Andi turn from her position at the edge of the crevasse and start toward them.

"Clark?" Daiyu asked.

"The vice president," Miranda said it simply.

Daiyu couldn't find her voice. She remembered the American vice president's death clearly enough; it had been international news. International news about a horrible *accident*. Did even General Liú know that it had been murder?

Miranda was continuing blithely on, "But those posthumous acknowledgements do not change their lives or mine. What purpose do they serve?"

This odd woman had been well enough acquainted with the vice president to discuss her own parents with him. Who in hell was she? Hell. There was a laugh. Her own name, meaning Black Jade, was so close to that of Hell, *Diyu,* had always intrigued her—especially during her time with Zhang Ru. Looking down at the twisted corpse of the pilot, she now wished for no association at all. This pilot had been through hell indeed.

"It mattered to my former copilot," Andi spoke up. She'd moved close enough to have overheard the last of the conversation. In fact, with a momentary lull in the wind, she'd probably been close enough to overhear everything. "The posthumous medals increased the level of continuing financial support his wife and child received."

"Ah," Miranda said, "that makes sense. Perhaps this man has a wife who will benefit by his being made a Hero of the Russian Federation. It is their highest honor after all."

"His wife is a cheating bitch," Nikolas had left the warmth of the Hagglund and stepped up from behind Daiyu though she'd tracked him from the moment he'd slammed a vehicle's door. "A *Shluha vokzal'naja.*" *A train station whore*, she translated in her head.

Was Nikolas Romanoff really the hapless bureaucrat he presented? That seemed unlikely if he'd been sent to secure this crash site.

Why had the Russians sent him?

Why had General Liú Zuocheng sent *her*?

He must believe her capable enough to manage this situation, so she would *be* capable enough.

She had to get down onto that plane, but Holly and Mike had refused when she admitted that she wasn't an experienced climber. Had never once in her life done so much as a hike that required being roped up, though she didn't say that. They had also refused to let Miranda or Andi join them.

If that plane lets go and drops, it will take all of our skills to survive.

And yet, for their team leader's sake, they had gone down to the plane at the risk of their lives.

Daiyu also noticed that Miranda hadn't blinked at Romanoff's Russian epithet, whereas Andi had looked perplexed. She reminded herself to be more careful. Daiyu had discovered that Andi spoke Mandarin. Miranda spoke sufficiently fluent Russian to understand the curse, did she also speak Mandarin? *Take more care about who is near you the next time you call in, Daiyu.* She'd spent too much time in a monolithic culture, where everyone shared Mandarin or Cantonese, and privacy was a myth. Among representatives of America and Russia? She must exercise immense caution.

"Holly?" Miranda called on the radio.

"Miranda?" Holly sent it back as a teasing question.

"Yes, this is me. Not a recording of me."

Daiyu spotted a smile on Andi's face though Miranda looked perfectly serious. Yet another piece of whatever this woman was. Somehow the pieces must fit together.

"What's up, Miranda?"

Miranda started to look up at the sky, but stopped herself, apparently having fallen for that a few too many times. She was both simpleton and brilliance wound together.

"In the cockpit, look for signs of a sonic boom."

"*Inside* the plane?"

"Yes."

15

HOLLY DIDN'T WANT TO RETURN TO THAT GRISLY CRYPT. THE blood hadn't degraded to a dried rust brown, it had been flash frozen bright red. The copilot's guts had sprayed across most of the control panel and been preserved with such disturbing vividness. The navigator's blood had sprayed over his smaller set of instruments and all of the windows below as well.

All of it perfectly preserved as garish red.

Mike had helped bag the bodies, but she'd seen his jaw muscle jumping with how tightly it was clenched. It would be a cruelty to send him back in to answer Miranda's question. Furthermore, he was their human factors specialist. Though he'd learned a lot since he'd first joined the team, he wasn't a technical boy. The implications of subtler technical indicators continued to pass him by, despite three years on the team.

And there was that damn number again. With Mike. Together. Three years. She'd never—

Holly chopped off the thought as thoroughly as whatever

had chopped off the navigator's leg. She'd already spent the whole flight from Vancouver grinding on that particular impossibility. Being with one man for—

Shut the fuck up, mate! She got moving.

They'd initially entered the fuselage through the topside hatch forward of the wings. It opened into the aft edge of the cockpit, affording them easy access to the bodies. They'd photographed everything for Miranda, then sent the bodies aloft. With care, she'd managed to access the lower, navigator's cockpit through the hole punched out by whatever had hit the plane. The narrow passageway that would have led back to its own door into the cargo bay was blocked by a ridge of ice that had punched through the hull.

Holly had scrambled down the cockpit stairs, which had been quite awkward with the plane's tilt and roll. The plane was robust enough that the hatch into the cargo bay worked, and swung inward smoothly.

The load had been all cargo, no more bodies that she'd been able to see. Bits of the cargo had come loose, but most had remained in place. All she could see was pallets of foodstuffs chained to the deck despite the rough ride.

Overly conscious that if the plane tumbled into the crevasse, no safety rope was going to save them if they were inside, they'd hustled back through the hatch the moment they were done with the bodies. If the fuselage fell, the safety rope would only serve to smash their bodies against the inside of the hatch, and that would be the end of them. But untying would only be an invitation to disappearing into the depths.

She'd escaped that cockpit of red hell intact. Together she and Mike had climbed along the top of the plane, punching their ice crampons into the skin with each step for traction. It was barely sufficient, but they'd managed to reach the open end of the cargo bay where the tail had broken-off. They'd check the cargo bay from the other end to see if there were any bodies farther aft.

Then Miranda had called.

Sonic boom in the cockpit? Wouldn't it show up in the pictures? Probably not. Mike had taken area shots showing the crew's final positions and the main line of damage: top of cockpit, copilot, and the deck. She'd taken photos of the navigator, the big notch out of his seat, and the exit path through the lower deck and fuselage with nothing but the shadowed crevasse below.

Someone had to reenter the cockpit and she wasn't going to let it be Mike. Instead, she had him belay her rope. Sitting on her butt, she slid back down the length of the plane, making the descent down the fuselage much easier than the climb.

"Arrest!" She shouted before she reached the cockpit hatch.

Mike belayed her sharply from where he'd anchored himself with a pair of ice screws sunk into the crevasse wall. If the plane fell now, there was at least a chance of a safe arrest.

"I'm okay," Holly reassured Mike as she turned to look at something that had caught her eye. They'd been too busy concentrating on the security of every step as they'd ascended to look aside from the topmost curve of the fuselage. "Tension!"

Mike took up every inch of slack as she climbed three laborious steps upslope toward his position, then she shifted over to the side.

The roll of the tilted fuselage had hidden a *second* hole.

Bracing one foot on the plane and the other on the crevasse wall, she looked down into a hole much like that one that had punched through the cockpit. Except it wasn't circular. It was longer than it was wide—as if someone had punched a hole the size of a slab of cold ones. She could use a couple of beers about now.

Her hand light revealed a missing section of a major structural member, and then the inside of a fuel tank, with a matching hole down through the cargo bay and out the bottom. Her flash picked up the ice wall extending down below the plane.

Holly keyed the radio. "Found another hole, Miranda, punched through the primary wing-box cross member and the main fuel tank two-plus meters starboard of center. I'm guessing that explains the engine flameouts. I'm photographing it, but whatever hit this plane buggered it bad. That's two holes drilled straight through top to bottom. That takes a serious bit of doing."

"We'll check the wing and tail again for other punctures." From her tone, Holly knew that Miranda wouldn't have missed anything the first time but was trying to stay busy up there with no way to get down to visit the wreck.

"Good idea, Miranda. I'm headed to the cockpit." Best way to keep Miranda calm was to let her do something, anything. "On belay, Mike?"

"On belay," he confirmed.

She managed to clamber up the hull's curve to balance on the top of the fuselage again and continued down to the cockpit. She hooked a boot on the edge of the hatch and called *Off belay*.

Down in the cockpit, she looked past the gore.

A sonic boom in a confined cockpit. What would that *look* like?

There were cracks in the windshield that she'd assumed were from the crash. But when she rubbed a gloved hand over them, they were bowed outward, not inward.

Numerous instrument dials had the glass out of them. She hadn't noticed it because of the gore, but also because the glass had been smashed back to powder by the blast.

Only a few instruments, on the pilot's left side outlining his final shadow, remained intact.

One was a tracking needle for a seventy-five-megahertz ILS beacon. Standard kit at older airfields. Could the pilot have followed that one surviving instrument all of the way down? Perhaps Progress Station used the same industry-standard frequency.

No point in asking Nikolas Romanoff. If he was out of Moscow, he wouldn't know rubbish. She'd try to get the helo pilots aside later to ask. She had no read yet on what the Chinese woman did or didn't know.

Zhang Ru's *wife*. What daft idea had them sending her here? No. That asshole was dead and gone. That was *not* why they'd sent her. Which mean what?

Wang Daiyu, not as General Zhang Ru's wife, but as a CMC operative whose previous assignment had *been* Ru? With Ru six feet under, she was still a CMC operative.

It sounded like a joke of an idea. Except now that she'd had it, a twisted sense of logic said maybe she had the right of it.

Which posed the question of how much power had been concentrated in Daiyu's hands? And more importantly, why? Most importantly, by whom?

Once Holly crawled back out onto the top of the plane,

she had to lay down on the top of the fuselage for a minute. She couldn't find the energy to lift her legs clear and left them dangling into the cockpit. Nothing up there but a slice of blue sky between ragged ice walls. It wasn't the cold, the altitude—or the feeling of the six stories of ice that seemed to lean in over and snuff her and the plane forever—that kept her frozen in place. It wasn't the unknown fifty or a hundred stories of narrowing icy canyon that lay below them.

Mike waved tentatively.

She waved back, but made no move to get to her feet.

For the first time in hours, perhaps days, she felt the spec ops soldier in her finally waking up—despite her current state of sleep deprivation.

Russia had sent an FSB bureaucrat to secure their plane —except he wasn't quite that either. Nikolas Romanoff not-related-to-Czar-Romanov owed her a few explanations. He'd come all of the way from Moscow or he would have been there sooner than they were. It was plausible, at least marginally, that the powers that be had sent him simply to investigate the loss of one of their planes. Marginally.

But a Beijing-based CMC operative? Who did *Daiyu* work for?

And then Holly remembered sitting in at a conference in Brunei. She'd arrived late and her main task had been hauling Andi back from the edge of a panic attack—which was never good in someone suffering occasional bouts of PTSD.

But Miranda had been talking to a general. Not any general, but rather General Liú Zuocheng, the senior vice-chairman of the Chinese Central Military Commission. If Daiyu was taking her orders from him...to come to

Antarctica about this plane currently trying to freeze her butt despite the thick snow pants?

The only explanation of Wang Daiyu's presence was that far more was in play here than an aging Ilyushin-76 Candid cargo jet. And Daiyu's high status completely knocked the I'm-merely-a-petty-bureaucrat feet out from under Romanoff.

Holly studied the slit of blue sky far above. There were answers up there—on the cold surface. But wheedling them from two professional government operatives seemed unlikely. Then she thought about the disastrous second Cold War forming up with Russia, that was fast shifting from cold to active. Add to that the trade wars that were constantly escalating between the West and China.

Right. Her chance of getting a straight answer from anyone up there was less than zero.

Which meant...

She sat up and looked down between her knees into the cockpit. No. The answers weren't in that bloodbath.

As she looked upslope toward Mike, her eyes ran the length of the fuselage. Three meters high and wide, twenty long. Sixty-six feet of fifty thousand kilos of cargo.

Romanoff and Daiyu weren't here for the crash. They were here because of what the plane was carrying.

Shoving to her feet, she waved at Mike. He waved back. She slapped a hand over her mouth to indicate silence.

He tipped his head in question, but didn't key the radio. Good man. Which was the problem with him. Beneath all of the smarm and his shady past, he was a good man. If he wasn't, she could have brushed him off without hesitation. Super annoying!

Holly spun a hand over her head, pointing straight up. Not a climber's signal, but rather for a crane or winch, *Hoist!*

As he pulled, she trusted her crampons on the battered top of the fuselage and ran up to join him at the high point of the wreck. Revealing no degree of common sense, she hugged him when she got there.

"Glad to see you too," he whispered in her ear.

"Yeah, that." She *was* relieved that he was safe, not trapped in the cockpit aboard a plane ready to fall at any moment. "We've got a problem."

"The cargo. Figured that one out for myself."

"It means that we'll be shifting cargo around aboard an unstable plane."

"Not an idiot, Holly."

No, Mike definitely wasn't that either.

In unison they glanced upward. No one was leaning over the edge to watch them at the moment—good. They made a quick job of reworking the lines, anchoring themselves as far as she dared along the canyon wall. If the plane did break free due to their jostling around inside it, and it fell nose first, and the gods and goddesses were smiling down on them, there would at least be a chance that they'd be yanked out the open stern by their lines and not dragged into the depths of the crevasse.

Together they swung down through the gaping hole at the rear of the plane where the tail had broken-off and entered the cargo bay that was tilted and rolled to the side like the floor of a carny funhouse—so very not fun.

16

GENERAL LIÚ ZUOCHENG STRODE THROUGH THE WHITE-marble, three-story lobby of the Eight-One building—the headquarters of the Ministry of National Defense of the People's Republic of China. The early morning sunlight streamed in through the high windows backing the two mezzanines that wrapped around the lobby. It lit the exhibits with the last daylight they'd ever see.

For this moment, he was simply one of the many citizens come to see the great aircraft displayed in the lobby. His pair of bodyguards had learned that they were to hang back so that he at least had the *feeling* of anonymity for a few minutes at the start of each day.

He passed the old single-engine prop planes without a glance. The towering missiles and the massive Xi'an H-6 strategic bomber were of no interest to him either. Instead he crossed beneath the outstretched wing of the World War II Petlyakov Pe-2 light bomber until he had a clear view of the Chengdu J-7, strung from the ceiling with heavy wires so that it looked ready to fly through the lobby. Licensed from the Soviet Union MiG-21, China had built thousands of these jet fighters. As a young first lieutenant, he had flown one during the Sino-Vietnamese War of 1979.

Four weeks. The entire war had lasted one day under four weeks. It hadn't kept Vietnam from crushing the Khmer Rouge despite China's misguided backing for the bloodthirsty Pol Pot. Nor had they driven Vietnam out of Cambodia, where they'd continued to interfere for another decade. However, the war *had* proven that the Soviet Union's long arm didn't quite have the reach to protect Vietnam from China's wrath. Small comfort for the sixty thousand killed and wounded on each side, or the hundreds of tanks and armored carriers destroyed in a mere twenty-seven days.

That had been his sole battle experience. Yet it had transformed him.

Born in the Year of the Goat in the Wood phase, he had grown strong and vital in the wilderness where his family had lived as poor trappers. Twelve years later, when the Year of the Goat returned on the Chinese zodiac, it was in the Fire phase. He'd been plunged into the heat of the city and the Young Pioneers youth branch of the Communist Party. Many had discounted him for his goatness—supposedly peace-loving and resistant to change—to their detriment.

By the time he turned twenty-four, the Earth Goat year and the Sino-Vietnamese War, he had indeed been in transition. The passage of Metal and Water had seen him through the five phases, first harvesting, then consolidating his power. The cycle had begun again in 2015, during the next Wood Goat.

That year, at sixty, he had reached that pinnacle of Executive Deputy Leader of the Central Military Commission and been there ever since. The CMC constituted the controlling power of the entire military. Only one position ranked as more powerful, but he didn't wish to run the country. The President knew that, trusted that in him.

And he truly didn't. In his position, Zuocheng never had to meet with world leaders and negotiate trade agreements... though on occasion he strategically created disagreements.

All he'd ever cared about was embodied in the Type 81 Short Rifle, the first ever produced solely by Communist China, and the Chengdu J-7. The rifle had become his at nine years old, when a brown bear had attacked his father. Neither of them had survived. For the three years before he'd gone to the city, his skill with his father's rifle had fed his mother and sister.

Earth Goat to Wood Goat, twelve years that had led him from rifle to fighter jet. Now hypersonic missiles, laser weapons, and aircraft carriers were his tools. His heart and soul had been given to the shaping of the Chinese military from an unstable ragtag force left behind by Mao, into one of the most powerful in the entire world.

Zuocheng sighed. Past times had *not* been simpler, he knew that. Only memory made it feel that way. Yet the present complications were most annoying.

Their supposed allies, the *New* Russians, were acting worse than the Soviets that they now so disparaged. The Russian Federation was dying under the weight of failed dreams and staggering corruption. And it was not going to die quietly—a matter they were proving in thick blood and shattered cities on the western border with Europe and the former Eastern Bloc. They had grossly miscalculated there. Yet they survived, struggling on, unaware they were already dead. That created opportunity for the wise man.

Opportunity. The name he had given his own Chengdu J-7, so many years before. He had tried several times to find the old plane, until he had understood that it was merely an indulgence in an unrecoverable past. A past where he had thought that he could make an ally of his fellow pilot Zhang Ru.

How had he ever been so naive?

What Daiyu had uncovered, and what Chen Mei-Li had reported through his own granddaughter, were horrors that he'd thought only the Russian FSB capable of. He had considered butchering the man himself; Father had taught him all that was needed. Gutting Ru would have been no different than dressing a deer. But Daiyu's need for closure had outweighed his own preferences.

He had put her in the way of far worse than he could have imagined when he'd placed her in Ru's path. Yet, by remaining until the end, she had also proven her absolute commitment to China, the party, and himself. He had rewarded her with enough of Ru's wealth to set her up for life.

For four weeks, she had reorganized her new-found prosperity as well as quietly integrated the balance of Ru's holdings into Zuocheng's own. Then she had placed her sister—a wise businesswoman and former vice president of the Bank of China (Hong Kong)—as the manager of both properties.

Wang Daiyu passed the test he hadn't been aware of placing upon her, when, in four weeks and a day, she had arrived at his office. She hadn't asked for anything; that day, she had simply been waiting in his outer office when he arrived.

It had been two months since then. To be realistic, she

was undertrained to have her first field test. But when the Antarctic crash had happened, an undefined instinct had him sending her to the ice continent anyway. The problem was remote enough that he could deny involvement if anything went wrong. And it was low enough priority that it should be easily within her abilities to make sure nothing did. A propitious beginning of the next phase in their working relationship.

Except now she had reported the arrival of a Nikolas Romanoff—*Colonel* Romanoff, the head of Russia's entire Antarctic program. That was most unusual. And he'd spent much of the night contemplating its meaning.

Leaving the Chengdu J-7 jet to hang from the ceiling in peace, his bodyguards closed in on him as he turned for the secure elevator. He waved them off once the door had opened. He wouldn't be ascending into the upper ten stories of ministry offices to the top echelons of the nation's military. Neither they nor his guards were allowed to go where he was headed.

Once he was inside the elevator, his biometrics allowed him to descend to the fifth subbasement—a level that showed on no building plan or elevator panel. It was here that the Central Military Commission did most of its work.

The President of the People's Republic was the chairman of the CMC. When he attended meetings, they met in the grandest room on the top floor of the Eight-One Building. Eight-One, August First, 1935. The declaration by the Communist Party for all Chinese persons to unite against the Japanese. Even that foul weasel Chiang Kai-shek had been forced to join the Second United Front upon the 1937 Japanese invasion.

When the President didn't attend a CMC meeting, the six

members met in the basement. That was where the real
work was done. They didn't need a fancy conference room
with a sweeping view of central Beijing. Ever since he'd
taken over as deputy leader, they met in a small room
appointed with hardware rather than hardwoods. Like the
American Situation Room, an entire globe's worth of
information was gathered and summarized for
consideration here.

Unlike the American's emasculated chiefs of staff,
anything short of a full-scale war could be directly launched
by the six CMC members. They also had the black ops
Falcon Commando Unit at their sole command. For a war,
the law stated they must consult with the President first. For
lesser operations, Zuocheng rarely bothered him.

The recent shakeups—replacing half of the faces in the
room—made all of the occupants unsettled. He
acknowledged each in turn: his deputy chair, three generals,
and an admiral. The youngest was fifty-five and the eldest
was but two years his senior. Not all bloodied warriors, as
there simply hadn't been active wars to offer that
opportunity. But all were good men who had faced down the
enemy in one form or another.

They awaited him in silence as he sat and checked the
status screen to make sure their subbasement room was fully
secured. It was. Not even the data service teams or attendant
comm techs could hear them at the moment.

Did he trust Wang Daiyu's abilities?

He did.

"An...ah. An *opportunity* may have arisen in Antarctica."

The others exchanged glances.

"The West?" Admiral Chen asked.

Liú Zuocheng shook his head.

He was glad to see that the slowest one in the room took only seconds to start smiling.

"Last night I created the framework of a new operation. Today we will finish its preparation. I've called it Operation Ice Thunder."

17

MIRANDA FINISHED INSPECTING THE TAIL SECTION, LOCATING nothing of interest that she didn't see the first two times. Still no emergency locator beacon. And she'd already recovered the Flight Data Recorder.

The first-pass inspection had indeed revealed no unexpected damage, neither did her second. The engines had caught against the snow during the forceful belly landing. By the way the wing had deformed at the roots, the metal had been weakened with each fresh *dit* as the plane skipped upon the snowfield, until it had finally sheared. The angle of the final twist on the strained structural members indicated that it was the plane's dive into the crevasse, adding a new, rotational shear force, which had severed the wing from the fuselage.

The wing's position on the snow was commensurate with this assessment. The one that had fallen into the crevasse would only have needed to remain attached for an additional few seconds to be taken over the edge. In fact... yes. She could see the mark on the snow where the other wing had briefly followed a trajectory different from the fuselage before its momentum had carried it over the edge.

At Holly's behest, she and Andi began inspecting the wing more closely.

As a former military helo pilot, Andi's specialty didn't overlap well with large Russian cargo planes. On investigations like this one, she primarily served as Miranda's assistant. Miranda missed Jeremy, though it had been six months since he and Taz had gone on to form his own team in Washington, DC. Their two years together had passed so quickly. But Andi was incredibly good in her own way, even when there wasn't a helicopter involved.

Andi sat cross-legged on one of the wings while Miranda paced the length of its surface for the tenth time searching for anomalies that couldn't be explained away by the impact with *terra firma* itself—or in this case *glacies firma.*

"Miranda?" Andi was sitting near the root of the wing, where it had broken off the airplane. As Miranda approached, she leaned forward and tapped a small hatch. It was the inner wing fuel tank inspection port, big enough to allow the insertion of an inspector's head and a flashlight.

"What are you thinking?"

"Holly said the hole was punched into the starboard side of the main fuselage wingbox and destroyed a major structural member. What if whatever hit it was also damaged? Might something have scattered sideways, but below the outer surface of the wing?"

Miranda tried to imagine how she hadn't seen that. She needed to focus. Everything here was so distracting. Her first-ever crash investigation had been in deep snow and cold —she remembered it vividly as it had been her own crash in her dead father's four-seat Mooney 201.

But the cold Idaho mountains had been nothing like Antarctica. The air here was so dry that simply breathing parched her throat. And she kept turning to look for references. No conifers, not anywhere on the continent. And Whoop Whoop Skiway lay above the Vestfold Hills, nothing to see but the plain of ice. The closest mountains that rose tall enough to break the frozen surface lay five hundred kilometers over the horizon to the west and two thousand to the south.

All that was here were a plane's wing and tail, the crevasse, the Aussie Hagglund and snowmobile, and five shacks plus an array of fuel drums that formed the terminal. At this distance, only the parked Russian helicopter really stood out. The foreignness made her feel dizzy and slightly nauseous each time she looked up. She quickly looked back down at Andi as soon as she caught herself searching once more for anything familiar.

Broken wing. Familiar. Andi Wu. Familiar. Good. Both were good.

A glance to the side. No sign of Holly or Mike.

"How are they doing?" Miranda asked her.

"Can't tell. The extreme cold was killing the battery life. I've tucked it inside my parka to warm it up. Do you want me to check?"

"No. Save it for later if we need it." Holly and Mike would report by radio if necessary. Their radios were kept warm inside the parkas except for the headset they each wore under their hoods.

But they were down with the plane where she should be. Where she couldn't go. The idea of having her life supported by nothing but a rope, perhaps a piton driven into a friable rock with unknown lattice discontinuities or an ice screw cranked into a surface of equally doubtful interstitial integrity... No, she'd never liked the idea of climbing.

How must Holly and Mike feel facing those dangers for her? Nervous as well? But they'd shown no hesitancy about doing it together.

"Couples are supposed to do new things together to create stronger bonds, aren't they?"

Andi shoved back her hood to look up at Miranda. "Um, I guess so. Sure. I've heard that. What did you have in mind?"

"I want to take a rock and ice climbing course." Miranda could feel the knot in her stomach. "No, I don't. But I should. That should be me down there." She could barely manage a nod toward the blue slit of the crevasse that lay a bare ten paces away.

Andi glanced over as well but turned away quickly. "I'd rather learn to sail."

"I can teach you that. I have a nice boat stored on the island that I never use."

"That's a date then."

Miranda had to puzzle at that. Had they ever had a date? They had worked together for six months and then become a couple, living and working together ever since. "We never had a date, did we?"

Andi laughed. "A little late for that."

"Is it? I think we should go on a date. Couples always do that and I wouldn't want you to feel bad because we never dated."

"Wow, Miranda!"

"What?"

"Did you just project what another person might be feeling? How did that feel?"

Her autism usually only let her guess at other's feelings

intellectually. But with Andi, she'd simply felt that there remained a lack. "I..." Putting emotions into words continued to be a challenge as she didn't know what to say. So, she returned to her initial premise. "I think we should go on a date."

Andi's bright laugh seemed to go out and skip across the ice much as the crashing plane had: laugh, *dit,* laugh, *dit.*

She hoped there was no *dah-*crash at the end.

"Okay," Andi declared. "We'll go on a date—restaurant, movie, hold hands, the whole bit. Maybe we'll both get lucky afterward."

"I don't think there is a high factor of luck involved. We have been sleeping together for months now."

"True." But Andi's smile made Miranda hope that she did *get lucky* after their date anyway. "What does that have to do with ice climbing lessons?"

Miranda had no idea. Returning to her original statement had clarified the date conundrum. Perhaps the same methodology would apply to the climbing course. "That should be me down there."

Andi stared at her long enough that Miranda could no longer focus on her face, despite it being Andi's. She looked over to see that the climbing lines leading down into the crevasse were twitching lightly but were otherwise slack, showing that Holly and Mike were moving about but not returning. *And* not dead.

"No, Miranda. No, it shouldn't be you in the crevasse."

"But—"

"I'm going to stop you right there, though I know you hate being cut off. We each have our own expertise. That's why we're here. Well, one of the reasons."

Her cheeks reddened by more than could be accounted

for by the cold. Which might mean something if Miranda's brain functioned differently but, she sighed, it didn't.

"You have to let each of us use our expertise. You already make all of us feel inadequate as it is."

"I do?"

"Duh!" Again that laugh sallied forth like... Some metaphor she couldn't conjure up, but not like a crashing airplane, which had been inappropriate in retrospect.

"Duh?"

"Yes, Duh! With the exclamation point. You're the best crash investigator there is, anywhere. We're all trying to keep up with you most of the time."

"That sounds...lonely." She'd spent years coming to terms with there being only one of her. Then this team had gathered around her and she'd been less alone. Despite Jeremy and Taz leaving the team to go to Washington, DC, she'd felt less alone now than most of her life.

"It does. So, drop the dangerous rope climbing classes, unless you actually want to learn."

Miranda felt around inside her head. A glance toward the open crevasse did not...excite. Nor did she feel fear, which her childhood therapist had said was easy to mistake for excitement. She felt... *Ah!* "That's why I was feeling nauseous. You're right, I don't like the climbing idea. Okay. Let's look inside the wing-tank maintenance hatch." It was good to be done with two topics in a row—and so efficiently.

Andi nodded, not laughing this time but smiling as if amused.

Deciding it was better not to ask, Miranda unzipped her parka enough to reach the proper-sized wrench in her vest pocket. Then she set about undoing the inspection hatch.

18

"WE ESCAPED."

Holly lay on the ice close by the edge of the crevasse. She managed to rock her head sideways enough to confirm, again, that Mike had made it clear of that icy dingo hole as well and lay beside her. With each tilt to the side, the snow under her hat creaked. Every turn made her skull feel tighter and tighter.

All the wishing in the world wasn't going to make his continuing survival less important to her.

"You're a pain in the ass, Munroe."

"Not surprised. Not all sweetness and light yourself, Harper," he mumbled.

"Me? I'm cute and charming."

"Drop dead gorgeous—"

"Which is why you like having me in your bed."

"—and a *major* pain in the ass."

Holly was less sure about the first part. But the second part? Oh yeah. She'd made a life career out of being a major PITA—except she'd tapped out of her military career as staff sergeant. Being a Staff Sergeant of PITAness didn't have quite the same ring. Though she was sure that her mother, her schoolmates, and her military mates first in the regular Army and then in SASR would have been glad to grant her the promotion.

Now? The kind of shit they'd uncovered on the Ilyushin Il-76 cargo jet down in that crevasse? *That* was a pain in the ass on a whole new scale.

She tipped her head back against the squeaky snow enough to see what the others were up to. Andi was sitting on the one wing and waved. Miranda knelt a few feet from Andi and had her head inside the wing.

Freddy and Marla were walking over from where they'd been working the winches on the Hagglund crawler to pull them out of the pit. Wang Daiyu joined them from where she'd been pacing about to keep warm. Nikolas Romanoff descended from the Hagglund where he'd probably been talking to his bosses on whether or not to send in one of their bombers.

"Showtime, Mike."

He groaned. "This is going to be so much fun." But he pushed to his feet and held out a hand to help her up. "We need a signal jammer to keep those two from reporting home until we figure out what's going on."

Holly ignored his hand and slapped her various pockets, then her chest. "Crap, left it in my other bra."

Mike made a predictably salacious comment about his willingness to go to the ends of the Earth to fetch it for her.

"Hello! Already at the end of the Earth."

"No, there's the Russians at Vostok Station—"

"More Russians? Screw that."

"—and beyond them you'd hit the South Pole. Many wonders yet to behold."

"God I hope not." Mike's hand was out so she used it to pull herself to her feet—and to knock him once more onto his butt as she did so. The ice chill that had penetrated the mighty red parka seemed to stick to her spine as she regained her feet. Not a real surprise after what they'd found in the cargo bay.

"Damn it, Holly," Mike grumbled from where he sprawled on the ice. Maybe she'd tipped him over harder than she'd meant to, but she didn't need anybody. Did she?

Holly unsnapped a spare line that led from her harness over the lip of the crevasse and handed it to Marla as she and Freddy arrived.

"Freddy, if you could hop on the snowmobile to pull the other lifting line. And Marla, if you could pull on this one in unison using the Hagglund, there's something below I want to bring up here." *Like hell she did.* "It's heavy so go slow, and watch my signals for when to go slower than that. Mum's the word, mates," she whispered the last.

That earned her raised eyebrows but also a cheery, "Righto!" Bless the Land of Oz. There were bits and bobs of it she missed. The easy willingness to let questions be answered in their own time certainly didn't exist in the US.

The two Aussies crossed paths with the approaching Russian and Chinese contingent. They might only be one of each but the power they could each call on was terrifying. She couldn't resist glancing aloft at the achingly blue sky and wondering if she'd be able spot a Russian bomber *before* it blew her out of existence.

Holly wished she could hide that danger from Miranda. Not half a chance in— Holly looked around the Antarctic ice sheet that ranged for thousands of kilometers to the South until it became the north all over again. Was *this* Hell frozen over?

Miranda might not understand people but she didn't miss much else.

Holly signaled to Andi to come on over, also pointing at Miranda who was still had her head down inside the wing.

Andi tapped Miranda on the shoulder, though it took her several tries to first get Miranda's attention and then convince her to stop inspecting whatever she'd found.

Holly should have been more conscious of not switching tracks on Miranda. She always took it hard. But this time there was a reason.

Andi apparently convinced Miranda. The two of them climbed off the wing and walked over to join the group well back from the crevasse's edge.

"Greetings, boss," Holly gave her a palm out Australian salute. Miranda, not knowing quite what to do with it, flapped her hands for a moment, then said, "Hi."

But she hadn't done it for Miranda.

The moment Andi glanced at her quizzically, Holly tipped her hand palm down as if shading her eyes. It was the military sign for keep a look out. Andi didn't so much as blink. She didn't need to.

Andi didn't react overtly. She made three subtle changes that showed her absolute understanding. She shifted so that she had a clear view of Daiyu and Romanoff. Her position also placed her in the perfect position to tackle Miranda aside if harm came her direction. Finally, she slipped off a glove and tucked it into her pocket where no doubt her sidearm had been placed for easy access. She made the whole thing look smooth and natural.

"What have we got?" Romanoff started toward the crevasse edge but Holly blocked his progress.

"Not without a safety line, mate."

"Well," Mike then stepped in before she could stop him. "We found a lot of fried bananas."

Which made everyone, including her, laugh— awkwardly, but a laugh. She should know better than to worry about Mike making a misstep. He never did when the pressure was on, so why did she have so much trouble trusting that? The answer to that and a fiver might buy a half-pint in a pub.

"There were also burnt blocks of bouillon, and a few other culinary catastrophes. When pickle jars, ketchup, or mustard are frozen that hard, they tend to bust open. Cold enough down in that crevasse to blow a couple cases of vodka as well." Though Mike had recovered an unbroken and apparently rare bottle now stashed inside his parka. She wouldn't be able to tell the difference from bottom-shelf by-the-gallon—she was a beer gal. But if he wanted to ply her with three-hundred-dollar-a-bottle Beluga Allure Vodka, she'd let herself be lured—later.

Marla and Freddy watched her from close by their vehicles. Must be ready.

She twisted an ice screw into the surface well back from the edge, then snapped a short line from it to Mike. She snapped her own safety line to it, then handed it to Mike to pay out.

"On belay," she announced.

"On belay," he agreed. "Be careful, Babe."

She'd *babe* him one right in the snoot—another time. Signaling the others to stay put, she strode over to the edge of the crevasse so that she could watch what was happening.

"Tension!" she shouted when she could see over the edge.

Mike snubbed the line.

She then signaled Marla only to start towing on her lifting line.

The first box, which they'd tied onto the new nine-millimeter haul line, slid out of the open rear of the cargo bay and began the six-story ascent from the fuselage to the surface.

She eased the relatively light crate over the lip of the crevasse and then unclipped it from the haul line, keeping it here by the crevasse edge and not letting it be dragged over to the waiting group.

The line continued down to the main object. She waved for Freddy to take up the slack on the other line. As planned, they came under tension together. Each line was rated as safe to two and a quarter tons, forty-five hundred pounds.

The big if: did the snow machines have sufficient power and traction to drag the four tonnes of the second item to the surface? Four thousand kilograms, eighty-eight hundred pounds—it was going to be dicey. It was at the rated limit of the combined lines.

The Hagglund was heavy enough to move forward at a plodding pace, but the snowmobile was light by design. With a double fist-pump, then a hand slashing ahead, she signaled Freddy to go for all he was worth. Soon, a rooster tail of ice and snow was shooting out from behind his machine.

Holly wished she was with the others, close enough to read the expressions on Wang's and Romanoff's faces, but between Mike and Andi, they'd have it covered. Or at least she'd have to *trust* that they did.

Damn that word to back o' Bourke and beyond!

With the demise of her old SASR unit, she didn't trust anyone. Not all the way. Not even Miranda. Because her own team had gone down so hard, Holly couldn't trust that Miranda wouldn't end up suddenly dead one day and the best three years of her life would also end that abruptly.

She then looked at Mike, keeping the others well back from the equipment and straining ropes.

Holly looked away quickly.

The big case continued to ascend slowly. The line from the Hagglund doing most of the work, the snowmobile picking up what slack it could.

But when the case reached the edge of the lip, they couldn't haul it over the ninety-degree turn of the edge, no matter how they struggled.

Time to apply a dab of physics.

She hurried back to where everyone was waiting.

"What is that you found?" Romanoff asked.

Could he not know? "It's labeled as a large telescope."

He grunted. She should introduce him to Barty. Good thing Mike wasn't a grunter, she'd have hammered him for that.

She hurriedly divided them into two groups at the center of the lines stretching from the case caught at the crevasse's lip to the straining vehicles. The lines were stretched so tightly they were humming in the freezing air.

Holly took Andi and Miranda with her, and ducked under the two parallel lines until they were facing Mike, Daiyu, and Romanoff across the middle of the lines in two groups of three.

Now that they weren't standing next to each other, she had to shout to be heard over the roaring of the two machines. "Grab the line. Pull sideways, away from each other, perpendicular to the line."

"What does—"

"Questions later," she shouted at Romanoff. "Pull...*Now!*"

Each team began pulling. The power of triangles; she hoped it worked because she didn't have any other ideas.

By pulling sideways at the center, with limited force they could vastly increase the tension on the line. The danger was, too much tension and it could snap the line. That's why she'd had Miranda and Andi on her side.

If the line snapped, she was going to do everything in her power to make sure that the whipping ends didn't kill them.

19

MIRANDA WISHED SHE KNEW THE SHAPE AND EXACT WEIGHT OF the second object they were pulling out of the crevasse. It was difficult to calculate the force moment-arm that would be sufficient to induce failure in the lines.

There were too many simultaneous unknowns, including that line manufacturers only provided minimum breaking strength of lines, never *likely* limits. They did provide a rating for number of allowable falls on a UIAA scale of height and weight of arrest but that didn't seem applicable in this situation.

She was leaning back against the line, pulling as hard as she could, but it wasn't moving.

"This is fun," Andi managed between clenched teeth. "As much fun as your gym."

A curious comment, as Andi was the one who had developed their shared workout routine. As a former Special Operations pilot, she constantly strived to keep them pushing the edge. Miranda had never been in such good condition.

Which gave her an idea.

"Pump the iron," she managed, wondering how she could be so out of breath while standing on the ice and leaning back against a line.

She and Andi started it, then Holly joined in.

Pull-release. Pull-release. Pull-release.

Their muscle fibers tired rapidly under sustained tension. But the brief release allowed momentary blood flow that increased oxygenation and flushed away lactic acid buildup.

The trio on the far side matched their rhythm.

It would also jostle the case slightly, perhaps rocking it enough to crest over the edge.

The Hagglund groaned and the snowmobile sounded like a grinder as it dug its tracks deeper and deeper into the surface.

They were either going to snap the lines or—

Miranda sprawled backward onto her butt. At first she thought she *had* miscalculated and snapped the line. Before she could apologize to Holly, she saw the large object resting on the lip of the crevasse.

There was no doubt about what it was.

20

"YOU SHIPPED *WHAT* ON THAT PLANE?"

"Are you questioning me, Captain Turgenev?"

"That's *Major* Turgenev, sir." Artie to his friends, of whom Army General Murov, the commander of the FSB, was definitely not one.

"No. Turgenev."

Turgenev swallowed hard. What had he done to lose a rank in an eyeblink? And what had he done to end up here at six a.m. on a bitter Moscow December morning? The sun wouldn't be up for three more hours.

He'd thought he'd make Lieutenant Colonel for sure when he'd introduced Aloysha Novikov to Lieutenant Colonel Kurchenko. But Kurchenko was sloppy. Screwing a pilot's wife hadn't been what had taken him down. Rumor said that he hadn't cut in his own superior, Colonel Romanoff, for a share of a major bribe. A fool's mistake. Goodbye, Kurchenko. Turgenev's own path to that seat should have been clear.

He knew that Aloysha had targeted Colonel Romanoff

after Kurchenko's abrupt disappearance from sight—his own suggestion and introduction in exchange for any information she learned. But her attempt to seduce Romanoff had fizzled like a ten-year-old firework for unknown reasons. Turgenev knew that it was the unknown that killed a man, but he couldn't unravel what had gone wrong.

Rumor said that Romanoff was now in Antarctica. And with Kurchenko disgraced, detained, and probably deceased, he himself was the nearest throat for General Murov to wrap his long fingers around despite the numerous ranks that separated them.

Turgenev had never been inside the Lubyanka Building before. Was it true that the windowless prison on the top floor was now a museum, or was he about to be dragged out of General Murov's office and incarcerated there to the end of his days? Maybe in a cell next to Kurchenko so they could rot out the rest of their lives in shared misery.

Artemy Turgenev looked around in case it was the last day of his freedom. Though he tried not to *look* as if he was looking around.

General Mikhail Murov's office radiated power. Perched on the third floor, it commanded a sweeping view of Lubyanka Square, all quiet at this hour, lit only by streetlights and the occasional delivery truck.

Inside, the walls were ornately paneled and painted a stately ivory. Though the room was large, his desk was not. A rich, dark wood with two guest chairs. Nearby stood a conference table to seat ten, facing several large television screens—all currently blank.

Then he looked at the man in the two-piece pinstripe suit. Anyone who didn't know his face would walk by him without a second glance. Murov waited, and Turgenev could hear how fast that ticking clock raced.

"I'm sorry, General. I didn't intend to criticize the choice of cargo sent to Antarctica, I was merely taken by surprise. That's all, sir. Until this moment, I thought it was loaded with foodstuffs and mechanical parts for the ongoing improvements at Progress Station."

Murov appeared to be slightly mollified. "I've been informed, Turgenev, that the plane has two rather large holes punched through it from top to bottom. Now it lies down a crevasse in Australian territory. Explain."

Turgenev considered everything he knew about the dead pilot. He and Fyodor Novikov had flown together for years before he himself had climbed out of the cockpit and into the upper ranks. The man had been the rock of the 196th Transport Aviation Regiment.

The general's scowl slowly deepened with impatience.

Turgenev swallowed hard and began thinking aloud to distract the general. "Every pilot award went to him, sir, and no one argued. Captain Fyodor Novikov was not imaginative. Nor political. But if he was the pilot, it was a given that your plane was coming home."

"Not in this case." Murov's expression eased slightly, moments prior to spelling his own doom, but Turgenev couldn't breathe any more easily.

"Two holes you say, sir?"

The general waved a hand at the green-felt blotter on his desk. "This size, I'm given to understand. Through the cockpit and the central fuel tank."

He knew the weapons of the Russian Federation well; his brother worked in arms development and kept him informed. Maybe he'd be interested in Aloysha now that

Fyodor was dead? They would be a good match, actually. Of course, convincing her that there was any advantage to sleeping with a scientist rated well below unlikely. Her loss, as his brother had a sterling future.

"From top to bottom? That implies immense kinetic energy to punch such a large hole all the way through without an explosion that would have killed the plane instantly. The Il-76 is a remarkably robust aircraft, General, especially around the central wing-box tank. That implies that it was fired at close range, or..." Turgenev stumbled to a halt.

The general raised his eyebrows.

"But that's impossible. To target a plane in a storm with a railgun or a hypersonic projectile from space—" he didn't know how to finish that sentence. "Not us, sir. I wish it was, but it's not us. The Americans, perhaps?"

"The Americans dispatched a *civilian* air-crash investigation team."

"To inspect their own handiwork?"

The general shrugged.

"It doesn't quite fit, does it, sir?"

The general studied him carefully, then spoke with a flat tone. "The Chinese sent an envoy of the Central Military Commission. A colonel."

Turgenev whistled in surprise. It was all he had in him.

The general waited again, without the unnerving scowl.

"Are the Chinese capable of such an attack? I've heard no such reports, General, but they are very careful. Perhaps it is up to this person to evaluate their success, or to finish the job."

General Murov studied him for a long moment. "I need answers fast, *Lieutenant Colonel* Turgenev. Do not contact

Colonel Romanoff in Antarctica; I am in contact with him and he's dealing with the Chinese colonel on site. I need corroboration. Explore the Chinese angle. Use anyone you need to, but do not tell them why. You report directly to me. If I do not hear a report from you every six hours, you will... regret the oversight."

Artemy Turgenev's next moment of awareness was standing in the busy hallway a story below General Murov's office and taking a breath.

He wasn't dead.

Or arrested.

Three ranks, from major down to captain, then up to lieutenant colonel, in as many minutes. And the most dangerous assignment possible. Success—and the general might elevate him past his most coveted dreams. Failure— and he would find out exactly what had happened to Kurchenko.

21

"ANTARCTICA IS NOT A MAJOR GLOBAL AGGRESSOR."

Drake wanted to snap back at her wry tone. But berating the Director of the National Reconnaissance Office was not the path to marital bliss.

"Therefore, I don't have a lot of surveillance eyes beyond the Arctic and Antarctic Circles," Lizzy continued. "And we don't take a lot of pictures of ice, so our surveillance birds in polar orbit aren't creating a wonderful backlog of images for you."

"I don't care about the backlog. I care about the last thirty-six hours."

"Drake..."

She didn't need to say anything more. He swallowed it down, "Sorry."

Lizzy had come to the Pentagon and he'd ordered in delivery Chinese food, because there'd been too many pizza nights of late. The *minute* President Cole's second term ended, Drake was done. He didn't count the days remaining —yet. Maybe he'd start tonight.

Logging into the NRO's system, Lizzy displayed one of those 3D orbital maps of satellite tracks weaving the globe in an all-encompassing fish net. It always made him feel claustrophobic, caught in a net.

Was that what he was going to do when he retired after forty years in the military, fishing? At nine years younger, Lizzy would be at the NRO for a long time to come. He'd never thought about that before. Would his life become cleaning house and preparing dinner while waiting for her return home? Only if she wanted to risk a poisoning—most of the meals in his life had been paid for by the Army.

"There," she'd reduced the number of tracks circling the globe. "We have three birds that made a total of nineteen passes over Prydz Bay in the last thirty-six hours."

With a speed that proved she'd adapted to the video age much better than he had, the feeds from all three were soon playing at high speed on different screens on wall.

"At least there aren't any issues with nighttime."

He remembered why the moment before asking. It was high summer down there. "Then why are we seeing nothing but white?"

"A severe storm blanketed the area for half a day. The Russian plane went down while trying to fly through that storm."

The white shifted and slid across the screens, making him slightly nauseous. Too much of General Tso's deep-fried chicken in sweet-and-spicy sauce.

"There!" Lizzy stopped the feeds, wound one back, and zoomed in.

"Where?"

She placed a red circle on the screen around a tiny smear

he never would have picked out. "It's the infrared signature of the plane's engines."

The image scrolled forward and back several times.

"It's only a brief gap in the storm, but the heading, speed, and heat signature are a good fit for an Ilyushin-76 headed from Cape Town to Progress Station."

Drake tried a steamed pot sticker to settle his stomach. As soon as Lizzy set the screens moving ahead in their whirling white blur, he knew it was a mistake.

With abrupt snips from the three feeds, she slowly rebuilt the final flight of the Russian cargo jet.

22

As the group approached the objects on the brink of the crevasse, Miranda wished she knew *less*. It was new experience.

All of her life she'd protected herself by knowing *more*, as much as possible. On nights when she couldn't sleep due to the strangeness of having someone in her bed night after night, she would slip into her office to study the newest information on aircraft. In her youth she'd focused strictly on American civilian aircraft. Her early twenties had been mostly involved with learning about foreign civilian aircraft, but also adding on US military aircraft on a case-by-case basis.

Now, her needs were being stretched in so many directions: helicopters, drones, military aircraft (both domestic and foreign), and lately the weapons that could bring them down.

Weapons like the two sitting where they should never be, on the lip of a crevasse in Antarctica.

"Please tell me those aren't what I think they are?"

Miranda hoped Andi was asking someone else because if she said what they were, it would make them too real.

In answer, Holly walked over to the smaller case that they'd initially lifted from the depths. The Russian label stated it was a sterile sounding probe for Lake Vostok. The world's fifth largest freshwater lake had been discovered three kilometers below the icecap under Vostok Station in the middle of the continent.

"It caught my attention because it says no one except authorized personnel may open it."

Nikolas Romanoff snapped out. "So, of course, you opened Russian private property, contaminating sensitive scientific equipment."

Holly knelt in front of the case, "Of course I did." She flipped it open, reached in, and extracted a moss green tube as big across as her forearm and five feet long. It had a pair of handgrips like a rifle.

Romanoff stumbled backward when Holly swung it onto her shoulder and pointed the tube at his chest.

"Tell me, mate. If I pull this trigger, will it release a scientific sounding probe, or will a 9K333 Verba Willow surface-to-air missile punch a hole through your chest before it blows you to hell?"

Romanoff tried shifting out of the way, but Holly tracked him easily.

"What is that thing?" Freddy asked. "It looks like a bazooka."

Holly lowered the weapon and tucked it once more into the case. "Know what MANPADS are, Freddy?"

"Uh, no."

"Man Portable Air Defense System. This is a fourth-generation piece of nasty that can take out a plane flying six kilometers overhead. It wouldn't slow down but a mite if it passed through our Russian pal here."

Miranda turned to look at Nikolas Romanoff, or at least his chin. She was lousy at reading expressions anyway, and strangers' eyes were always so confusing that she never looked *wholly* at them.

"Militarization of Antarctica is a direct violation of the Antarctic Treaty System."

"I will not speak of how much the Russian Federation could not care. These are but minor weapons to protect our stations' sovereignty against Western aggressors."

Holly reached into a pocket of her parka. "We also found boxes of rifles and a couple caseloads of these," she pulled out a grenade and tossed it to Romanoff, who fumbled to catch it.

Holly and Mike walked over to the long metal tube, the one that their collective efforts had barely managed to retrieve from the crevasse. They pulled off the endcap, but Miranda had already recognized it; she'd simply hoped that it didn't contain what she thought it did.

Seeing the nose cone of the contents was sufficient.

Nine meters long and half a meter across.

An SS-N-30A Kalibr cruise missile.

At least now she knew the weight of the object. Twenty-three hundred kilograms of missile and approximately three hundred for the casing. She'd estimate that the dual lines had been strained within eighty-four percent of their breaking limit, plus or minus seven percent. She must remember to tell Marla and Freddy to not attempt reuse of those lines in any climbing safety capacity.

Wang Daiyu smiled strangely after she glanced inside the tube.

Miranda pulled out her emoji reference, but couldn't find her smile anywhere.

Andi leaned close, "It's exactly what she expected, and that pleases her for an unknown reason."

She checked the emojis again. None of the images bore labels that matched such a complicated range of emotions. Emotions were *so* tricky! She'd *never* get the hang of them.

But she knew one thing for certain, "This is not an appropriate weapon for small station protection as you claim."

Holly was nodding, "Twenty-five-hundred-kilometer range. Placed at Vostok, you could target the Americans at both the South Pole Station and McMurdo. Five-hundred-kilo warhead—at least the ones we saw down below weren't nuclear-tipped—but they be plenty nasty. Call it a three-hundred-meter kill radius, along with heavy injury and damage out to a kilometer. Now that'd screw up a station through and through."

Romanoff pulled out his radio but spoke too fast and quietly for Miranda to catch. Holly took a step toward him, but he tucked it away before she could move closer.

"We will be reporting this to the other Antarctica Treaty System members," Miranda told him. Though she didn't think the committee had ever faced the need to take punitive action against one of its members other than minor environmental fiascos—mostly at abandoned Russian stations.

She didn't need to see anything else here. With that checked off in her mind, her thoughts returned to the broken-off wing.

"There's something I want to show you, Holly." And she led the four of them toward the wing.

Daiyu followed them and the Australians began cleaning up the climbing gear and the lines that coiled and twisted across the ice like frozen snakes. Miranda smiled to herself, rather pleased with the metaphor. She let her eyes follow their definitely snakelike winding paths until she spotted Romanoff standing at the edge of the crevasse without a rope.

"Hey, that's not safe."

If Romanoff heard her, he didn't turn.

Perhaps it was because he couldn't hear her over the sound of the approaching helicopter. The Russian Ka-32S Helix had taken off from the far end of the skiway and was flying to land near him.

Romanoff made a jerking motion in front of his chest, while he faced the crevasse. Then he raised a hand high, before throwing a fist-sized object down into the opening.

Holly had been close enough to hear her warning however. After turning to look and watch Romanoff's actions, her shout was rather different.

"Run!" Holly grabbed Miranda's arm.

The others who had continued a few steps toward the wing were soon trying to keep up as Holly sprinted ahead. Miranda was glad for Andi's running habit—they ran at least five kilometers each morning they were on the island. She dug in, though she wasn't quite sure why she was, and managed to retain her balance despite Holly's impetus.

"...three, four..." Holly was counting under her breath.

At five, Holly tripped Miranda and sent her tumbling to the ice. In the same moment, she dove on top of her, driving all the air out of Miranda's lungs.

There was a distant pop of noise that Miranda hoped wasn't someone's knee.

Then the ice bucked beneath them.

Three, four, five times it tried to heave them into the air.

Each successive shockwave exceeded the one before.

A blast wave tumbled them all a dozen meters over the ice, knocking Holly off her.

Miranda turned in time to see fire explode upward out of the crevasse, a sheet of yellow-orange flashing heavenward, a garish, living brilliance against the stark white ice and blue sky.

That's when the sound caught up with her, as if her ears were running a quarter lap behind. Miranda did *not* take the time to congratulate herself on another metaphor.

The ice groaned against the onslaught. Bright shearing and cracking sounds like an ice cube dropped in hot tea, but a hundred times louder—which wasn't a metaphor but rather a parallelism.

No fire followed the initial blast. There would be little burnable on the plane down in the crevasse. Once the explosives aboard fired upward, only the aftershocks would be of consequence.

That's when she focused on Nikolas Romanoff.

The helicopter, mere feet from landing, had been knocked aside by the force of the blast. The pilot was exceptional and managed to avoid digging his rotor blades into the ice. But he over-corrected. Or perhaps there was a backdraft.

The helicopter tumbled sideways and disappeared into the crevasse. It didn't re-emerge.

Romanoff scrambled up on all fours, then managed to

regain his feet as he began running away from the crevasse when the next blast knocked him off his feet again.

He braced on his hands and knees—as the ice began to crumble beneath him.

Like a wave rolling outward from the crevasse, or rather downward into it, the lip began moving rapidly in their direction.

First the case of 9K333 Verba Willow MANPADS tumbled off the edge and disappeared. Then the big tube of the Kalibr cruise missile tumbled into the hole.

Romanoff made it to his feet again.

At the same moment, fifty meters farther from the crevasse, Andi, Holly, and Daiyu were grabbing her and Mike. They half dragged, half ran them farther from the unfolding disaster.

"Cut them! Cut the lines!" Holly was shouting to Freddy and Marla.

They slashed at the hauling lines on the Hagglund with knives.

The big snow machine was being dragged backward. Until they'd severed all except one line. That one snapped in complete silence, at least silence compared to the roar behind them. The Hagglund stopped moving backward. The snowmobile was still tied to the missile. It weighed five hundred pounds. The missile and launch tube weighed over five thousand. There was no contest.

The big missile struck something below, ice or the plane, it didn't matter.

The five-hundred-kilo warhead and enough solid rocket fuel to drive the missile across twenty-five-hundred miles went up in a single blast.

The last thing Miranda saw before being knocked from her feet again was Nikolas Romanoff, or at least his silhouette. He was a dark blot leaning into a sprint and highlighted by a fresh sheet of fire behind.

Then the ice beneath his feet erupted.

23

"What the hell was that?" Drake had stopped eating and wished he had a beer, but there weren't a lot of late-night bars in the Pentagon. Then he'd spotted a flash on one of the screens while Lizzy happened to be reading her fortune cookie: *You will find great*—

Lizzy dropped her fortune half-read, reversed the current live feed, then played it again on Slow.

The angle was bad, Davis Station was barely above the horizon. Lizzy had retasked every satellite that passed anywhere close to focus on Davis.

In slow motion, a multi-stage explosion roiled upward out of the ice. It rose in a long, flat sheet like no explosion he'd ever seen—and back in his days as a 75th US Ranger, he'd seen a lot of them. The fire disappeared as the satellite passed it edge-on, then showed it once more.

"No mushroom cloud," Lizzy said.

"So, not nuclear or large thermobaric," Drake agreed. "Is that as big as it looks?"

Lizzy called up a scaling tool on the screen. "At least two hundred meters high and half a kilometer wide."

As the view receded behind the satellite, they could see that the now fading explosion was fan-shaped. A great semicircle standing edge-on.

A secondary flash went up, brighter than the first.

Again the fan shape.

Then it fell behind the horizon as the satellite continued along its ninety-minute orbit.

"When's the next pass of anything in that area?"

Lizzy rattled on the keyboard for a moment, "Thirty-seven minutes."

Drake grabbed the phone and dialed Miranda.

24

NOTHING REMAINED OF THE ILYUSHIN-76 CANDID.

The hand grenade that Nikolas Romanoff had tossed toward the open maw left by the broken-off tail section had been highly accurate. He had spent uncounted hours of his youth as a ball boy for his mother—fetching and tossing stray tennis balls. She had ultimately ranked top twenty-five globally, her powerful serves were considered to be the best in the sport.

For his tenth birthday present, she had publicly declared that achievement was a large part his doing for the endless hours he'd helped her. It continued to be one of the proudest days of his life.

This time he would have been better off missing the throw.

He'd known there were three other SS-N-30A Kalibr cruise missiles aboard. Unknown to him, Mike and Holly had left behind the missile tube that they had initially opened while they were aboard to inspect the contents. Instead they'd lifted clear one that was still sealed.

Romanoff's grenade, after ricocheting off a desperately needed element for Vostok Station's old heating system, had bounced into the Kalibr's open tube before exploding.

The shrapnel, not energetic enough to punch through the tube or into the other rockets, easily penetrated the skin of the missile itself a meter above the rocket motors. Only three of the thirty-two fragments also penetrated to the solid-fuel core.

It was sufficient; the fuel ignited.

Uncontrolled by a rocket nozzle, the core burned far faster than designed. Initially sucking in oxygen through the three small penetrations, it rapidly melted the containment case providing a flood of fresh oxygen to the reaction.

Within the first fifty milliseconds, the fuel was fully involved. A rate of burn so catastrophic couldn't be contained.

By the end of the next fifty milliseconds, the first tenth of a second, the overpressure within the fuel tank spiked.

Flashover from fire to explosion required an additional twelve milliseconds.

The open end of the launch tube proved an insufficient release for the rapidly expanding firestorm.

When the first missile's fuel exploded, the other two remaining missiles were struck with far more highly energetic shrapnel than three tiny squares of an F-1 fragmentation grenade.

Before the next two-tenths of a second had passed, the second and third missiles had exceeded the limits of restraint offered by their now punctured launch tubes.

The HE explosive warheads—primarily RDX, one of the best explosives in the world for shattering both casings and any structures it might encounter—had not yet become involved. It was inherently stable, but could be triggered by a sufficiently large shock. That was unnecessary in this case.

In seeking to escape the severe overpressure, a portion of the rocket fuel fired out the first missile's rocket motor nozzle. It wasn't sufficient to fly the missile effectively, but it was enough to drive it hard against the far end of the launch tube containers. The impact destroyed both the safety mechanism of the warhead and the radar element of the proximity fuse.

It did not destroy the contact fuse.

Slamming through the thin endcap, the missile struck a four-tonne pallet of rice in fifty-kilo bags. It might as well have hit the steel hull of a warship. As designed, the contact fuse sent its signal deep into the heart of the RDX, and five hundred kilos of high-energy explosive puffed four thousand kilos of rice in the next thirty-seven milliseconds.

The explosion had sufficient force to trigger the other two warheads—an additional thousand kilos of RDX—and the disaster expanded from there.

In turn, the hull suffered the same fate as the missile tubes—a blast of fire out the missing rear of the cargo bay insufficient to relieve the pressure of the building explosion —and the top of the hull was blown apart.

But the lower framing kept the plane held in the crevasse's grip. Falling ice from the edges of the opening high above speared down, knocking the remains of the hull lower, but not quite dislodging it.

Not until the edge crumbled enough to undermine the weapons that had been so laboriously hauled to the surface.

The small, shoulder-mounted Willow surface-to-air missiles simply tumbled down into the depths.

The fourth SS-N-30 Kalibr cruise missile slid free from

its tube as it fell. Nose first, it struck the block of frozen bananas—now as hard as steel—and exploded.

What was left of the Ilyushin-76 Candid fell into the dark depths of the crevasse. No pieces were big enough to catch on both walls as the plane's fuselage had, until the gap was significantly narrower.

The missile had struck vertically, nose down. The engine and rocket fuel in the final missile stood nine meters—three full stories—above the airplane's hull when it ignited. With no restraints around it except for the thin casing of the missile, that blast slammed outward, shattered the sidewalls of the ice crevasse with a massive hammer blow.

That was the blast that had thrown Nikolas Romanoff up and forward as Miranda watched.

For a brief moment he had the sensation of flying, driven by an oven-blast of wind.

As he fell back to earth, he could see the ice crumbling away beneath him.

He had managed to gain enough distance from the original crevasse that he didn't plunge into its much-widened maw.

Instead, he fell into a field of shattered ice pinnacles that sliced through his body more easily than his mother's tennis serve.

He was wholly unaware of the tube falling into the unblocked crevasse or of the uncut line that had been attached to it to haul it to the surface. However, he did manage to look upward as the Australian's snowmobile was dragged backward into the ice field.

The last thing he ever saw was the undercarriage of the snowmobile that killed him.

25

MIRANDA'S PHONE RANG.

It was the first sound to shatter the vast silence.

The explosion had not been followed by fire as there was nothing of substance below left to burn. A few stray wisps of smoke emerged from the crevasse, perhaps the Russian helicopter's fuel, but no more.

The agony of the groaning ice—did a personification count as a metaphor?—had also subsided into silence.

One by one, each person sat up and looked around at each other but no one spoke. It was as if sound had ceased to exist on the high ice until—

Her phone rang again.

She answered but couldn't think of what to say.

"Miranda? Is that you?" A male voice. "Are you okay?"

Was she? She hardly knew.

"Miranda?"

"We're..." she managed, then looked toward the field of shattered ice. "We're going to need a new Russian." Did this negate her mistake of revealing to Romanoff that she spoke

Russian? She hoped so, because an angry Holly was more than she could handle at the moment.

There was a strangely choked laugh on the other end of the line. "How about the others?" Drake. Drake's voice.

"What others?"

"Who else is with you Miranda?"

She had to look around to remind herself. "Holly, Mike, and Andi." Andi was crawling toward her across the ice. No one was standing. "Marla and Freddy."

"Who?"

"They're Australian. Antarctic Program."

Freddy was holding a handful of red snow against his cheek. Marla reached into the Hagglund and pulled out a medical kit.

"And Wang Daiyu. She's Chinese."

There was a brief silence during which Miranda noticed that the tail and wing of the Il-76 were gone as well. She hadn't seen those being swallowed by the disaster. And the crew's bodies, too. Their final burial place would be in the ice, until the glacier eventually moved out to sea in the distant future.

"Wang Daiyu?" Drake had paused long enough that he must have looked her up. He made it sound important.

"Yes. Did you want to speak to her?"

"Um...no. Tell me what happened. I'm here with Lizzy."

"Hi, Lizzy."

"Hello, Miranda. That was quite a fire."

"It was. Though as nothing is burning, I believe that *explosion* would be a more appropriate noun to select."

Again one of those weird conversational pauses. "Did you want me to keep speaking?"

"Yes please. Can you tell us what happened?"

This was good. She pulled out her personal notebook and made a note that a pause could be a silent invitation to continue a communication. She left a question mark in the column that denoted whether this was a standard rule or simply an occasional usage methodology.

"Miranda? Are you there?"

"Yes. We were investigating a Russian Il-76 that crash landed at Whoop Whoop Skiway. It was a good landing under the circumstances, or it would have been if the hadn't been for the final *dah* in NHA. The plane fell into a deep crevasse, jamming into place twenty meters below the surface."

"The final...NHA...never mind. Did the crew survive?"

"One lived to the surface, but probably not much longer."

"That was over thirty-hours ago, so—"

"Between thirty-five and thirty-nine hours."

Drake sighed deeply before continuing, "—what caused the explosion now? It was so big that we picked it up with one of our satellites."

"Seismographs should also pick it up, at least in Antarctica. I would estimate that between the rocket fuel and warheads it should register as at least a four-point-one magnitude ice quake on the Richter scale."

"*What,* Miranda. *What* caused the explosion?"

Miranda turned to Holly and Andi. "He's getting that tone." That too was progress. She used to want to fold up and hide when someone used that tone with her. Now, she knew how to deal with it. She held out her phone.

Holly grabbed it before Andi could. "No, Wu, you'll yell at the Chairman of the Joint Chiefs. Won't help a bit."

Andi's face was indeed a good match for the frowny

emoji complete with flushed cheeks and grinding teeth. All that was missing was the steam coming out of her ears to make it anger/fury. Oh, another metaphor, emoji to human this time. Andi was indeed livid. Miranda was unclear as to why.

"Drake, mate, Holly here. Staff Sergeant Holly Harper of Oz's Special Air Service Regiment, retired of course. You remember me, don't ya, mate?" She was using that broad Strine accent that said she gearing up for a fight.

Miranda figured it was better if she removed Andi from the vicinity of that battle.

26

Miranda's own balance remained unpredictable despite managing to stand. Andi rose as smoothly as the athlete she was.

Daiyu tipped her head in a way that Miranda didn't understand, but Andi waved for the woman to join them. The three of them moved across the ice to join Marla and Freddy, who were untying the short ends of the lines that they had cut from the Hagglund as the falling missile was dragging it toward the crevasse.

Freddy had a large bandage on his cheek, but it wasn't red with fresh blood. At least not much.

Mike hooked a good line from his waist to the Hagglund. He took a probing pole and began working his way toward the now much wider crevasse.

"Don't any of you others go wandering off more than ten meters without being roped in," Marla told them. "We've checked only that much around us. We'll have to remap the whole area for new crevasses before it will be safe to move."

"How long will that take?"

"Well—" Freddy started then quickly rested a hand on his cheek.

"Don't speak, Freddy." Marla patted his other arm. "You're held together with bandages and glue until the base doc can stitch you up."

He nodded carefully.

"We didn't lose the ground penetrating radar, but it's back at the huts. Freddy and I were about to rope up and work our way there. We could land the helo now. But a plane? Days, maybe weeks if we find a problem with the present skiway, before we dare bring one in here. With the ice shelf down at Davis melting out, that's going to be a real problem."

"That's a pity, maties," Holly strolled over and gave Miranda back her phone.

She was glad to see that the call was disconnected. She unzipped her parka long enough to tuck it into an inside pocket to keep the battery warm.

"Why? Because Freddy may have a pirate scar for the rest of his days?"

"Aw, and it was such a pretty face." Holly's teasing accent was far broader than Marla's.

"I always—" Freddy clamped his mouth shut as his smile turned into a grimace.

"The worry is that McMurdo is scrambling a Skibird in our direction with all due haste."

"No. They can't. We don't know if it's safe to land," Marla protested.

Holly waved toward Miranda's pocket. "You're welcome to call the Yanks' Chairman of the Joint Chiefs of Staff. That's four stars on his shoulder. Not many folks dare to argue with him."

"You argue with him all the time," Mike returned from the crevasse edge, re-coiling his rope as he progressed. She assumed his headshake meant there was nothing left to see in the churned ice field beyond the edge.

Miranda decided that she wouldn't miss Romanoff— he'd caused the explosion that had killed him, after all. That struck her as an exceedingly shortsighted action. But as she'd been taught to never speak ill of the dead, she kept her thoughts to herself.

"Sure," Holly unhooked Mike's line from the Hagglund. "But that's me. I'm special."

"And you're always glad to tell us all about it," Mike noted as he bound up the line and set it beside the other gear that had survived.

"Right-o, mate. I'm an obliging sort of gal thattaway. Comes from being a pure-blood denizen of the land of Oz."

"Give it up, Mike," Marla was smiling. "She incorrigible even by Oz standards. You need a rational gal like me. What's a pretty man like you doing for the next couple decades?"

Mike smiled and opened his mouth.

"Aren't we missing the point?" Miranda cut him off before he could speak. That wasn't really interrupting, was it? She had the sneaking idea that they'd all be glad to banter until the sun went down, which was a month away. She didn't have a month.

"The point is," Andi spoke up, "that the New York Air National Guard is going to be landing a Hercules LC-130H Skibird here as soon as they can."

Marla was shaking her head. "Reg, if they can land, do we have enough fuel to send them back where they came from?"

Freddy also shook his head, though very carefully.

"No worries, as Holly would say," Miranda hoped she had that right. "The LC-130H has extended range tanks. It will probably fly from McMurdo to Scott-Amundsen Station at the South Pole. There it can top up its tanks enough for the entire return trip. It will be approximately a seven-hour-and-forty-four-minute flight, not including preparation or the refueling stop."

Miranda stopped.

"Why does everyone look at me like that when I remark upon flight times?"

"Because," Mike gave her a sideways hug, "not everyone memorizes the distance between every airport for the fun of it."

"What do they do for fun? I've never understood pure recreation as a reasonable pastime."

"Maybe we can come back to that one later, Miranda."

"Okay, if you think that's best. But why is Drake sending us a plane, and such a big one? There are only four of us. We could easily return the way we came. I don't think we're going to get more data and I do have samples I want to get back to DC."

"I pointed that out to him but he wouldn't say why." Holly squinted at her. "What samples?"

"From the aft strike that hit the plane's wing box and central fuel tank. It sent numerous splinters into the wing tank, creating hundreds of punctures."

"That's why you were wearing the wing as a hat. Very stylish by the way. I mean—"

"Exactly," Miranda could see the flipped perspective, but Holly looked befuddled by her confirmation. It didn't matter. "I was able to collect numerous samples that I deem to not be original equipment in the Ilyushin-76's manufacture." She pulled several baggies out of a sealable pocket she'd discovered over her left breast. She was coming to appreciate these parkas. The largest object was under half an inch. "More than enough for a spectroscopic analysis as well as a thin-slice microscopic inspection if necessary. And we have the flight recorder in the back of the Hagglund. We'll know much more after we get back to the lab."

"We can't have the runway ready in time," Freddy mumbled, barely moving his jaw. "And the iceway down at Davis is already marginal for the Basler. Never carry a Skibird."

"Please allow me to offer a solution," Daiyu had kept her silence throughout the conversation. "The skiway near Zhongshan Station is easily big enough for your Hercules Skibird to land. China would be glad to fly you there in our Snow Eagle 601 parked at Davis. Our station is a mere seventy kilometers away from Davis; simply reroute your Skibird to there. We will gladly extend every hospitality while you wait. We also have plenty of fuel if your aircraft needs it."

The solution seemed sensible enough.

Holly was tipping her head one way and then the other, perhaps trying to look at it from various angles.

Miranda tried imitating the gesture, and only discovered that her neck was quite sore from the battering by the explosion.

27

Lieutenant Colonel Turgenev prayed that he had his rank at the end of this meeting. The Lubyanka Building unnerved him badly.

"What do you mean we need a new operative in Antarctica?"

Turgenev wished he hadn't decided to make his report to General Murov in person but he deemed it too important to trust to any other channel. In today's Russia, anyone might be listening in, vying for any advantage. Face-to-face was far safer.

"Per your instructions, I did not contact Colonel Nikolas Romanoff. Have you heard from him?"

Murov's grim expression said that he had not.

"I have, however, been in contact with Progress Station Manager Viktor Petrov. He has reported that neither Nikolas Romanoff nor the Helix helicopter he had requisitioned have returned."

"And why did you feel it necessary to track Colonel

Romanoff?" Murov's question held all of the edge of a death sentence.

Turgenev didn't answer the question directly. "Instead, Petrov reported that a Chinese Snow Eagle 601 airplane, one that had departed the Progress Skiway shortly after Romanoff, had returned. It left with one passenger and came back with five, one Chinese and four Americans."

Murov's face flushed dark red and Turgenev wondered if he was about to die on the spot.

"Nothing on why?" he finally ground out.

"No, General."

"Anything on the Americans themselves?"

"One had unzipped her parka. Beneath it she wore a vest labeled NTSB. The National Transportation Safety Board is the American team responsible for investigating air crashes."

Murov eased infinitesimally. "That fact was confirmed by Romanoff. I ordered him to investigate the Chinese woman, a Colonel Wang sent by the Central Military Commission, and to dispose of the plane and any who had boarded it."

Turgenev didn't have to say anything aloud. They shared a look that said Romanoff had screwed up and perhaps died in his attempt to destroy the plane. Or was he their prisoner? No, he hadn't come off the plane.

Murov sat in grim silence for several minutes.

Turgenev was careful not to move a single muscle to avoid disturbing his thoughts, or attracting any attention to himself.

"What else have you learned, Lieutenant Colonel?" Murov's addressing him by rank said he might yet survive this.

"I was able to confirm the woman's, Colonel Wang's, arrival time at Zhongshan. It was a mere five minutes prior to the departure of the Snow Eagle en route to the Australian station at Davis. I traced flights back as well as I could. There is a high likelihood that she departed Beijing within the same hour Romanoff departed Moscow. I have been unable to prove any other connection than timing between the two."

"And you suspect?"

"I have considered many things, General. Moles in our Antarctic program," he was careful to not suggest anyone within the FSB itself, "on behalf of the Chinese. Moles in the Chinese CMC who informed us. Informants at Davis Station. Each scenario is presently no more than highly unlikely conjectures."

"And?" Murov wanted his opinion. Turgenev forged ahead.

"Those each are so unlikely—a mole risking being caught for such a seemingly trivial occurrence as a lost cargo flight—that it would be much simpler to trace back to the root cause, the crash itself. It took me seven hours to report the crash to Colonel Romanoff as he had left absolute orders not to be disturbed."

If it turned out he wasn't dead, Murov's look said that Romanoff's career was over.

"By that time, the storm had blown out and the Australians must have noticed the crash. They called in the American crash-investigation team. Perhaps they called the Americans instead of their own people knowing that it was a dangerous political situation, our cargo plane crashed in Australian territory."

"And the Chinese?"

"I found one unconfirmed rumor that the CMC had a prior dealing with what may have been the same investigation team involving a Chinese military jet that crashed in Taiwan. If this is so, might they have a working relationship? Perhaps limited to informational updates, but a relationship nonetheless."

Murov sat back heavily in his chair, the first sign of weariness he had shown in Turgenev's presence. "The Chinese cooperating with the Americans?"

"Not unlikely. The West *is* their largest trade partner. Despite any other animosity, the West might cooperate on such a basis as their relations with us sour."

Murov glared at him.

"Your pardon, General. I try to follow such relations. My father was also interested in them." And he had been a good party man. Murov was a careful man and would surely have looked into Turgenev's background. To any thinking person, it was impossible to deny the miliary conflict in the former Soviet Bloc and the threats to end all cooperation on the International Space Station. The cancellation of Soyuz launches for other nations must be costing billions. Of course, it was an era in Russia where thinking was a dangerous trait.

"Recommendations, Turgenev?"

And here he was being asked to think. There was no other option.

"The Americans can not easily depart Zhongshan Station without our knowing. The Chinese icebreaker supply ship has arrived but that seems unlikely as a route of departure. That means they must leave using our shared skiway at Progress. The station master will keep me apprised of any changes."

General Murov stared at him in silence again.

Turgenev again did his best not to show anything. He'd done well, hadn't he? Please tell him he'd done well.

"Keep me informed of any developments. Try to find out what happened to Romanoff. Make sure the plane was disposed of. You may base your operations from Colonel Romanoff's office on the second floor. Especially let me know if the Chinese woman or the Americans move so much as a finger. Report to me, only to me. Anytime day or night."

Turgenev rose to his feet, saluted, and left before the general could change his mind. Romanoff's office. Perhaps one day he'd have Romanoff's rank and power as well.

This time he managed to breathe again as he took the stairs down to the lower story.

28

"WHY DID YOU DO THAT?"

Daiyu managed not to cringe at the tone in General Liú Zuocheng's voice. Zhongshan Station rarely had sufficient bandwidth for video calls. Now she wished that she hadn't demanded that they clear all other traffic for her to make one as his glare only emphasized the annoyance of his tone.

The secure communications room could fit two chairs, but not three. One more could stand, but not two. She sat alone, after chasing out the technician once he had made the connection and closing the door on the irate station master's face.

"The Americans were departing the area, whether or not I was with them. This created a window of opportunity. I only sought to make time for you to instruct me regarding your wishes." *Keep it ever so humble, Daiyu. That is how you have survived so long.* "They can be allowed to depart by themselves when their plane arrives. Or I can accompany them as you deem best."

"And you do not know why their general sent them such

a plane across the entire width of the continent?" Was Zuocheng's scowl easing?

"Neither do they. Their Miranda Chase asked to fly back to her American labs by the route they arrived and was overruled."

The general was correct in many aspects, bringing the Americans here was a problematic decision. It would be far too easy for them to see the bare fingertip-hold Zhongshan Station had on Antarctica. Surmising the devastating impact upon the station's supplies if the Skibird did indeed require refueling would also be obvious.

For the third year in a row, the *Xue Long* icebreaker supply ship had caught in hard ice thirty-five kilometers from the station and not entered the bay to unload close by the shore.

Station Master Hu had given her a long lecture about the poor placement of the station. Yes, it was in one of the rare, bare ground oases on the continent. But unlike the Russian station across the narrow peninsula that separated them, Zhongshan was placed in a deep embayment mostly barricaded by rocky islands. The geography might keep sea storms at a distance, but it had been discovered too late that it also trapped the ice close to shore.

And he'd protested that they weren't allowed to ask for help from the greedy Russians. Despite the two stations being so close together, relations had deteriorated until the sole point of cooperation was China's lease of use on the Russian skiway. They desperately needed to build their own, though it would be far less conveniently placed. The closest good site was high on the ice plateau.

The sea ice was too fractured between Zhongshan and the ship to make a road. All of the one thousand tonnes of supplies would have to be transferred by helicopter. All nonessentials would be left aboard.

That included spare fuel.

The rare large cargo jets were required to carry round-trip fuel. To fully refuel an American Skibird, at any price per liter, could prove disastrous over the twelve months until the next voyage of the *Xue Long*.

Matters were so dire that many scientists who had anticipated a long summer's research would be flown out to depart on the icebreaker. The winter crew would be painfully slim, fewer than ten, perhaps only five. If the Skibird needed a full refuel, there might be *no* winter crew. If the ship was delayed next year, they might have to abandon the station by air for lack of heating oil.

Yet that was not what the Americans must see. With the ship in, fresh food was plentiful. Accommodations for the six hours they would be here had been created by emptying individual's rooms into a neighbor's room and assigning both occupants to work double shifts. The rooms were warm and clean, each big enough for a single bed, a tiny desk, and a small set of drawers. The ones she'd requisitioned for them —and herself—had private toilets and showers.

She had decided the station master could report the entire array of complaints to his superior and they would never reach the general's ear, nor would he care if they did.

"How soon does their plane arrive?"

"Five hours, General. They are currently refueling at their South Pole station."

There had been long delays reaching here. First the Australians had to survey an area for safety before calling up their helicopter. That in turn had been busy working to service their own supply ship. The logistics to travel a hundred kilometers in Antarctica from Whoop Whoop to her plane at Davis to Zhongshan Station had required six hours. During her days as a star ultra-marathon runner for the People's Liberation Army, she'd been able to run that distance in under seven hours.

He stared out of the screen at her. Liú Zuocheng was the polar opposite of her dead husband Zhang Ru, may the bastard rest uncomfortably in hell. Ru had been stocky, constantly full of bravado, strong as an ox, and greedier than any pig ever born. Zuocheng's thoughts were as long and quiet as his face. His words moved slowly. When he did act, only those closest too him would see it happen. The delicate, silent puppet master.

She would take that lesson herself and remained in silence while he planned.

He eventually offered a ghost of a smile, "I believe I have a call to place. Remain where you are."

And he was gone.

29

He'd been having a gloriously pleasant dream. He and Lizzy had been curled up together, her slender body spooned inside his as they lay on a vast, perfect field of ice. It wasn't cold at all. Only the two of them, together in the vast silence, without any disturbance.

Then a harsh ring and the ice beneath them fractured explosively.

By the second ring, Drake was awake, in bed, holding his personal phone, and shivering.

The moment before he answered, he noted that the caller's ID was blocked. Only Lizzy and his three kids used this number. Lizzy was here beside him, grumbling about being woken up but not fully awake. The kids didn't use blocked numbers.

The only other person who had this number was dead— at least he hoped to God that report was accurate. And his number had always been blocked.

"Hello?"

"Good morning. I am sorry to wake you." The voice was

familiar. Chinese. Male. With the perfect non-accent of American English as spoken in the Pacific Northwest, especially compared to Zhang Ru's heavy Chinese accent. Pacific? Yes, that was the last place he'd heard this voice. Across a table, at the far corner of the Pacific.

"Good morning, General." Liú Zuocheng. "May I suggest that we encrypt this call using the name of the country where we last met?" The only time they'd ever met, Brunei.

They both did so.

"I hope that you do not mind my using this number, General," General Liú stated. Despite the encryption, neither of them were using their names. He must have obtained Drake's private number from Zhang Ru.

"What is the state of the prior holder of this number?" Half test and half begging that—

"In a place his remains will never be discovered or mourned." Zuocheng replied.

"Then I am glad to speak with you, despite the hour." He went to move away to not disturb Lizzy further. She snagged him by the back of his pajama bottoms and kept him on the bed. Then she wrapped herself around him from behind. This wasn't the moment for— She rested her chin on his shoulder so that her ear ended up close by his phone. Right. He eased the phone away enough for them both to listen without the audible change of switching to speakerphone.

"I would like to discuss an interest we have. It is *not* in common." Liú replied.

"This should be good." What little tact Drake could usually muster continued to sleep comfortably on the soft pillow.

"I would like to discuss failed states."

"Libya? Somalia? Texas?" The last didn't earn him so

much as a polite chuckle. Please don't let this be about Taiwan.

"I should have said a *failing* state."

"That doesn't narrow it down in the slightest: Myanmar, the Congo, and again Texas." Still no chuckle, but a poke in the ribs from Lizzy—a sharp one, like *shut up.*

But then Lizzy shifted to his other ear and whispered, "Russia?"

He echoed her comment as she shifted once more to his other shoulder to listen.

"Most astute."

"And you say that we have an interest, *not in common,* regarding this country?"

"Regarding this country's actions and assets on a certain continent."

Russia was heavily involved in at least four of the seven continents: Asia and Europe, especially former Soviet Bloc countries at the moment, Africa through the use of their Wagner Group mercenaries—and Antarctica.

Miranda had mentioned a Wang Daiyu. A quick lookup had revealed almost nothing. Wife of Zhang Ru. Former (?) Army, division and rank unknown, skills unknown. He'd sent a note to Director Clarissa Reese to see what the CIA had on her; he should have marked it urgent.

Ru was dead and Daiyu was in Antarctica, which meant—

Half asleep was his only excuse. Daiyu wasn't merely Zhang Ru's widow, she was General Liú Zuocheng's tool. She had reported to him about events in Antarctica, and he had called Drake.

"You have spoken to your operative there regarding what my team found on the Russian plane." Drake wanted to test the waters. He'd read reports that the Russian President was working to convince his Chinese counterpart to withdraw from the Antarctic Treaty System and open the continent to mining. Militarization would, of course, be the first step in Russian thinking.

"Yes, I've spoken with her. And while we are not wholly averse to an alternate scenario for the use of Antarctica, we find the arming of stations to...lack finesse." Zuocheng had definitely understood the question.

Lizzy shifted to his other ear again. "Especially as the Zhongshan Station is five miles from the Russian Progress Station."

"I can see how any tactical changes at Progress Station could be worrisome." The real question remained, what was Zuocheng, and by extension China, after?

"Are you also aware," Zuocheng asked, "that Russian involvement in Antarctica has fallen from more than twenty stations to a mere five on the continent?"

"Five that now have unknown degrees of Russian preparation for military control of Antarctica." He was fully awake now.

"Yes," Zuocheng sounded thoughtful. "*Unknown*. It is such an interesting word to use about a land that in itself is so filled with unknowns. Like the reason you have sent one of your precious LC-130H Skibirds racing across the breadth of the continent to gather up a *civilian* air-crash investigation team."

It had been a gut-reaction decision while he was speaking with Holly about the cause of the explosion—four Russian Kalibr cruise missiles where they were never supposed to be. What else was already there?

He'd called President Cole immediately afterward,

catching him on the way to bed. Roy confirmed the action, as Drake himself didn't have the power to make orders, only to advise.

Drake hadn't been happy when the plan shifted to land an Air National Guard asset at a Chinese station. Less so again, when he'd discovered that the Chinese station used a Russian skiway, but he'd deemed that to be low priority when the logistics were explained. Now he was less sure.

The question was, how far could he trust Zuocheng? More than Ru, which meant marginally more than not at all.

"What are you asking?"

"I would like to suggest a small detour for your team."

"To where?"

"Why doesn't this sound good?" Lizzy whispered in his opposite ear.

"Nothing occurs at Progress Station without our awareness. It lies a mere eight kilometers from our station at Zhongshan and we are confident in our knowledge of their actions. A station, I might add, that exists to little purpose except to support Vostok Station."

Lizzy merely tapped his other shoulder without removing her ear from beside his phone.

Yes, it was definitely the other shoe.

"If our Skibird were to..." Drake paused.

"Perhaps declare an emergency."

"...and place a top aircraft investigation team..."

"Along with an individual who has afforded your team services at our Zhongshan Station."

"...along with your aide. She might then report any observations without arousing suspicions."

"Precisely."

Drake turned enough to look face-to-face at Lizzy. Even

in the dim bedroom, lit only by the small nightlight in the bathroom, he could see that she was thinking hard and fast. He knew her first-level answer already as there was such minimal information on Antarctic activity in general. Add on the limited number of satellite passes, which hadn't previously targeted those remote stations, and he knew the intel-gathering part of Lizzy's NRO brain was in high gear.

But she would also factor that desire out to give him advice.

He himself was leaning toward agreeing unless she thought of a strong negative.

Merely for the chance of starting a bridge with the CMC's senior vice-chairman, it was tempting. Perhaps weaning the PRC's leadership from the Russian Federation —that too could have global consequences to America's advantage. The Russians had done the groundwork for him in Eastern Europe, by proving that a massive *quantity* of strength was not the same as a *quality* of strength combined with an opponent's intense commitment. Definitely a content lesson for the PRC regarding any move against Taiwan.

Lizzy's head tip said she didn't see any obvious crevasses for him to fall into.

All that meant was that, if a crevasse of Chinese manufacture awaited them, neither of them could see it. It didn't mean that it wasn't there.

General Liú had waited patiently, unlike Ru who was always in such a hurry.

"General, pending approval, that is acceptable. We may instead couch it as an Antarctic Survey inspection team."

"Yes, that is perhaps a more reasonable option. It would allow a wider access to their station."

Drake was thinking fast, "Perhaps you could have your Zhongshan Station Manager provide an instructional tour to both my team and your representative to assist them in presenting a convincing appearance." His bet was seventy-thirty against.

"I will suggest that immediately."

Drake lost, but it also told him that if the Chinese were militarizing Antarctica, they hadn't done so at Zhongshan —yet.

"We will be in touch," and Zuocheng was gone.

Drake cursed. General Liú could obviously call *him,* but he'd left Drake no way to call him back. He couldn't exactly dial the CMC headquarters in Beijing and ask for the man by name. Unless Liú retained Zhang Ru's phone.

"Okay," Lizzy slid beside him, so they sat hip to hip on the edge of the bed. "What do you think his hidden agenda is?"

"Hidden agenda? I'm worried about his *unhidden* agenda of an inspection team entering Vostok."

"The team will handle that. But as a Japanese person—"

"And Scottish and Italian."

"—and three-quarters Japanese—"

"Which looks incredibly good on you, by the way."

"You're my husband, you're biased."

"True. True." He slid a hand around her waist to pull her close enough to kiss her atop the head. That he'd been lucky enough in his life to marry two such amazing women only made the second one all the more dazzling. He had been so sure that his heart had died along with Patty.

"As a Japanese person," she hummed softly for a moment under his kiss, "I can promise you that any self-respecting Asian person will always have a hidden agenda."

"Anything I should know about you?" he teased her.

"Oh no, I'm always an open person about my hidden agenda. For example, it is too early to wake the President when the Skibird has yet to reach the South Pole Station. Perhaps if we briefly clear our heads with some other activity, we will feel wiser about General Liú's plan." She slipped free enough from his arm to shed her nightgown over her head.

"Briefly?" Drake pulled her closer. "I have a very difficult time thinking about doing anything briefly with you, Lizzy."

What happened next—however brief—was definitely high on his own unhidden agenda.

30

MIRANDA HAD NEVER ENJOYED SLEEPING IN STRANGE BEDS BUT
it seemed to be an essential element of working as an air-
crash investigator. She never slept well during investigations,
but how much of that was her drive to solve the crashes and
how much was it the strange bedding? She always traveled
with a full-length flannel nightgown, socks, and her own
pillowcase. That usually helped.

But not tonight. Today. Whatever it was in a land of
constant sunlight...late afternoon in Zhongshan Station.

Each of their rooms were identical. A single bed with
drawers beneath, a tiny desk, and the most efficient shower
and toilet arrangement she'd ever seen. Everything at
Zhongshan was spotless. Not clean, like Australia's Davis
Station, but spotless. When they'd arrived, one man had
been running a dust mop along the hall, another following
close behind with a damp mop.

No, the problem wasn't the efficient spotless room, the
comfortable bed, or the time of day. She'd become unused to
sleeping alone. These beds were too narrow for two, even

when she and Andi were the two. These were narrow pallets intended for sleeping and space efficiency.

For the first time in her life, Miranda was happier with someone than being alone. Was there a deeper meaning that she was supposed to understand? Perhaps it was one of those things Tante Daniels had tried to teach her to simply accept.

Sometimes it's okay to simply be in the moment, Miranda.

She was unsure what her autism therapist-turned-governess had meant by that, though this situation did sound as if it fit that statement in some way. Another parallelism?

Knowing that sleep would continue to elude her, she dressed, put everything back in her pack as neatly as the room's condition dictated, and went exploring.

Zhongshan had half the population of Davis Station, but was perhaps a quarter of the size. Everything here was scaled to the task at hand. At Davis, the beds were fully twin size and two people could curl up together on them. And everyone had their own room. Here, there were year-round rooms with individual beds, and rooms with bunk beds for the summer-only staff.

At Davis, they'd eaten in a spacious complex. A long table down the middle of a room, a luxury seating area, a bar and pool table. There had been a separate pub complete with a bar. Here, eating occurred at cafeteria-style tables placed in neat rows. Meals were served buffet style with no individual plating. Every space was neat and of minimal size.

She could come to appreciate the efficiency. It was the opposite of her spacious home. Yet her home did offer privacy. How would she feel if her house guests were crowded close to either side of her bedroom at night? Or if there was only a small lounging area and a smaller dining table?

Perhaps minimalist efficiency had its place.

She tracked down the outer door where her parka was hung, shrugged it on, and moved outside. The midafternoon heat had driven the temperature several degrees above freezing, feeling quite comfortable after the chill plateau skiway.

Like Davis, Zhongshan stood on bare ground close by the icy shore. Unlike Davis, there were so few buildings that their purpose was easy to identify. The two largest were the living quarters and the research labs, standing side-by-side with a small connecting tunnel between.

The communications module was easily identified by the towering antennas that could cover the local area. The garage looked like a garage, a metal red-and-white building conveniently located at the back of the research building. On one high point was the main radome that would provide the primary connection to a geosynchronous satellite and the Chinese mainland.

The purpose of the last building eluded her. The other high rocky bluff near the station was topped by a green-and-white striped hexagonal structure that rose and expanded upward like a chunky flower bloom for three tall stories.

"It is our space physics observatory," a man said from close beside her.

She turned to see that he was older, and watching her carefully. "Good to know."

"Do you like our station?"

"It is neat and efficient. I like that very much. It makes part of my mind," she pictured the smiling emoji in her reference notebook, "happy."

"Good, I'm glad. We worked hard to make minimum impact on the land. I have worked to make our stations here in Antarctica be the number-one best."

"Well...good job."

They stood together in silence for a time, facing the open bay. A helicopter flew in from beyond the ice, laboring over a heavy sling load. No conversation was possible as it lowered and set the container next to several others.

Four workers who she hadn't noticed before moved over and released the sling load within moments of the helicopter's arrival. Before it was out of sight, forklifts were already shifting the load into the building it had been placed beside.

Her relationship with Andi was undeniably efficient. Andi translated the world for her in many helpful ways—defender and buffer against the battering of others' emotions. It was also undeniable that sharing a bed each night had definite advantages that were far more efficient than the long gaps between lovers she'd typically had over the years.

But was efficiency enough to justify continuing a relationship? It didn't sound...nice.

Was there a deeper meaning than mere efficiency?

Did feeling better when Andi was nearby count? Perhaps being happier than she'd been before? Ever?

Or was this one of Tante Daniels' *be present* times of her life? And she should simply stop thinking. She wasn't good at that.

It was normally the kind of question she could trust to Andi. But since it was about Andi, Miranda suspected that would not go well.

She wished she could scream out her question and hear

an answer. It felt as if her insides were being battered by a series of *dit-dah* and *dit-dah-dah* that she would never manage to translate. How was she supposed to know what was the truth?

The man beside her stood, watching the helicopter disappear over the horizon.

"Yes, all very efficient," he spoke with absolute surety.

31

Hu Min liked this quiet Miranda Chase. He was content to stand with her, finding joy in the first quiet moment of his day and letting the sun shine upon their faces. Moments like this were so rare and precious.

His day had begun badly and only become worse as the hours passed.

He had argued with the Daiyu woman, without any luck, when she had landed with the latest transport and commandeered his Snow Eagle 601—Zhongshan Station only had the one this summer. With it, he had to balance the demands of Taishan and Kunlun Stations much further inland. With it gone for an unknown amount of time, he'd been helpless to act.

His good fortune had continued to die when the brainless supply ship's captain, who hadn't been scheduled to arrive for three more days, radioed. Instead of pulling up to the station, he'd stopped far out on the ice and announced he was here. Except he wasn't. The bastard refused to risk his ship in the bay. Wasn't the *Xue Long* built to break ice? It wasn't fragile.

Instead, he parked across thirty kilometers of rotten sea ice that no snow machine could safely traverse. That meant every load had to be transferred from ship to shore by helicopter—which was off serving three different field camps today. Then at the far end of its run, it hadn't returned for hours.

Anything that isn't unloaded in five days, I'm taking back to China.

The key technicians Min needed for the most fragile equipment unloading were marooned five hundred kilometers inland at Taishan Station because his Snow Eagle was gone.

Then, when Daiyu had finally returned his plane, she'd brought four *laowai* with her and demanded the five best rooms at Zhongshan Station. That it was summer and they were at capacity didn't faze her for a moment.

He'd also had to negotiate with the arrogant Russian station manager at Progress so that the Americans could use his skiway. He quoted an exorbitantly corrupt fee. Out of time, he told the man he would have to negotiate directly with the Americans after they landed.

He'd managed to warn the Chinese-American about what the fee *should be,* hoping she would tell their pilots.

Min had a set of well-paid eyes and ears at Progress, but he wished he could be there to hear the negotiation himself. In his limited experience, Americans alternated between spreading money about as if it was more common than water, and being *Ji zei.* They followed no rational balance like a civilized Chinese person would. He hoped they were as stingy as a chicken thief.

After that, Daiyu had taken over his communications room for an hour. When she'd finally unsealed the door, there had been a massive queue of calls from the useless ship's captain, a marginally lower counteroffer from the Russian who at least had enough brains to *not* want to deal directly with the Americans (too bad for him), and another from Taishan Station saying that they needed the technicians for two more days—the plane was already halfway there.

Before he could answer any of them, the lunatic Wang Daiyu had dragged him away.

"I need an immediate class for the Americans on how to conduct a station inspection."

When he'd refused, she'd shown him her authorization. He'd never seen an ID from the Central Military Commission before. Couldn't she have shown him that in the beginning? Not that it would have made his life any easier, but he'd have known to curb his anger sooner.

She'd then sent him, like a servant boy, to find the missing *laowai*.

And he had found the foreigner, standing in a moment of peace and beauty that the Buddha himself would admire. They had shared the moment and his day had finally shifted.

Everything that had been broken, now fit. The plane was fetching his technicians, the unloading had begun. And neither the Americans nor the CMC were here to judge him and take away his station.

An hour later, his face hurt from smiling at the *laowai*. It was so strange that they were the one thing that had gone right today.

Every aspect of a proper inspection was gathered and

cataloged as if they'd been doing it for years, though he was certain it was all new to them. The woman he had shared the moment of joy with hadn't spoken again. She held silence as if it was a gift. For her, nothing had to be repeated or clarified. If he skipped a step, such as the waste-heat recapture in the power generation plant, she would simply point to indicate her question. Her nods when he'd explained were more as if she was confirming a guess rather than struggling to understand.

Her companions were also impressed by her perfect silence, looking at her again and again as if waiting for her to speak when there was no need.

He led them through proper spill containment around larger fuel tanks and catchments for individual fuel drums. Environmental impact mitigators like the kitchen food waste dryer to only ship out the lightest amount, the wastewater plant releasing sterilized water into the ocean, the desalinization plant, and the wind generators. Construction considerations including everything from enclosure insulation (typically three feet thick in Antarctica) to proper disposal of old and deteriorating buildings.

Once he understood that they truly weren't secretly inspecting his station, he relaxed enough to give them tips on what to look for.

"Do not expect this from *older* stations. Yes, I have heard that your American stations are cleaner than most. But other countries..." And he went on to describe the few other stations he'd seen. Especially abandoned stations.

In the mid-2010s, the Russians had replaced the buildings at Progress Station. As they finished, they made a terrible mistake—burning down the new building and killing one of their people. It had now been replaced. But the wreckage of the older buildings and the new burned one had simply been shoved aside, though by treaty it should be demolished and removed. The ice by their station had been black for half a season when they'd decided to dispose of the waste by burning it more. The construction equipment had not returned to Russia, but rather been left to rot along the shore.

He knew he was rambling but it was such a relief to see fresh faces. Zhongshan only supported sixty people in the summer and twenty in the winter—during a busy year. And never knowing who would say what to who back on the Mainland, every thought was carefully considered. He'd been on The Ice for nine years, been station manager for six, and had learned caution. Yet these people seemed to be no threat.

"When was Vostok founded?" the pretty American-Chinese had asked. Wu Andi reminded him so much of his daughter—he stayed with her family on every leave—that he'd addressed many of his remarks to her directly. The few times he'd tried a joke in Mandarin, she'd looked confused, so he'd stopped. Though occasionally there was an inscrutable half smile that said she was either laughing at him, or understood the language and secretly laughed with him. He preferred to think the latter.

But she had asked the key question. They were targeting the Russians.

He couldn't resist glancing at Daiyu. After so many years on The Ice, he knew a few truths and most of the secrets. Her face remained so carefully neutral that, though the question sat on the tip of his tongue, he didn't dare ask it. Instead he answered the *laowai's* question.

Most of their names were so strange that he didn't dare

trying to use them: Miranda, Holly, Michael. They had such hard American sounds in their names. For politeness, he never attempted any of their names. Only Wu Andi came easily to his tongue but addressing one by name and not the others would be as impolite as mispronouncing their names.

"Vostok. It is building in 1957, one of first stations not on Antarctic Peninsula or norther islands. They want the South Pole but you Americans building there year sooner. Their station most old and horrible. They building a replacement. But they be Russia. Everything late, many delays, broken delivery ships, and much, much corruption. If new station arrive, how long to finished, or ever made? After so many time, they do make foundations last year. New modules coming, but much crews needed to assemble."

No reaction from Daiyu. He turned back to Wu Andi.

"At Vostok, ignore new work. Look at what left behind. Much lie under the snow. Their station buried many times. Tunnels, many tunnels under snow, connecting one place to other place. If they take you above snow, on top of ice, they hiding what is between places. Look close. Look close."

That would teach the Russian Progress manager to try and make a fool of him with the Americans.

He eyed Daiyu again. She was from the CMC. If he was right, that spelled a whole different type of problem for the Russians. He must start his own preparations. He had an advantage. Every Chinese scientist and technician ever assigned to The Ice was first and foremost a military soldier. Russia, like the Americans, was foolish enough to send pure scientists. And their technicians might have been happier in a Siberian Gulag. They had proved to be very open to recruitment.

32

"BEST SPORT EVER?" CAPTAIN ANTONY *CAP* CAPRA ASKED OVER the plane's intercom.

"Soccer!" No question where their new loadmaster Bob *Footie* McAllister had earned his nickname. It was his rookie year on the Skibird but he was adapting well.

"V-ball!" Ginny Markos declared. Her third year with the 109th Airlift Wing, but the first on his plane.

"Volleyball?" Footie scoffed. "That's so wrong."

One look at *Stretch* Markos said it was so right. Their flight engineer was five-eleven of pure athlete. She could also troubleshoot any LC-130 system blindfolded. If not for that gold band on her finger...because, damn! Move over, Serena Williams.

"Two strikes," Cap announced.

"What's up, Cap? Football? Baseball?"

Stretch groaned, "Those aren't real sports. A bunch of lunkheads banging their heads together until someone gets TBI'd—guess they weren't using their damn brains anyway.

Or a bunch of goofballs standing around scratching what they got while waiting for something to happen."

"Harsh, Stretch. Seriously harsh. Basketball?"

"No. No. And, yet again, no. That's five downs and no yardage. Jackie?" Cap didn't need to turn to his copilot. For seven years she'd been flying Skibirds with him for the New York Air National Guard. They'd tried getting it on at one point, but it hadn't stuck. Didn't mean she wasn't pure joy to fly with.

"The best sport in the whole world is the internationally recognized sport of..."

"Airborne Boondoggle!" They shouted in unison, then traded a high-five across the cockpit.

The LC-130H Skibird hummed in agreement.

The two back-seaters groaned in unison.

"Nothing better in the whole world than flying, folks, especially when it's anywhere new. Come on. Tell me the last time you crossed an entire continent made of ice? Daylight the whole way. I'm telling you. Nothing better."

He scanned the readouts, though the plane would warn him of anything wrong faster than he'd be able to notice it. Jackie was currently pilot in command, which also didn't take much as they were on autopilot. With the upgrade of the Skibird fleet to an all-glass cockpit, it was actually trickier to drive a car. The big LCD screens had replaced the ranks of dial instruments. Now it placed exactly what they needed to see at their fingertips.

As long as they stayed high enough to clear the occasional mountain peak that jammed up through ten thousand feet of ice and low enough to not freeze the fuel—unlikely in midsummer—they were good. That didn't mean they weren't vigilant, it was a key safety protocol. But

Lockheed Martin had built over twenty-five hundred Hercs in more variants than could be counted on all of the fingers of the four-person crew. They had it down.

For this flight, the National Science Foundation, who ordered all US flights on The Ice, had scrounged together a quick twenty-five thousand pounds of cargo at McMurdo. They'd dropped it at the South Pole—unloaded on the hustle—and only needed a third of a load of fuel to top off all the tanks. They were traveling fuel heavy-cargo light, which made the plane handle like a go-kart and an utter dream. It also meant that they could cross the continent twice and not care about fuel.

When Footie and Stretch had gone to do their periodic walk through the plane, Jackie flipped the intercom to Pilots Only.

"Hey, Cap. What's up with those guys?"

No question who Jackie was talking about. It wasn't their two new crew. They'd slid into place like they'd always been there. Two months into the season they never missed a step.

But in lieu of cargo, they now had four US Marshals in the back. He hadn't known that there were *any* law officers on the American Ice. There were. Four of them—three at McMurdo and one at the South Pole. He'd been ordered to bring them all. The three men and one woman looked serious, too. Day jobs: machine shop, firefighter, telescope maintenance, and heavy equipment driver. Night jobs? US Marshal. And these weren't commercial flight guys with badge, handcuffs, and a hidden ankle piece. They'd come aboard with heavy bags that clanked when they hit the deck. When one guy had opened his duffle, Cap caught sight of a bulletproof vest. These were serious people.

"Kandahar flashbacks?" Before shifting to the Skibirds,

they'd both put in their fair share of air time in the dustbowl. Huge wear and tear on the equipment. Doing combat landings and takeoffs—screaming through the vertical airspace ruled by MANPADS as fast as possible—cut a third out of the life of a plane. They'd also dressed in layers of armor and prayed no one shot their asses off with a sniper rifle.

"Shit man," Jackie concurred.

They had their own gear aboard. Just because they flew over Antarctica, and had skis in addition to their wheels, didn't mean they weren't military. They flew for the 109th Airlift Wing, and if any foreign actor was coming for them down here on The Ice, they'd be ready.

33

HU MIN'S QUESTION WAS ANSWERED AND HIS WISH FULFILLED because Daiyu and her four *laowai* needed a ride to the Russian skiway. That meant they probably weren't coming back or they'd have commandeered a vehicle to leave at Progress Skiway—whether or not it was convenient for him.

Daiyu had also requested several items from the Station's weapons locker.

He'd tried backdooring the question of what she was doing, "Why now?" *What happened that you are taking on the Russian stations?*

Daiyu had looked around, but he'd been careful to ask when they were briefly alone near the tracked Nanji snow vehicle. It was very, very similar to the Swedish Hagglund, but with improvements by China's best polar science engineers.

"You know the Russian Kalibr?" Daiyu kept her voice low.

"No! Those bastards!" A cruise missile in Antarctica?

"Four of them were stopped en route to here at Progress.

We don't know why yet, or if more are already here. But be ready."

Min had stood up straighter. "You inspect Vostok. Min will watch Progress."

She had offered a sharp nod as her pet *laowai* came out of the station and loaded into the Nanji.

It took seven kilometers of rough road to reach the Russian skiway. Over the final rise, a big surprise awaited him. They could see Progress Station in the distance from their perch. He stopped to stare.

He'd heard that the Russian supply ship was in as well. That it had managed to come within a kilometer of the shore was most annoying, but that was not what was important.

What he hadn't heard was that a massive cargo ship had come with it. Min pulled the binoculars out of the glove compartment and focused on the distant ships.

Yes, stacked on the cargo ship's deck were scores of bright steel shipping containers—with windows in the ends. Great piles of them were already stacked on the shore. He only saw one of their Helix helicopters helping with the unloading; he didn't see the other one anywhere. But they had three snowcats scuttling back and forth across the ice dragging their loads on skied sleds. May the *Xue Long* captain roast in hell.

"The Russians have finally managed to deliver the modules for the new Vostok Station. They will need to be dragged over fourteen hundred kilometers of ice in massive tractor trains and assembled, but they are here."

He handed the binoculars to Daiyu and she too spent a long time gazing at the ships.

"An incredible asset," he ventured.

She nodded without looking away.

"But why here instead of Mirny?" And then he remembered. "The fire! Mirny burned down half their station two years ago. Of course, Progress burned down their own new station building back in 2008, immediately after they finished it." They had managed to reconstruct one big building, but reports stated that it was painfully overcrowded.

Then, as she handed the binoculars to the *laowai* in the rear, she leaned close to whisper, "Unless I personally tell you otherwise, do nothing until those ships are unloaded and gone."

In his estimation that would take at least a day more. "And after?"

Wang Daiyu shrugged, then waved him on.

Min put the Nanji in gear and descended toward the skiway.

His day was improving.

Taking a lesson from Daiyu, he had informed Taishan Station that his technicians were going to be on the Snow Eagle the minute it landed. Only if Taishan behaved would he send the technicians back to finish their repair of the power plant. And not before the *Xue Long* was unloaded. That it meant shutting down half of their equipment wasn't his concern. Their station would have heat and food—for now that was enough.

He decided to take one further risk after they had arrived and were awaiting the arrival of the American plane. "Do what you must with their warrens, Daiyu. Do not damage their foundations for the new station."

Again, her terse nod. "Do not let the *Xue Long* depart before the Russian ships."

"The *hún dàn* captain said he is leaving in five days

whether or not I have my supplies. How am I supposed to do that across thirty kilometers of crappy sea ice that I know he can easily break through?"

Daiyu pulled out her phone and sent a text message. "He may be a bastard, but he will shortly receive orders that he will be moving forward directly to Zhongshan and will not be departing without your clearance."

Did she truly have such power? Or did she have it simply because she *acted* as if she did? Min had spent too much time attempting to placate others. From this woman, he had received a lesson about when to simply inform them of his decision.

Min bounced on his toes several times and felt the warmth surge into his chest. Today may have started terribly, but it was fast becoming the best in his years as station master. The yin and yang of life curled together. It was an excellent time to be alive.

If the *Xue Long* was indeed going to be on the move, he would offer his own helicopter to aid the Russians unloading their ships. Yes, far better than letting it sit idle. Perhaps the cargo ship could be fully unloaded by this afternoon.

The tall blonde *laowai* heard it first. It had been less than ten minutes since their arrival when she twisted to face south. The American airplane came into view from over the high ice. It was strangely unimpressive. It was a third smaller than the Ilyushin-76s that both Russia and China used to supply Antarctica, when the bay ice was hard enough.

Again, China was far too reliant on the Russians. Someday he would see nothing but Xi'an Y-20 cargo jets arriving here. They might be built from stolen American C-17 Globemaster III plans, but they would be Chinese built.

And better stolen from the West than purchased from the Russians.

However small it might seem as it descended toward the ice, the modified Hercules LC-130 was the largest ski plane in the world. What he could do for the other stations with a Skibird at his call. And rumor said that the Americans had ten of these. Envy struck deep in his soul. If he had *two* of those...but he didn't.

Viktor Petrov, the Russian Progress Station Manager, arrived on his snowmobile at the same time the Americans landed. They traded friendly nods, and Viktor took that as an invitation to reopen the discussion of landing fees for the American airplane.

Min carefully made no commitments, answering as often with a shrug as a word. Viktor looked sad when he understood that it was out of Min's hands and now up to him to salvage what he could. Not that any fee he collected would be recorded anywhere other than Viktor's wallet.

Everyone watched the plane land and taxi in silence.

Viktor tried another question as the plane slowed in front of them, "Have you news of my other Ka-32S Helix helicopter or Colonel Nikolas Romanoff?"

Min didn't but was fascinated that Viktor had managed to lose a fifty-five-million-yuan helicopter, over eight million American.

"Both dead, and the pilots." The Miranda Chase woman spoke as if she was discussing the temperature.

"And the supply airplane that I was expecting?" Viktor asked quickly as the Skibird slid toward them over the snow.

"Destroyed," she replied from that place of such peace, nipping off the word as no more was needed. She then turned to face into the wind of the plane's propellers as it turned tightly in front of them and presented its rear to them.

Viktor gave up.

Min could only gaze at her in wonder as the plane rocked to a final halt. Death and destruction had surrounded her, yet her clarity was so pure that not even the pushy Viktor Petrov dared breach the bastions or her perfect serenity. A Chán Buddhism master ready for instant action and therefore needing to take none. He must learn that for himself. Though he doubted he'd ever succeed, he could at least strive.

The Americans didn't come out the side door below the wing. Instead, they lowered the massive rear ramp as if they were going to load up pallets of gear and not a mere five people carrying their own packs.

Two men and a women stood on the ramp in gray flightsuits with parkas pulled on but not zipped. A pilot must be at the controls, as the engines were running and the propellers beat the air with a low drone. Four men stood behind them, visible as silhouettes in the shadows of the vast cargo bay. Their stance made it clear that they were military as well.

"Ah," the big man at the front took in a deep breath and huffed it out. He spoke loudly enough to be heard easily over the running engines. "I was hoping that your air here in East Antarctica was more exciting than ours, but it smells the same—cold and dry."

And he gave a belly laugh that Min found easy to join.

He alone strode down the ramp, but didn't step onto the snow. "Are you one of my five?"

Min could only shake his head. The man was so confident. Of course, he was a tall blond American in command of such a beautiful aircraft. He also stood with a towering black woman and red-haired man. Min had seen a few blacks before, though none so striking, but he'd never seen red hair. It was the color of the lucky red dragon painted over the door of his grandson's bedroom and he could only gawk.

"Maybe next time," the blond man shook his hand as if they were old friends.

Daiyu led the four *laowai* up the ramp.

"No, wait," Viktor protested. "I must board for a customs inspection and a landing fee. We can also sell you fuel if you need it."

The big man looked amused, "This is a pickup, not a delivery—no boarding and no customs. Don't need fuel—it's a small continent after all."

Antarctica wasn't. If it was a country, it would be the biggest in the world after Russia. The American was rubbing their vast capabilities in Viktor's face.

"And a landing fee?" The big man winked at him.

That finally shook Min loose of his temporary paralysis. He was worldly enough to know that Americans thought a wink to be friendly and conspiratorial. In China it was a vulgar invitation for sex. He was now sure that the plane's commander had received Min's warning. He managed to return the wink.

"I crossed the entire continent to fetch these folks. That sounds like an emergency to me. Can't see charging anyone for anything in an emergency." He waved a hand upward and the ramp began to rise, carrying him aloft. "Thank you for assisting in this crisis. Need to get a move on before my skis stick to the ice." Then he turned and strode into the aircraft as the ramp continued to close.

While Viktor was spluttering in protest, the engines roared to life and a heavy propeller-driven wind blasted against them. Taking a hint from the commander's actions, Min let the wind drive him over to his Nanji snow tractor.

By the time Victor recovered, the plane was underway with a great shooshing sound of the skis sliding over the snow.

And Min was underway back to his station to start preparing for whatever was about to happen.

34

ARTEMY TURGENEV TRIED TO TAKE IT IN. HE WAS SITTING IN Colonel Romanoff's Lubyanka Building office as if it was his own—at least until the man was found. It was no grand affair, but it was an office in FSB headquarters. And in General Murov's wing, a placement of high prestige.

His window didn't face Lubyanka Square like Murov's, instead it looked inward at one of the many narrow courtyards, but it had a window. He could see the helipad perched high on the opposite side of the building, which would be interesting to watch for VIP arrivals and departures.

A major, his own rank until yesterday, sat in an outer office waiting for his slightest command. It was nearing midnight, but the man was there. What had Romanoff been up to that he was staffed around the clock?

Turgenev began organizing his notes. There must be a way to trace—

The harsh buzz of his desk phone had him nearly leaping out of his chair.

"A Viktor Petrov is calling you," his new aide stated over the intercom.

"Um, thank you." That sounded weak. He shot for a more brusque tone, "Patch him through."

No verbal response, merely an audible click. Good.

"Petrov?"

"The Americans have left and they took the Chinese woman with them."

"Left? Left for where?"

There was a long enough pause that he wondered if the connection to Antarctica had been broken. "I don't know, sir."

In the palm of his hand! He'd had them in the palm of his hand and now they were gone?

"What aircraft were they in?" A helicopter or small plane would most likely mean they were going back to Davis for an inscrutable reason. He didn't know why they'd come to Zhongshan Station in the first place.

"An American Skibird."

Turgenev hit the back of his new chair as if he'd been punched in the chest by the President himself. They could go anywhere. American and Chinese together—cooperating!

"They said that my Helix Ka-32S helicopter and its pilots are dead. And Romanoff as well."

"Who said that?"

"One of the Americans."

It was both terrible and excellent news. The loss of a half-billion-ruble aircraft and three lives on the one side— and Romanoff would never return to oust Turgenev from his new office on the other.

"What else?"

"That's it. That's all I know."

More terrible news. "How is it, Petrov, that you have so failed in the simple task I assigned you?" How could he go to Murov with such incomplete information? Yet he knew he must.

"I tried. They wouldn't let me board the plane for an inspection. They were on the ground for less than five minutes, stopped for less than two."

"And yet you learned so little."

"I saw inside the cargo bay. There was nothing there. No equipment, no pallets of supplies. Three people in flying uniforms and four standing back in the shadows. That is all."

Four in the shadows? Military operatives? They would be if it was his flight. Combined with an air-crash investigation team, if that's all they were, and an envoy of the Chinese Central Military Commission. What could it all possibly mean?

"Describe them to me."

"Which ones?"

"All of them, you dolt."

Petrov's failure to observe details was staggering. The only ones who had made an impression on him were the big blond commander of the plane and the small brunette woman who had told him Romanoff was dead. "She might be the same one who was wearing the NTSB vest under her parka when they arrived. I think her name was Miranda Chase. Or Clace. Or something like that. Oh, and there was another small Chinese woman who stayed close to her."

"If you remember anything else that might save your skin, you will call me immediately, Petrov." He hung up before the man could respond.

Then he pressed the intercom to his new major. "Get me

everything you can on an American air-crash investigator named Miranda Chase. I need it in thirty minutes." He clicked off before the major could complete saying, *Yes sir.*

Turgenev rocked back in his chair. He could delay his report to Murov for as much as one hour. He had best know much more by then.

He had a thought and called back Petrov. "Which way was the plane headed?"

"South."

"Nothing more than that? Southeast? Southwest? Christ, man, from Progress Station almost everything is south in Antarctica."

He hung up on him as the man babbled that he hadn't thought to check so *minor* a detail.

Back to the major, "And get me a detailed map of all of the research stations in Antarctica, all countries." Again he didn't wait for a response.

Fifty-eight minutes to Murov. The man was notorious for always being in his office. There was no question that with the recent events, he'd be there in an hour.

He had no one to call. No one to text, *Am now Lt. Col. with inside office in Lubyanka Building.* He wished he did so that he could ask her advice.

A brief image of the dangerous Aloysha in that role, with his secrets in her clutches, almost made him laugh. At the moment he would trust to his own instincts.

Fifty-seven minutes to Murov. Twenty-seven until the major had to deliver on Miranda Chase.

Which meant he had twenty-six minutes to ransack Nikolas Romanoff's office and try to learn what else the man had been up to while commanding the Antarctic stations.

35

"WELL, THAT WAS FUN!" THE CAPTAIN HAD RETURNED FROM the cockpit now that they were aloft.

Holly had felt the shift from climb to cruise far sooner than she'd expected. She been aboard LC-130 Hercules when they were doing a hard climb, and this bird hadn't been.

"Why the low altitude?" Habit had her raising her voice over the four big engines, the American military didn't waste load capacity on sound insulation. The bare metal ribs of the hull structure were spaced a few feet apart up the length of the plane. Between most pairs were tucked heavy-duty apparatus: water (thirty person-days, refresh 1x per month), food (sixty person-days), raft kit (deployable, radio batteries refresh 1x per year), and on and on.

"First trip to Antarctica, lassie?"

"Not a dog, mate." She did her best to look completely at ease on one of the fold-down seats mounted along the side of the cargo bay, which experience had taught her was physically impossible. But no way was she giving him the upper hand in anything.

"Woof," the big man answered with a sly grin that said he was flirting but not seriously. "Captain Antony Capra of the 109th Airlift Wing at your service. And, yes, I'm distantly related to the Italian film director, so give me a break on that. Everyone calls me Cap since I was a kid in command of my first tricycle." Again that brief flash of a smarmy smile. "You know about the short climb, we topped at fifteen thousand. But you're missing something..."

Holly didn't mind the tease, but she honestly didn't know what she was missing.

Miranda apparently did, as always. "Vostok Station lies in an area commonly referred to as the Pole of Cold. It lies above eleven thousand feet and is one of the coldest places on Earth."

"You're shitting me." How had this happened to her? "Dammit. I want immediate transport back to under that nice warm quilt at your house. How cold?"

"Well, that's the issue, lassie," the captain had latched onto that, a choice she'd break him of soon. "A warm day there makes Siberia look like a tropical paradise. Current temperature is minus forty, which is the same in Fahrenheit and Celsius. Expected high of a balmy minus thirty-two, that's Fahrenheit. Smashed a lot of high heat records this last year—hit minus fourteen once. Hottest ever."

"And freezing is the issue," Miranda put in. "His fuel is AN-8, especially formulated for the polar regions. But despite that, AN-8 begins gelling into wax crystals at minus seventy-two. Temperature typically drops at a rate of five-point-four degrees per thousand feet of altitude. At minus forty on the ground, his fuel will freeze at roughly seventeen thousand feet—six thousand feet above Vostok."

"That would be bad," the captain agree easily.

"Yes, that would be bad," Miranda nodded.

"It's why those small Basler-converted DC-3s and Twin Otters are so popular down here. Mechanical controls. No major hydraulics to freeze. So, anyone want to tell me what's so important that I'm traveling empty across the whole continent to ferry you folks to the Pole of Cold?"

"In and back out. No leaving us there." Holly looked at the four men who had silently shifted close to listen, "And not only us, mate."

Cap offered a thoughtful nod.

Before she could jab at him—she definitely wanted to knock him down at least a few pegs—Mike eased forward.

"We're posing as an Antarctic Treaty survey team. All stations are supposed to be open for inspection by any other treaty signatory."

"And you're looking for what?"

"This for starters," Miranda handed over her tablet.

On it was a split screen. One was the long green tube resting on the ice with the missile's nose visible at the open end. The other was a shot of the cruise missile in flight.

"A five-hundred-kilo RDX warhead with a range over twenty-five hundred kilometers."

"I know what a Kalibr is." Captain Antony Capra was finally completely serious. "On The Ice? Here? Antarctica?"

"The one in the tube there, mate? Part of a set of four we destroyed... What the hell time is it anyway?"

"Twenty-four-hour sun will do that to you," Cap's voice was drifty as he kept contemplating the image.

Cruise missiles could be set to kill a lumbering plane like a Skibird as easily as they could destroy a research station.

"Time Zones are weird here below the sixtieth parallel south, too. Two a.m. for Zhongshan or Vostok. Heard you came from Davis, where it would be three in the morning. For this crew, it's eight a.m. McMurdo and South Pole time. Your call kicked us aloft about eight p.m. last night."

"Three a.m. here? Not where my brain is. How about Seattle?"

Cap stared at the ceiling for an eyeblink. "I'm thinking noon."

"No wonder I feel so wide awake." The two hours of sleep she'd managed at Zhongshan hadn't begun to make up for anything. "Well, we killed off a whole set of those missiles between breakfast and lunchtime yesterday. There were also a number of cases of the Willow surface-to-air chappies."

That took the last of the wind out of Captain Antony Capra's sails. Weapons like the Willow served only one purpose—killing planes.

"Sorry to tell you, pal. Yes, on The Ice. Russian aircraft."

"And the five of you are planning to stroll into a Russian Station to see if they're in a mood to kill you?" He looked aghast. He'd also stopped calling her *lassie*.

Holly shrugged, then nodded. "Got it pegged about square on, mate."

36

"No! No! AND NO! WHAT PART OF *NO* DON'T YOU understand?"

Miranda wished the captain wouldn't shout; it made him hard to ignore. At least he was fighting with Holly and not her.

"The *no* part!" Holly snarled at him. And her voice was softer, which was nice. Not dangerous-soft—yet—though getting there.

Should she warn the captain how hazardous it could be if that happened? No, best to stay out of it and not draw attention to herself.

"My people are *not* getting off the plane. That's final."

"Look, mate, if we do a razzle dazzle move, they won't be able to lock down fast enough to hide anything from us. Four teams of three: one of us, one of your crew, and one of these good old boys."

"Aren't you forgetting someone?" Daiyu said softly.

"No, you'll be leading one of the teams. I know that I can't separate Andi from Miranda in a situation like this.

Frankly, I'd rather Miranda stayed on the plane, but I know that won't happen either. Andi, if Miranda gets hurt on your watch, I'll be far more pissed than I am at Captain Antony Freaking Capra."

"Not gonna happen," Andi reassured her.

That was nice to know. Add protection to efficiency. Now two reasons that Andi was *convenient* to be in a relationship with.

The captain and Holly continued their argument.

The US Marshals were listening but also checking over their weapons.

Miranda wondered if that was another part of efficiency. Andi was a retired Special Operations Forces soldier, there would be no better protection to have constantly at her side. Only by keeping her mouth clamped firmly shut throughout the Zhongshan tour had she managed not to blurt out her question to Andi.

Was there more?

More than efficiency and convenience?

How was she supposed to know?

To distract herself from the question and the ongoing fight, Miranda began calculating the most likely energy propagation of the explosion at the Whoop Whoop Skiway. The givens of four Kalibr cruise missiles, four cases of Willow SAMs, and no remaining jet fuel were insufficient to account for what had happened. Adding what Holly had called *a couple caseloads* of F-1 hand grenades hadn't significantly altered the math.

In reviewing the feeds from Mike and Holly's helmet cams, she saw two more crates in the cargo bay she'd have liked to know the contents of. But neither Mike nor Holly had focused on them. They'd found the missiles and the MANPADS, then stopped looking.

Working the energy equations backward, to calculate the scale of those crates' contents, was proving difficult without a detailed model of how glacial ice fractured. Oh! She pulled out her phone.

"Thank God!" Holly snarled at the plane's captain. "Now you'll have the Chairman of the Joint Chiefs on your arse."

"When it's a safety issue, nobody overrules me about my crew."

The phone started ringing.

"Fine, how about her good friend President Roy Cole? You planning on telling your Commander in Chief that you aren't in the mood?"

The captain twisted to look at Miranda with narrowed eyes.

Miranda turned to stare at Andi's boots. That placed her back to the captain.

On the third ring, it was answered.

"'Lo?"

"Hello, Taz. Is Jeremy available?"

"*What?*" Holly shouted in the background. "You're supposed to be calling Drake or—"

Miranda plugged her other ear so that she could hear Taz.

"He'll be back in a minute."

Miranda glanced at the second hand on her watch. There was a silence. She hadn't been speaking but maybe this particular a silence could also mean it was her turn. "Um, did you solve the commuter crash?"

"An utterly ridiculous effort. We spent five days tromping

around the swamp, chasing off crocs and mosquitos that were twice *their* size."

"I was unaware of any bigger than the Australian elephant mosquito. It can only grow to one-point-three inches. An *Alligator mississippiensis* can grow to nearly six meters."

Taz laughed. "God I've missed you, Miranda. Okay, not *that* big, but plenty aggressive. Remind me never to meet one of those elephant types."

"It wouldn't matter. They live on sap and the larvae of their biting cousins. They don't bite people."

"Good to know. Anyway, we recovered every bit of that stupid plane before medical autopsy got back to us. Pilot was stone drunk. Probably passed out at the wheel by the flight profile. Not a thing wrong with the plane. Thankfully, it was a deadhead run, so the only person he killed was himself. Better off dead. Cleanse the gene pool."

Miranda considered the appropriate response. "At least you figured it out." She hoped that was better than pointing out that cleansing an eight-billion-person gene pool by an individual units was such an inefficient methodology that it would never be practical.

"We did. What are you working on?"

Miranda checked her watch and counted backward from four. At zero, she spoke up, "It's been a minute. Is Jeremy back yet?"

"It was a figure of speech, Miranda, not a precise prediction. But...Oh! Not far off. Jeremy!" she called out. "Miranda's calling for you." The sound quality changed indicative of a switch to speakerphone.

"Miranda! How are you? Is it too late to fly out to join you for Christmas?"

She didn't know where she'd be for Christmas. "Um, maybe. I need something as soon as you can."

"Sure, what is it?"

"I'm attempting to model an explosion inside the cargo hold of an Ilyushin-76, an older one based on the instrumentation. I'm so sorry, I don't have the hull number or aircraft ID."

A serious oversight. She'd have to recheck all of the videos to see if it had been visible anywhere. Though either side of the fuselage had been pressed against the sides of the crevasse and the name plate on the cockpit's console had been covered in blood and body parts. Perhaps it was okay that she'd missed it.

"Its fuselage was caught twenty meters down a crevasse, which had a top width of sixteen meters and an estimated width of one meter at a depth of a hundred." At least that where the other wing had caught after ripping off both engines during the fall. "True bottom is unknown."

"Uh..." But apparently he couldn't think of anything else to say.

Taking the silence as an invitation to proceed, she proceeded to describe the most likely sequence of the explosions and her most accurate reconstruction of the aftermath.

"Wow. What's the material of the crevasse? Basalt, sandstone, granite..."

"Ice."

Again one of those long silences that Miranda didn't know if it was up to her to fill.

"Ice?" Jeremy finally asked, solving the problem for her.

"Yes."

"Ice frozen over rock?"

"No. Only ice."

"Um, Miranda, where are you?"

"I'm on an LC-130H Skibird en route from Zhongshan Station to Vostok Station. I'm sorry I can't be more accurate than that without bothering the pilot." Which she definitely didn't want to do at the moment.

"Vostok. Like the one in Antarctica?"

"Yes." She couldn't think of what else to say.

Again, as always, Jeremy knew what to do. "Where was the explosion?"

"One-point-three kilometers due east of Whoop Whoop Skiway, about two hundred meters north of the midpoint. It's hard to be certain of that in the snow. My problem is that I can't make the math work for the force of the explosion. I'm sending you my calculations, though I haven't been able to access any seismography data, which may not be relevant because I don't know about—"

"—wave propagation through ice with air gaps caused by crevasses. Also the transmissibility speed—"

"—of sonic waves through an inconsistent crystalline structure." Jeremy was the only person ever who she could have broken conversations with and not lose her place. Andi's thoughts were too different. They made her think harder, making it difficult to maintain the thread. Holly and Mike's thinking were too foreign and their interruptions always sidetracked her completely.

"Anything else?"

"There are at least two objects that weren't identified in the cargo hold. I included the images but I doubt if they're sufficient for more than basic size calculations. I'm trying to back calculate what they might have been as they definitely enhanced the explosion."

"Russian?"

Miranda considered. It had been a Russian plane, but might someone else have placed the unknown objects on that plane? Was that why Daiyu was so interested in the cargo? Or had the Kalibr weapons been a sufficient motivation to dispatch her?

Occam's Razor stated that, lacking other givens, the simplest answer was the most likely.

That would imply that the crash of a Russian aircraft in Australian territory was sufficient for the Chinese to send in an individual, exactly as it had been sufficient to send in Holly and the rest of Miranda's team. That conclusion implied that Daiyu was *not* specifically investigating an additional package placed on the aircraft by the Chinese.

"Yes. Russian."

"Okay, I'll get back to you."

"Sooner would be better."

"I'm on it, Miranda."

"And about Christmas?"

"Yes?"

"I don't know where we'll be."

"I guessed that. Be careful, Miranda."

"Okay."

Miranda hung up and didn't hear anything else. People were no longer arguing over the deep roar of the big Allison T-56 engines. She liked the deeper, steadier sound of the Collins Aerospace eight-bladed propellers that had replaced the old four-blade Hamilton systems. They had also cut maintenance for blade-seal failures from thirty-six hours to two. She wished she'd been a part of that recommendation.

She turned on her phone's camera, flipped it to view her own face, then raised it to look over her shoulder.

The captain had gone forward to his cockpit, which was a relief for several reasons. A tall black woman from the plane's crew was listening in, but not speaking. Daiyu and her own teammates were talking with the four US Marshals in hushed voices.

Miranda turned off her phone.

37

"HOW LONG?" VICE PRESIDENT SARAH FELDMAN ASKED AS SHE strode into the Situation Room.

Drake rose to his feet. "Not long enough. I should never have agreed to this."

Lizzy didn't argue and Drake wished she would.

"How long?" President Roy Cole asked as he came in close behind Sarah.

Drake, halfway back to his chair, rose again.

"They'll be landing in under an hour," Lizzy answered for him.

"What are we expecting to find?" Roy waved them to both sit.

"Expecting or fearing?" Drake pulled up the image on his laptop and fed it to the array of screens at the end of the oak table. "We know for a fact that a Russian Ilyushin-76 plane was struck out of the sky with a kind of hypersonic projectile. Not ours, I checked. And I can't see the Russians shooting down their own plane, which leaves China. No one else is close to being able to do that. And with the required targeting, I don't know that we could have either."

"Not the news I'm looking for Drake," Roy stood by his usual seat at the head of the table but didn't sit.

"Because the strike didn't destroy the plane, we were able to inspect the contents. We saw four Russian SS-N-30A Kalibr cruise missiles en route to Progress Station. Also a wide array of grenades, rifles, and MANPAD surface-to-air missiles—their 9K333 Verba Willows—very nasty. Their Russian investigator lost his life during his successful effort to destroy the evidence, after it had been photographed. We can only assume that, had he survived, he would have done the same with the rest of the team we sent down there."

Roy Cole grunted as he settled into his chair at the head of the table.

"We can give the abort, sir. We haven't notified Vostok Station of our intended visit."

"And how are you getting around that?"

"Surprise at the communication breakdown that should have told them to expect a visit from a friendly inspection team."

"Are you recommending an abort, Drake?"

"I wish I knew, sir. And that's what's worrying me. If we send in Miranda Chase's team, even with support from the US Marshals, and it's a non-starter, then we're fine. If we send them in and discover that the Russians have been arming Vostok as a forward military base put in place to threaten our own stations? I can't see sending civilians into that hornet's nest."

Cole had laced his fingers together in his lap. "Yet this was your idea."

"Actually, Mr. President—"

Cole turned to his VP, "Hear that, Sarah? When he calls me Mr. President, you know there's trouble."

Sarah nodded sagely. She'd been an astute choice for VP after Clark had been murdered. Enough so to almost make Drake sad that he'd be retiring with the end of Cole's second term. Almost. She would make an interesting President.

"Actually, *sir*—"

Cole smiled at him, "That's so much better."

"It was at the request of General Liú Zuocheng of the CMC."

Drake was pleased to see at least Sarah was taken aback. Roy Cole rarely showed his emotions, except now he was tapping his forefingers together. It was his only tell, one that Drake had learned the hard way that the President did *not* use while playing poker.

"It seems that your time in Brunei was not wasted."

That one meeting had averted an international crisis or at least a trade war that might well have escalated into a shooting war. It had also built a narrow bridge with the senior vice chairman of the CMC.

"Do you think your people can handle it?"

"Damned if I know, sir. Ms. Harper and Ms. Wu are both former Spec Ops. Even a green beret like you must know what that implies."

Cole's ghost of a smile said that Drake would pay for that disparagement of the President's former regiment. But Drake had been a 75th Ranger and was ready for whatever might happen in their long-standing rivalry.

"However," he continued more seriously, "that leaves Mike Munroe and Miranda. We also don't know the capabilities of Colonel Wang Daiyu."

"The Chinese must think her capable if they sent her in

with no additional backup," Lizzy spoke up for the first time since the President's arrival.

That wasn't making Drake any happier about sending Miranda into harm's way.

"How much time to put together a sufficiently armed team and prepare them to look like an innocent inspection?"

"Other than being a treaty violation of its own? A week minimum. And a month or two would be better, allowing them to learn the station layout, build a mockup, and practice. Then we would need to locate the personnel, train them for the mission, then deploy them to Antarctica. And we'd want to deliver the asset with a backup in place. Mind you, that's a backup when the nearest station in every direction lies eight hundred miles away. The only one anywhere close is the French-Italian station at over three hundred miles. Oh, and I should mention that Last Flight is probably mid-February, six, perhaps seven weeks away."

"Last flight?"

Lizzy spoke up again, "That's the last service flight for the year. By March it's too cold to fly to Vostok due to a high chance of the fuel freezing and causing the plane to crash."

Roy studied the images of the Kalibr missile on the screen and continued to tap his fingers together. It was when they stopped that—

"Bottom line, Drake?"

"Bottom line, *Mr. President,* I've spent the whole day trying to come up with a better solution than sending in Miranda's team. Frankly, I don't have one."

Cole nodded. "I was afraid of that. Okay, I'm going to give this mission a go." Then Roy called out to the room monitors, "Get me the captain on that plane. Try Miranda Chase's phone if nothing else works."

They *did* have to go through Miranda's phone.

"Captain Capra here."

"Hello, Captain. President Roy Cole here. I'm authorizing this flight into Vostok as directed by Miranda Chase and Holly Harper."

"Yes sir." The man's voice sounded impossibly tighter than Drake's felt.

"I want your people on the ground for one hour max. Any excuse you want: an urgent call for the plane, that your wife is having a baby—anything. Cover what ground you can in that hour. See what you can. Get the hell out. If we need to escalate from there, we will."

"Yes sir."

"Best of luck, Captain. I want to hear from you the moment you're aloft."

"Yes sir." And the connection was gone; only silence remained in the Situation Room.

Drake could only pray that he didn't hate himself in the morning.

There were four digital clocks on the wall: Moscow time (02:06), Beijing (07:06), DC, and President (which matched DC's 18:06). On one of the screens a new timer blinked on: Vostok Station, Russia, 05:06.

It was already morning there.

38

MIRANDA HAD NEVER LANDED ON SKIS BEFORE BUT THE sensation was similar to a wheeled landing. The relative flexibility of tire rubber traded for the hardness of the skis created a near one-to-one offset with the exchange of the harder paved runway for the compacted snow-and-ice surface. It was a sound more akin to landing on water pontoons.

Tire squeal was supplanted by a bright shooshing sound of the ski. In the hands of the Air National Guard pilot, there was no bounce or skip. Taxiing seemed more laborious, requiring a continued deep bite by the variable pitch propellers. There wasn't much else of note.

The file of what was known about Vostok Station itself was surprisingly thin for a station nearing its seventieth year. There was more published about the new station built in Russia in 2019 and only now arriving in pieces after three years' delay than about the existing station.

She, Andi, and a US Marshal were Team One. Holly, Mike, and Daiyu would be leading the other teams. The captain had conceded to Holly to let his engineer and loadmaster join two of the teams, with him and his copilot remaining aboard to keep the engines idling. Putatively it was against the cold, but it would also support an immediate departure.

"Remember," the captain announced over the PA as he taxied toward the buildings, "we're at thirty-five hundred meters, that's eleven-five in feet. That's a thousand higher than the highest town in the US."

"We have a village at five thousand meters," Daiyu whispered to her.

Miranda's nod of acknowledgement appeared to be all that Daiyu was seeking. How curious to live so high, knowing that a trip to lower altitudes could induce reverse altitude sickness.

The captain continued, "You've come straight up from sea level. It's also one of the driest place on earth with less than an inch of snow every year. So, stay hydrated and don't so much as think about running anywhere. I don't want to be stuffing any of you into the hyperbaric chamber."

Miranda glanced forward. Strapped to the forward bulkhead of the cargo bay was a portable chamber, like those used in deep-sea diving accidents. A person could be put in the chamber and pressurized to a lower altitude.

"You all have radios. Use them. We'll be listening. Footie and Stretch, stick with the teams that remain closest to the bird. If we need to bail, I want you two aboard and I don't give a good goddamn what the President said." Miranda didn't know if his tone shift meant he was joking or not, but she wouldn't ask.

Miranda didn't know what Roy had said to the captain. But when he'd returned her phone after the call, it had made him look at her thoughtfully—she'd checked that against her emojis (straight mouth, squinted eyes, furrowed brow, and a question mark above his head that she now understood was symbolic and not literal). It had been such a specific match, one she'd never made before, that she had confirmed that with Andi.

Convenient!

They taxied to a stop.

Again, they used the rear ramp and not the small passenger door.

"Display of power. It's much more impressive," Andi explained when Miranda glanced her way.

Very *efficient.*

Miranda wanted to cry.

Eight Russians were waiting for them, alerted no doubt by the captain requesting permission to land. That was a significant portion of the population as the station's maximum reported capacity was twenty-five people.

"Welcome to Vostok Station," one of them stepped forward and called far too loudly in heavily accented Russian. "I am the station manager here, Oleg Sidirov, but people are calling me Ollie."

Miranda wondered at his bare face and partially unzipped parka. Everyone on the Skibird was wearing the multiple layers specified by the Gen III Extended Cold Weather Clothing System: two layers of undergarments, a fleece jacket, a full layer of trousers and jacket, and the parka. The were additional layers to the system but, as they'd be active, the plane's loadmaster said that they'd be excessive. They also all wore neck gaiters pulled up to and tucked under the edge of their goggles, and woolen hats pulled down over the tops. She supposed after a winter spent here, minus forty was unremarkable.

"Greetings, mate," Holly stepped into the lead. But Miranda could only tell it was her by her accent; Mike and the crewwoman they called Stretch were equally tall and equally heavily clothed. The US Marshals were easily distinguished because their parkas looked hard used.

Miranda appreciated Holly taking the lead. Her only practiced greeting line—*I'm Miranda Chase. Investigator-in-Charge for the NTSB*—wouldn't be appropriate under the circumstances. She understood that, but hadn't thought to develop a lie. Lies were always confusing and she didn't like them; they always made her feel all sticky and in need of a shower.

Holly could do it like a professional and always made it sound so effortless. Miranda would have to ask for lessons. But she didn't want to unzip three layers to reach her notebook to enter a reminder, even if the pen could work in this cold. Inappropriate to ask and unable to write it down trapped her in rather a dilemma.

"Sorry you chaps didn't get notice of our visit. That's government for you, isn't it?" Holly rambled on happily.

Miranda wanted to check her watch but it was under multiple layers as well. The captain said he was leaving after precisely one hour, no matter who he left behind. She estimated that there was a sixty percent chance he was joking, plus or minus thirty percent—a margin of possible error that invalidated her estimate—and she hadn't asked Andi. Either way, time was wasting.

Ollie smiled at Holly. "Yes, those is governsment."

"No worries? We don't get over this side of the continent

often and thought it would be rare luck that we could drop in on you folks."

"Yes, it is okay."

"Don't want to freeze our engines," Holly hooked a thumb over her shoulder indicating the plane with its spinning props, "so we'll keep 'em idling while we do a quick peek-and-howdy if'n you don't mind."

"We have nothing to be hiding," Ollie offered another smile.

Something not quite right with it. She turned to ask Andi if the corners of his mouth indicated undue tension, but then turned away. Andi being an efficient part of her life wasn't enough reason to be in a relationship. She was sure of that. And Mike was standing on the far side of too many people to walk over and ask.

"You come at an awkward time. Our station most old. Next year we have *new* station. Come, I show you foundations."

"Nah, mate, rather tour the old place. That will give us a baseline to judge your new station by when you've got it all spiffed and shiny. Make you look even better for putting it in place."

Ollie shifted from foot to foot. That meant *nervous,* didn't it? But it also could mean *excited anticipation.* How was she supposed to tell them apart?

"Come," he finally called out. "I will show you our station. We are most proud of it."

Miranda couldn't see why. Perhaps once, but now? There were two primary buildings the size of a double-wide trailer home. Paneled in alternating strips of peeling beige and peeling light blue, they were decidedly unattractive. There was a window in each four-foot-wide panel, but many of these were boarded over. A large snowdrift had inundated one end to well above the windows.

Two tall towers at either end of the station were for the ice core drills. The captain had parked the plane in the middle of the skiway close by the closer drill building. These towers were equally shabby, but far more impressive. The drills had pulled up near continuous cores going down through three kilometers of ice covering half a million years of climate data to be analyzed.

That could be a fascinating project. It was one of the first ideas she'd ever had other than investigating air crashes that sounded interesting. If it was simply her and quantitative analysis of thousands of meters of ice cores, she wouldn't need a companion to interpret other people or political motives for her. Cold ice, pure data. It was incredibly attractive.

From her perch high on the ramp, she could see that there was one more building whose top was level with the snow. A pit had been dug around it, but it must require continual maintenance to not fill in again.

Andi gave her a brief shove. The others were already in motion from the plane toward the closest building.

Once she stepped off the ramp, she almost tumbled over.

"It takes time to learn walking in the wind," Ollie said as he propped her upright. "It never stops here. Five meters per second so much of time. Today is ten. Many time twenty-five. Always from south, you know."

Ten meters per second was over twenty miles per hour. And it was loaded with snow crystals that rattled against the hood of her parka so like a storm of BB pellets that she understood why Ollie had been shouting.

"Come. We get you inside."

Climbing the five steps to the entry winded her slightly because of the thin air. They entered through a double-door airlock two-by-two because three wouldn't fit. Airlock was too grand a word, it was no better than the mudroom at her house. But the first door blocked the wind and snow. The second—

Again she stumbled, backward this time instead of sideways, and almost exited the second door backward. Despite the filtering cloth of the neck gaiter, the smells were an assault.

Miranda knew that the South Pole Station allowed two two-minute showers per week—she'd heard that a scientist transferring from McMurdo, which had no such limit, had overrun her first shower by seven seconds and been heavily teased about living in luxury. Well, it was a luxury Vostok clearly did not share. The smell of scorched oil was also so thick on the thin air that she was glad her stomach had been too scrunched up to eat much of her one meal at Zhongshan Station.

The room itself was surprisingly dark. After she removed her shaded goggles...it remained dark. Three unblocked windows, in a room that should have eight, allowed harsh sunlight into the dark-paneled room. No lights had been turned on, perhaps to save power during the daylight.

A crammed bookcase stood at one end, partially blocked by a meter-tall handmade Christmas tree. To the left was a small kitchen from which the worst of the grease smells were emanating: they were serving a breakfast of coffee, porridge, sausage, and thick slices of Russian black bread. The middle of the room was filled with wooden tables that the cheapest American diner would have thrown out years before.

Six to a table, the men of Vostok Station were staring at them aghast. One mumbled, "Women!" in a voice stretched thin with surprise. Scanning, she saw they were all men. Longer hair and beards were the norm. The other end of the room was a small sitting area of worn chairs, a sofa, and a few games on a low table. It would be uncomfortable with the winter population of thirteen. The summer population of twenty-five were crowded using both the dining and the lounge area. The addition of the eleven people of their *inspection* team, increasing the station population by half, made movement impossible.

39

Turgenev rested his forehead on his desk and wondered if it would still be his come dawn. It was two a.m. and he'd sent the major home. As far as he knew, his entire floor, his entire wing of the Lubyanka Building was deserted.

His sacking of Romanoff's ex-office had revealed little. Petty corruptions, a few bank accounts that Turgenev had quietly emptied, but nothing damning that he could leverage. When he had the major unlock Romanoff's office safe, it was sad. A few blackmail items that were barely worthy of tossing into the burn bag.

The map of Antarctica had revealed nothing of real use either.

Due south from Progress and Zhongshan Station lay the two other Chinese stations, Taishan and Kunlun, and the Americans' Amundsen-Scott South Pole Station. All arranged like neat pins in a row with five hundred to a thousand kilometers between each. These seemed likely landing sites because of the two Chinese women Petrov had reported boarding the American plane.

To the southeast lay the most direct route to the hub of most American activity on the continent, McMurdo. This also seemed a likely destination as the American Skibirds were careful to never park at the South Pole due to freezing.

What had worried him was that also to the southeast, within a mere forty kilometers of their best route, lay Vostok Station. It seemed unlikely that the Americans would go there, but it was the only other Russian Station along one of their possible routes.

He had tried to contact General Murov, but his aide had insisted that Murov could not be disturbed. The so-called *special military operation* in Eastern Europe had spiraled into further chaos than normal yesterday and Murov was meeting with the President. The aide took a message, but that was all.

Back in his office, Turgenev had studied the thin file assembled by his own aide.

Miranda Chase.

At first glance, an air-crash investigator for their civilian agency. He had to read the dossier on the NTSB several times to convince himself that while they might know of problems and dangers, they had been granted no power to fix them. They must wade through bureaucrats to achieve any changes. It made him feel marginally better about the challenges he'd encountered in his own career. Red tape wound around every corner and corruption was often the only avenue to achievement. It was said that the Americans didn't have the latter option, though he found that unlikely.

Yet in her work, Miranda Chase herself avoided publicity with the skill of a top operative. She slid in and out of investigations leaving behind no more than rumor or the occasional photograph.

The attack on Air Force Two in Turkey, there was an image of her in the background. She was so nondescript that she was only truly identifiable by the tall blonde woman who was rarely far from her side.

A Chinese mainland jet crashed on a sandy beach in Taiwan.

A helicopter crash at an American airshow.

An airplane crash on a remote desert island in the Pacific.

At the scene of the helicopter crash that killed their Vice President.

Rarely her name, never a good photograph, but that distinctive blonde and, he now saw, a tall man with dark hair. Others were in some photos but not others. It was hard to be sure. A tiny, dark woman who might be a Latina. A Viet man. And lately, twice, a small Chinese woman.

Was that the woman Petrov had seen? Was she a secret liaison between whatever American agency this Miranda Chase truly worked for and the CMC?

He raised his forehead enough to bang it back down on his desk.

Skibird.

Miranda Chase.

Colonel Wang Daiyu of the CMC.

Unidentified Chinese operative.

The crashed Ilyushin-76 filled with missiles.

Zhongshan Station. Vostok, Kunlun, Amundsen-Scott, McMurdo.

Nothing fit.

Another thump jarred loose no new ideas.

He was a dead man when—

"Is that helpful, Lieutenant Colonel?"

Turgenev bolted upright to see General Murov standing in his doorway. He jolted to his feet and saluted. "I wish it was, sir. I truly wish it was."

40

GENERAL LIÚ ZUOCHENG SKIPPED HIS MORNING RITUAL IN THE lobby of the Eight-One Building. The venerable Chengdu J-7 would have to fly alone in the great lobby.

He had only gone home for a few hours last night, causing great consternation among the Ministry of National Defense minions. But there had been a great deal to set in motion—on such very short notice—which he had seen to personally to avoid any unforeseen problems.

He checked his watch. If his calculations were correct, Wang Daiyu and her team of *friendly* investigators should have landed in Vostok Station five minutes ago. He did not expect to hear from her for at least ninety minutes. There would be no satellites overhead except for the occasional passage of those for Iridium satellite phones. They, too, had spotty coverage when he needed it most.

Zuocheng went to his private office in the secure subbasement and told his secretary that he was available to no one.

It was not a luxurious underground cave. There was no bar. An electric teapot was the only comfort.

He powered up and unlocked the room's computer screens.

Two Xi'an H-6 long-range bombers had departed. They carried an immense load of fuel, and few, but incredibly powerful weapons—station busters. They were weapons of last resort in Operation Ice Thunder.

They were preceded by four Xi'an Y-20 strategic lifters: two as midair refueling tankers and two carrying a special cargo.

He checked their locations. Everything was in place, exactly as he had ordered.

But until he heard the results of Wang Daiyu's mission, all any of them could do was wait.

41

"WHAT WOULD IT TAKE TO GET DECENT SATELLITE COVERAGE down there?" Roy Cole was watching the Vostok clock as intently as Drake himself was.

He had no idea.

"We're currently running three systems," Lizzy knew, of course. She was the Director of the National Reconnaissance Office and was in charge of all Department of Defense satellites from launch to deorbiting. "NASA, DoD, and the UK Skynet system. With them we consistently cover thirteen hours per day at the South Pole, on a shifting schedule. Our best window from any single bird is five hours. If you're willing to authorize three more satellites, you will receive innumerable thanks and marriage proposals from the South Pole scientific community."

Drake watched the President's reaction. They'd been friends for far longer than Roy Cole had been in office, and the President's reaction was one he recognized.

He asked his question with a single word, "Rose?"

Roy's glare was answer enough.

Four months ago, Mrs. Senator Ramson had been widowed when her husband's hotel suite had been rammed by a stolen US military jet.

DC's leading socialite had since proven that to be the least of her skills. Rose Ramson had been selected by the governor of Utah to serve out her husband's term, and she was making more of a mark than Hunter Ramson ever had.

She had apparently also caught the President's eye, with good reason. Still stunning, though her Miss Utah pageant win was near enough four decades in her past.

And—despite her previous association with Hunter and the wildly dangerous CIA Director Clarissa Reese—Drake liked the woman.

Roy continued staring at him, but now there was a question.

Drake considered. He *did* like the woman.

"An invitation to the next reception in the Residence. To hell with what the newsies might say." He'd meant to make it a question, but it came out in his military voice.

Roy tapped his fingers together several times, nodded, then turned back to Lizzy. "Get me an estimate."

"A half billion apiece, full lifecycle cost, for a polar-orbit comm sat. Three times that for one with basic visual ability. Four billion for sub-six-inch resolution. Or—if you don't require optics, voice, and video bandwidth on any of the systems that private firms are launching by the thousands— we could lease that for a couple hundred a month."

"And why the hell aren't we doing that already?"

"Because the FCC and the competitors who are behind on launching their own systems are blocking the industry leaders from using the polar orbits beyond a few limited tests."

"You mean that I'm not going to know what's happening to my people in Antarctica because a stupid internecine tit-for-tat war between commercial vendors?"

Lizzy nodded.

"Tell me who I have to kill."

"I'll send you a list, Mr. President," Lizzy said cheerfully.

"I'm sorry, sir," Drake spoke up. "I can't let you do that."

"Go ahead, Ranger, try and stop me."

"I can't advise any action that includes the President getting his hands bloody, sir. Besides, we can't let a Green Beret risk dirtying his hands, can we? Not even a former one."

"Fine, I'll have Sarah do it. What are Vice Presidents for?"

"Better than mopping a floor any day," Sarah joined in. "Lizzy, send me the list. I'll get someone to take care of it. Congress has been looking for a target lately."

"In the meantime?" Cole stared at the screens at the end of the table.

Drake checked his watch. "They've been inside for nineteen minutes. All we can do is sit and wait."

42

"Vostok?" Murov's face went white.

Turgenev gripped the edge of his desk, bracing himself for whatever storm was about to be unleashed. He'd laid out everything he'd learned from that useless piece of trash Station Manager Victor Petrov. Then the few details he'd learned of the elusive Miranda Chase.

Together, he and Murov had puzzled over the scant data about the woman.

There were categories of people for whom existed minimal data. The majority, because they were so unworthy of note. Look up an old friend from grade school, and there might be no digital footprint at all beyond a yearbook photo, and perhaps a real estate symposium. At the other end of the spectrum, a select few were Special Operations soldiers who would also have no digital past because what couldn't be erased was left behind under a hidden identity.

Miranda Chase looked like the former but felt like the latter.

Finally, Turgenev had laid out the possible routes the American Skibird might take.

"I can't see how anything important connects. They'll pass over the two inland Chinese stations if they depart due south to Amundsen-Scott. McMurdo lies to the southeast, a third of the way around the continent's coastline. If they flew direct, it would pass them within twenty kilometers of Vostok."

And that's when Murov's pallor had blanched as white as snow.

"Contact Vostok. Immediately."

"I can't, sir. We have such minimal satellite coverage there, it is only a few hours each day. I won't be able to reach them for hours."

Murov's curse was deep and resonant. "That useless Petrov at Progress, can you reach him?"

"Yes sir. They are far enough from the pole to connect to a geosynchronous satellite over the equator." Turgenev explained as he keyed in the number.

"Petrov here. What do you want this time, Turgenev?"

Murov traded a look with Turgenev that said the man was definitely finished.

Turgenev nodded that the general would have no argument from him.

Murov leaned forward. "What air assets do you have there, Petrov?"

"I have a Ka-32S helicopter. The Chinese have loaned us theirs as well. We've just finished the unloading of the new station modules for Vostok. Who is this?"

Murov ignored him. "I want both to depart immediately for Vostok Station."

"They'll never reach it. They have a range of nine hundred kilometers if traveling with no cargo. Vostok is fourteen hundred."

"What else do you have?"

"Our only plane has been out of service for a month. The new engine arrived on the ship. My mechanic says that we can have it operational in five, perhaps six days."

"You've had no way to reach our Vostok Station for a month, you incompetent fool?" Murov glanced at him, but Turgenev shook his head. He'd known nothing of this in his prior position. He'd only been responsible for making sure the Ilyushin-76 cargo planes were properly scheduled out of Moscow and through Cape Town. Their contents had been Romanoff's responsibility.

"Perhaps we can borrow the People's Republic of China's Snow Eagle 601. It can cover the distance if there is an emergency."

"It's an emergency, you fool. Load up every soldier you have and get to Vostok immediately. They may well be under attack."

"By whose order?"

"Mine!" Murov shouted. "Army General Murov."

"I'm sorry, sir. I had no idea, sir. I'll—"

"*Now,* Petrov. And I expect you to be leading the charge." Murov jabbed the disconnect button hard enough that Turgenev was surprised the general didn't break his finger.

"There is a problem, sir," he said carefully.

"What is that?" And the general was once more fully under control. Had he ever been out of control? Perhaps it was all show. A most effective show.

"The American Skibird, if it did indeed route to Vostok,

would already be on the ground. Once airborne, the Snow Eagle will require three hours to make the crossing."

Murov's glare said that his anger definitely hadn't been for show.

43

HOLLY DIDN'T KNOW WHAT SHE WAS LOOKING FOR, BUT THIS
wasn't it. Being a personified grubby-Russian-guy magnet
looked to be a lousy career choice.

She wished she'd had Mike close, but he was off with
one of the US Marshals and the crewwoman called Stretch.
She'd ended up on the short team, only herself and Freddie,
the US Marshall who'd been maintaining the South Pole
telescope.

The place was only six buildings, but she rarely caught
more than a glimpse of the other teams. Vostok was a rat
warren that had evolved organically. The main buildings
weren't one-story tall, they were two stories tall—with the
lower story long since buried under the snow.

Descending the narrow stairs was like climbing down
into a pit. No natural light. The windows had been boarded
over before the snow had covered them completely.

No immaculate private rooms here. The beds were all
dormitory style: steel frame, sagging mattress, and piled with
massive layers of quilts against the chill that pervaded the

station. They were lined along both sides of the lower level, less than a meter between each bed.

She wondered if any snorers had been murdered in these beds.

From the lower level, a heavy wooden door opened into an ice tunnel. It was tall enough to clear her head and wide enough for two to walk abreast, if they weren't in their parkas. A thin light filtered down through the snow and ice cover. If one of these tunnels collapsed, that would be the end of anyone caught in it.

This tunnel split after a few meters. Daiyu's team of three, and a Russian guide, had continued straight ahead. She could hear their voices echoing back to the junction.

"They are going to old lounge. Place where we could relax," Ollie offered as he led her and Freddie to the right.

"*Old* lounge?"

"First building at Vostok. The heater not so good. Insulation very not good. It now excellent ice core storage and laboratory."

"You actually drilled through three kilometers of ice?"

"Russian engineering. We capture core all the way down."

She'd give him credit for that, it sounded bloody impossible to her.

The walls and ceiling of the tunnel were ice, not snow. It looked several inches thick. She ran a glove over it and it was as slick as a skating pond. Every few meters along the walls, niches had been carved. In one was an old ice saw. In another, an unnested set of Matryoshka dolls. A third had a hat and a fourth a piece of steak. Each one was coated over with a thick layer of clear ice—frozen in time. This Gallery of Despair followed them all the way along the tunnels.

"Our breath. It freeze on the tunnel walls. Very strong."

She wondered how many thousands of trips along this passage had been necessary to lay it down this thickly.

The tunnel ended at another heavy wooden door.

Ollie heaved it open but not before she noticed that another passage led to the left, but was now hidden by the wide-open door.

He waved them inside then pulled the door shut behind him, not that it made any difference. This building was no warmer than the tunnel, and it was nothing like the building they'd left. If she'd kept track of her orientation, she'd have known where they were, but the depressing dormitory had distracted her. Which made the inside of this building doubly surprising.

It was a massive machine space. There were long racks filled with five-meter sections of hollow pipe she could insert a fist into. Around the outside of each pipe was a raised spiral band.

"Core drills?"

"Yes. Yes. See? See this?" he held up a vicious looking piece of metal about six inches across. "This is bit."

Unlike any normal drill bit, it was open in the center. But the edge had three big teeth. He held it face-down and twisted it. It would carve a circular slot in the ice, the teeth chewing up a thumb-wide area of ice and feeding it past the bit through small gaps in the edge of the head. These ice chips would be whisked aloft by the spiral ridge on the outside of the pipes.

The cut out central circle would slide into the pipe to be safely taken aloft and stored in their *Old Lounge*.

The room, larger than the primary residential building, was filled with heavy equipment. It was all idle now, covered with a rime of ice so thick that restarting any of this machinery would take a miracle.

At one end of the building, the ceiling towered upward for forty or fifty feet. It was a crane arrangement for lifting the drill tubes from horizontal to vertical before feeding them down into the ice.

Ollie would have been only too glad to show them through every detail of the process. He was clearly excited by and proud of it, so she let him run on a bit.

"Lake Vostok. Two-hundred-fifty kilometers long, fifty kilometers wide. Number five freshwater lake whole world. We drill down but maybe life. Special life. Buried long, long time." He tapped his own chest. "Russian engineer. We drill so close that lake water, squeezed by pressure of three kilometers of ice, *whoosh!*" He shot a fist upward. "Water of lake break into our hole and freeze hard. We drill sample of lake ice but never touch lake. Heh? Heh?"

"Amazing!" She gave it to him, because it was.

Holly also noticed Freddie checking his watch. Time was definitely running. Holly made a point of taking a number of pictures as if to catalog the amazing engineering. She had Freddie take a picture of her and Ollie standing close by the drill hole.

"Our President declare whole building historic monument. Official."

"That's wonderful." As far as she could tell, the Russians tried to declare everything that wasn't moving as a historic monument. One of the crew chiefs told her that at Mirny station there was historic monument where someone had died two kilometers from the station.

Then she figured out why. By labeling everything historic, it saved them tearing it down after the new station building arrived. It circumvented the treaty, allowing them to leave everything to rot in place. Not the American philosophy. The single most iconic building of them all, the massive geodesic glass dome that had been the second South Pole station, hadn't been declared historic. Instead, they'd removed it and flown it back to the States to leave a minimal footprint on the continent.

"I wish I had time to see it all. But we have to keep going."

"Yes. Yes." Ollie looked sad to leave the frozen drill building. This had clearly been his baby. Past the door, he tried to shoo them back the way they'd come, again covering the other tunnel with the wide-open door.

"What's down that tunnel?"

"Which..." but then Ollie gave it up as a bad attempt. "It leads from Drill Building B," he swung the heavy wooden door closed and patted it affectionately, "to Drill Building A."

There had been two drilling towers visible, one at either end of the station. "Great! Let's go see it."

"This tunnel...not...good. Very not good. It, uh, collapse. No passage."

You're a crappy liar, Ollie my friend.

"Well, let's go up on the surface and walk over. I'd hate to miss seeing another drill as amazing as this one." She went to open the door back into Drill Building B as it had an exit out onto the surface.

Ollie held the door shut. "Uh, no good. Old structure. Not safe. Filled with snow drift. Nothing to see."

Gotcha! Holly didn't know whether to be pleased or upset. Well, they'd certainly found out what they came for. She had to remind herself that they didn't need to see the weapons stashed here. They were only supposed to find out if there were any—she had.

"That's too bad. Was it designated as a historic monument as well?" She waved for Ollie to lead them down the corridor back toward their starting point.

Then she had an idea. As soon as Ollie's back was turned, she flashed a signal to Freddie to head down the *not good* tunnel. With a fist pump for double time.

"Hey, Freddie," she called out loud. "Why don't you go out through this building and tell the captain we're finishing up here? I know he's worried about having enough fuel to get us on to McMurdo and doesn't want to idle the engines for too long."

"Sure, Holly. Sounds like a good idea."

Before Ollie could protest, Freddie opened the door to reenter the drill building.

She hurried Ollie along the corridor. At the first turning, she glanced back to see Freddie close the door, without reentering the drill building, and hurry down the *not good* tunnel.

44

THE VARIOUS TEAMS HAD REGATHERED IN THE CROWDED MAIN room of the first building they'd entered.

Holly's pulse rate was pounding from the altitude by the time she'd climbed the steps from the Dormitory of Despair.

Daiyu was talking when she and Ollie arrived. "I can't believe the amazing science you've managed here in such, ah, age-worn conditions. Your new station will be amazing by comparison."

"Warm!" One Russian called out.

"No snow in bed," another cried out. Then he repeated himself in Russian and the other men were laughing, perhaps a touch hysterically.

As Daiyu continued the compliments, Holly checked the other team members. Mike and Stretch gave tiny headshakes, as did the Marshal who'd been with Daiyu.

Andi held up a hand as if to wave from the far side of the room. But she kept her hand in a fist with the thumb upright along the side of her curled forefinger as she waved. American Sign Language for the letter A.

Drill Building A.

Holly nodded her agreement, then casually looked away. She counted out two more minutes, hopefully that was all the time Freddie needed, because it was all she could give him.

She called out to add her thanks and to offer them all an invitation to visit them at McMurdo—because there wasn't a chance in hell of any of them ever getting there. After a season trapped here at Vostok, they'd probably defect to the last man.

Once they were outside, Daiyu leaned close. "Thank you. I was out of nice things to say about that horrible place. Those poor people."

Holly nodded her agreement.

She spotted Freddie as they came around Drill Building B. Having doubled back, he was only now coming out of the door she'd told him to use. Thankfully, it was near enough to where the plane was parked that he shifted his pace as if he was doing a leisurely inspection of the Skibird.

Hopefully no one would notice the heavy puffing of his breath through his neck gaiter, creating clouds of vapor after his run along the *not good* tunnel. Luckily, he'd been the one stationed at the South Pole, which was only two thousand feet lower than Vostok. She couldn't have made the run at all.

Hands were shaken. Another group picture was taken. And another.

Promises were made to write a good report and send them a copy for their superiors. Then they were finally aboard.

The instant the ramp closed, Daiyu called out loud enough to be heard over the engines. "Did we find them?"

Freddie, too out of breath to speak, gave a thumbs up.

"This is your captain," blared out over the internal PA. "Sit your asses down and buckle in. You're about to learn what this plane can do."

Holly noticed that neither of the crewmembers walked to their forward seats in the cockpit—they sprinted.

They all buckled into their seats, extending belts to reach around the heavy parkas.

The engines didn't roar—they howled.

45

"Kandahar flashbacks?" Captain Antony Capra called out to Jackie. He was definitely having déjà vu for having already asked that question on the way here.

"Shit man," she offered the same reply as they firewalled the engines.

Every ten minutes they'd retracted the skis, letting the wheels briefly support the plane on the hard skiway, then lowered them again to keep them from sticking. Twice he'd fed enough power to the engines to inch them forward a few feet, scrubbing off any snow that was bonded to the skis themselves.

So, when he fed the power, the big girl practically stood on her haunches and leapt.

He didn't like this place. Didn't trust it any farther than he could throw it.

He certainly didn't waste time taxiing to the far end of the Skiway.

"Problem, Cap."

"What?" His big girl should be lifting her nose at any moment.

"Kandahar, thirty-three hundred feet. We're above eleven thousand."

46

"I was asked many strange questions about Drill Building A."

Ollie looked at the senior ice scientist as they watched the big plane race along the Skiway. "What kind of questions?"

"When and why was it decommissioned. Why did we build Drill Building B? They very much wanted to go down the tunnel from Old Lounge."

"What did you tell them?"

"That we never finished it." It was a better answer than he'd come up with himself.

"Did they then ask to cross the surface to go to the building?" Ollie held the outer door of the airlock for him.

"They did."

Ollie spun to stare at the plane. "*Pizdobol!* They're liars. They came for only one reason." He raced inside, leaving both doors open.

Men lingering over breakfast shouted their complaints about the break in door protocol. What marginal heat the old generator had bled into the living area blew out the pair of open doors.

He shoved them aside, flipped the sofa forward onto a low table, scattering a half-played chess game.

Snapping open the case he'd hidden there, he grabbed its contents and raced back through the door, knocking the senior scientist backward down the outside stairs.

47

"Jesus God, that was close," Jackie gasped out as the Skibird lifted.

"I'm going to kiss every engineer at Lockheed Martin." Cap was shaking—and he never shook. Instinct had told him not to power down and try again. He'd have had to taxi the entire the length of the skiway, then turn and run again because the wind was strong out of the south.

"Cold air. I love cold air."

And Jackie was absolutely right. In Afghan summers they'd always been fighting air thinned by high heat, creating low-lift scenarios on every load. Here the air was dense and stone cold, creating lots of lift for such a high altitude.

The skis had come off the snow less than a hundred meters from the end of the groomed and packed skiway. If they'd plowed into the soft snow past the end at takeoff speeds, they might have flipped tail over nose—an ugly way to die.

But they were aloft and clean.

Then an alarm Cap hadn't heard in years screeched to life.

48

OLLIE HAD SERVED EIGHT YEARS IN THE 6TH GUARDS TANK Regiment. It had been over thirty years since he'd fought in the Soviet-Afghan War but, when his tank had been destroyed out from under him, he'd grabbed a case of Strelas as he ran. The surface-to-air missiles worked on trucks of Afghanis as well as against airplanes.

This shouldn't be that different.

He aimed the 9K333 Verba Willow at the dark dot of the departing airplane. He wasted several seconds until he found it in the aiming scope. With the magnification, he could see its wings and tail section clearly, even the air shimmer of heat off the engines.

He'd been told that he must protect the greatest secret in Antarctica.

Depressing the trigger halfway created a clear tone, the weapon had acquired the plane. It wasn't too far away yet.

Ollie prayed he was doing the right thing. Colonel Nikolas Romanoff had called him personally before the first weapons shipment. He had that said keeping this secret was critical to continued state security.

Station Master Oleg Sidirov pulled the trigger.

49

"TONE! TONE! TONE! THEY HAVE TONE ON US." JACKIE called out.

A radar warning system had acquired the Skibird, and Cap was betting it wasn't a Vostok science experiment.

"Launch! We have a launch!"

"Prepare countermeasures."

"Countermeasures ready."

Cap considered. He had four kilometers on Vostok. If it was an older SAM, the missile would be subsonic and take at least fourteen seconds to span the distance. He'd cover another two kilometers in that time and be well beyond the missile's range. All they'd blow up was snow.

If it was one of their new rigs, eight seconds to reach him, and he'd be well within its range.

"Deploy countermeasures. Now! Now! Now!"

Jackie fired them.

The oncoming missile would see a spread of angel flares —so called because they shot wide of the wings to mask the engine exhaust and a great tail spread that would fall like a flowing gown behind his plane.

"Time since launch?"

"Three one thousand," Jackie began counting aloud, "Four. Five."

He nosed down hard but kept on straight to hide behind the flares. He didn't have much altitude but it was his best chance, and the dive gave him additional speed. The engines were firewalled for all of the good it was doing him.

The ice surface was a rippling expanse of white. No way to visually estimate how close it was.

"Five hundred feet, four hundred," Jackie was on it, now calling the readout from the radar altimeter.

At one hundred, he leveled before he buried his nose in the snow.

Looking ahead, he wondered if he dared go lower or—

"Brace! Brace! Brace!" Jackie shouted over the PA.

The flares had failed to distract the missile. He heaved up and left on the yoke to gain maneuvering room—when they took the hit.

50

"I have a visual," Lizzy announced. One of the screens at the end of the Situation Room conference table flickered to life.

It was like a horrible replay of watching the explosion at the Davis Skiway in his office yesterday morning.

Low angle. The world seemingly cut in two: white ice below, blue sky above.

And off to one edge, close to the white, a brilliant flash of yellow.

"Location. What's the location, Lizzy?"

"It's hard to tell at this angle. Not at Vostok. South. But not far south." She spoke in fits and starts as she attacked her laptop's keyboard.

As he watched, the angle improved, slightly. There was a familiarity to the look.

"Angel flares," Roy spotted it before he did but was absolutely right.

"The Russians fired at our Skibird and they deployed—"

A second flash of brilliant yellow-white bloomed on the screen. It was much more concentrated.

He prayed for a better angle but knew he wasn't going to get it fast enough.

Then the comm channel crackled to life. "Mayday. Mayday. Mayday. This is Skibird three-niner-three. We've been struck by a Russian missile at five kilometers south of Vostok Station."

"Get them back!"

"Not our role, Drake."

He didn't remember pushing to his feet or pounding his fists down into the table. But Lizzy was right.

"Roger three-niner-three," a deadpan voice came on the air. "Status? Are you declaring an emergency?"

"Hold," but the captain left the mic live. "Talk to me, Jackie."

"Firing bottle Engine Two," a woman responded.

"What does that mean?" Sarah Feldman asked.

Lizzy, being a former fighter pilot, answered before he could. "It means they had a fire in Engine Two, inboard engine on the left wing. The bottle is the fire extinguisher."

"Is that bad?"

Lizzy shrugged uncomfortably—far more uncomfortably than Drake liked.

"Fuel loss," the male voice called over the air. "Left wing auxiliary tank. Left wing inboard and outboard tanks. Close all left-wing fuel tank transfers."

"We'll lose Engine One," Jackie spoke.

"Acknowledged. Proceed."

"Engine One shutdown. Props feathered. Cabin air pressure loss. We've been holed."

"Roger. This is three-niner-three. Yes, we're declaring an

emergency. The left wing appears intact. Engines Three and Four are operational. Insufficient fuel remaining to reach any stations except Vostok. Don't plan on returning there to get shot again. Best estimate is we'll be a hundred kilometers shy if we try for South Pole station. Passenger status unknown."

"Roger, three-niner-three. Proceed due east-northeast for Concordia Station. Repeat, proceed to French-Italian station Concordia. We will advise."

Drake felt the blood drain out of his face. He suddenly felt a hundred years old.

Before he could collapse back into his chair, his phone rang loudly enough to make everyone in the room jump.

He'd turned in his service phone per protocol when he'd entered the Situation Room, but he'd forgotten about his personal phone.

He pulled it out and saw that the number was blocked.

Drake tapped the answer icon, then snarled into the phone, "I'm going to choke you to death with my bare hands."

51

GENERAL LIÚ ZUOCHENG NOW HAD THE INFORMATION HE needed.

"One moment, General Nason."

He picked up his other phone, dialed a number, and issued a simple command. "Operation Ice Thunder is a go." He hung up.

"My apologies. What is the reason you are going to kill me?"

"My people. They were just shot with a surface-to-air missile by the Russians at Vostok Station. You knew!"

"No, Drake. I suspected. I feared." *I hoped,* not that he would ever admit so aloud. "Did the plane survive? Are your people okay?"

"Yes, for now, and I don't know." Drake Nason was getting control over his voice. He cared deeply about his plane.

Or did he?

Zuocheng thought back to their one meeting in Brunei. There had been the CIA Director, who Drake clearly despised. But there had also been the curious woman who spoke with absolute certainty on all technical matters. Miranda Chase, a genius in a peculiar way.

Drake had cared about her a great deal.

And if he was following the events of a plane crash in Antarctica so closely...

"I hope that Ms. Chase and her team remain well."

"You'd better pray they are," Drake's tone was pure threat if she wasn't.

"We will hope for the best." Zuocheng took a calming breath. "Now please tell your President that we have come to the time when we have a mutual interest—again, *not* in common."

"Time for you to explain that one." There was a sound of his being switched over to speakerphone. "President Roy Cole, this is General Liú Zuocheng, Senior Vice-chairman of the Central Military Commission."

"Greetings, Mr. President. I would like to tell you about a minor operation called Ice Thunder that China is about to undertake. We ask that you take no notice and no action. I think after recent events, you will be amenable to this suggestion."

52

"STRETCH, FIND OUT HOW BAD WE ARE. FOOTIE, CHECK ON THE passengers." Cap had flown a Herk on two engines before, the plane was so overpowered that it could fly on one. But he'd never done it at fifteen thousand feet while hundreds of miles from the nearest safe airport.

"I would suggest landing soon. Concordia is much too far away."

Cap twisted around to see a woman standing in his cockpit. One of the investigation team. "Who the hell are you again?"

"I'm Miranda Chase, investigator-in-charge for the NTSB." There was blood on her parka. She looked at the stain herself. "One of the US Marshals is dead. Shrapnel punched through the hull and his back."

"Someone is going to pay. Are there other injuries?"

"Yes. Who would you send the bill to? And for how much?"

"You joking?"

"No. I'm not good at that."

"What *are* you good at?" Cap couldn't believe he was having this conversation.

"Airplane crashes. Which will include this plane if you don't set it down shortly."

Cap glanced at Stretch, who hadn't made it out of her seat. At a nod, she scrambled out and headed aft.

"Lady—"

"My name is Miranda."

"Miranda, we're in the middle of nowhere. There's no place safe to set her down."

She shrugged. "You're the captain, it's your choice. But I feel that I should inform you that either way we'll be on the ground in under ten minutes." No raised voice. No panic. Simply—

Stretch hurried back into the cockpit. "Cap. I have no idea why we're airborne at all. Get us out of the sky." She turned to Miranda. "How did you figure we'd still be aloft in ten minutes? There's no way."

Miranda nodded. "Yes, if the brace for mounting the external fuel tank to the underside of the wing is still sound, it will carry and additional three thousand pounds of the excess stress currently spread across the damaged wing's skin and structural ribs. I'd estimate now nine minutes and thirty seconds maximum flight time. Of course, that's maximum, which has a likelihood of under four percent. My calculation of median flight time remaining spans only three more minutes with a first standard deviation of—"

Cap tuned her out. "Everyone buckle up for a hard landing. We're going down." He keyed the radio. "Mayday, Mayday, Mayday. Skibird three-niner-three attempting landing at," he read out the GPS coordinates. They'd made good another twenty-five kilometers away from Vostok.

Hopefully that was out of range for a follow-up attack. No other choice remained.

He called for flaps.

His right wing swung upward as the extra lift of one wing wasn't matched by the damaged wing. "Kill flaps."

Jackie retracted them once more and he was able to level the plane.

"This is going to be so much fun."

Miranda sat in Footie's seat and snapped in the five-point harness like a pro. Footie must be in the rear with the passengers.

"Winds twenty-five gusting thirty out of the south," Jackie announced. She had the emergency checklist out and began calling best air speeds and rate of descent.

From three hundred feet, the latter barely mattered.

He began his flare when she called fifty feet. It was the same moment that the first ice crystals began pinging off the windshield. The surface itself was a complete blank beneath blowing snow.

Smooth ice?

Ski-breaking ridges?

A plane-eating crevasse?

They were about to find out.

53

"GENERAL MUROV," TURGENEV SAID THE MOMENT HE HUNG UP the phone. "One of my people, engaged to monitor all Antarctic transmissions, intercepted an American Mayday call made in the clear. It was bounced off one of their satellites. An LC-130H Skibird has been shot by a missile from Vostok Station and is going down on the ice."

Murov didn't react.

Turgenev knew what he would do if it had been his plane shot down and he was in charge. He'd blow Washington, DC, out of existence. Were the Americans about to nuke Moscow? If so, he was at Ground Zero or near enough to make no difference.

"Vostok shot down an American airplane over neutral Antarctica?"

Turgenev nodded carefully.

"I must speak with the American President. But first find me a way to speak with whatever idiot fired that missile."

54

Miranda's satellite phone rang as the Skibird's rear skis kissed the snow.

She answered it as the front ski touched down without a bounce. Any sound of the skis was drowned out by the fusillade of blown snow and ice against the windshield.

"Hello. This is Miranda Chase. This is me and not a recording of me."

"Hi Miranda," Jeremy spoke quickly. "I was able to model the explosion. You were right, the math didn't pencil out."

"I think I have another problem at this point," she huffed out a hard breath but her chest felt clutched impossibly tightly.

She tried another sharp breath.

It didn't help. There wasn't enough air at this altitude.

The captain reversed the propeller on Engine Four, the outboard engine on the right wing. Then began easing the prop angle on Engine Three. It should make them decelerate in a mostly straight line, despite nothing being visible outside the cockpit windshields.

"What's up?" Jeremy asked.

"We're in the middle of a crash landing in a Skibird LC-130H. It's going well so far."

"Then it isn't a crash because— Wait! You're *what?*"

"Eighty knots," the copilot called out. "Seventy. Sixty."

"Full flaps!" Miranda shouted out.

"Why?" But she noted that the captain had yanked back on the lever to extend them. She listened for the low grind of the flap motors. Yes, she could hear them.

"Because, when the left wing breaks off, we need lift to keep the right wing from digging into—"

Miranda felt the lurch before she heard it.

The left wing breaking and folding exactly as she'd expected based on the damage pattern she'd been able to see out the small inspection windows in the side of the fuselage. The missile had blown up below the left wing and close between the engines.

"The question now is—"

There was a hard bang. That shook the whole hull.

"The wing hasn't fully separated," Jackie called out to the captain.

"If it—" Jeremy started, but didn't have a chance to complete it.

The left wing must have folded fully against the fuselage because the plane lurched heavily to the right. The lost weight of the broken left wing, two engines, and any fuel weight remaining in those wing tanks caused the plane to want to roll onto its other side. If it did, it would dig the intact right wing into the snow.

At a present gross weight of approximately fifty tons— she was only able to roughly estimate fuel losses from the shrapnel-riddled left wing—times sixty knots of speed, it would create a disaster when nine million foot-pounds-per-second momentum was dissipated within moments.

Miranda braced herself...

But it didn't happen.

The wide stance of the skis and the timely deployment of the flaps on the remaining wing fought the overbalance.

The plane righted as it slowed.

"Fifty," Jackie called out their airspeed. "Forty."

There was another bang as the broken left wing struck the fuselage again, but it didn't separate.

Miranda twisted around to look through the open cockpit door back into the cargo bay.

The left wing, anchored at the top chord of the wing box, sliced into the fuselage like a scythe. A massive gash appeared in the side, directly through the port side seating mounted along the hull.

After she'd seen the damage that the missile explosion had caused to the wing, she'd had everyone move to the other side of the plane and strap in again. The only person seated to port was the dead US Marshal. Now he was dead and partially decapitated.

The plane shuddered to a stop.

"Kill Engine Four. Engine Three to idle."

Jackie echoed each of Cap's commands and then performed the action.

"Estimated runtime at idle?"

Cap tapped one of his screens. "At least eight hours. That's heat and electricity until tonight. Damn fine call on the flaps there, Ms. Chase."

"There's no nighttime in December this close to the pole," Miranda told him.

"Right, good. Who are you talking to?"

Miranda looked at the phone in surprise. It was clutched in her lap and a small voice was shouting at her. She raised it.

"We're alive, Jeremy." She looked back over her shoulder and saw the US Marshal's corpse. She tried to look toward the others, but Andi blocked her view as she raced into the cockpit and threw herself at Miranda.

"Are you okay? Are you hurt anywhere?" Andi pulled back and began checking her. "Blood! Where?"

"It's not mine, it's his," she pointed toward the seated Marshal.

"It's not yours? Thank God." Andi winced. "I mean I'm sorry there's any blood from anyone; I'm glad it isn't yours. Is that selfish of me?"

Miranda wanted to consider that statement. She *herself* was the one being selfish, keeping Andi close for efficiency and convenience. But Andi sounded as if she felt genuinely happy that Miranda was okay. That posed a different question, "How do I *feel?*"

"I don't know, how *do* you feel?"

Miranda hadn't meant to ask the question aloud.

Cap finished shutting down his station and unbuckled. "I don't care how you feel right now. If we don't get a move on securing the plane, we're dead. It's minus thirty-eight out there with another twenty or so of wind chill. A bit of shrapnel must have clipped my satellite antenna. Hope they heard the last message."

Andi looked at her.

"What?"

Andi pointed at the phone she'd forgotten about again. "Have Jeremy call Drake."

"More than efficient. Smart too."

Andi offered one of her smiles, then returned to the back of the plane now that she was sure Miranda was okay. She wanted to think about that, but decided that it better to answer the phone first.

She raised it back to her ear. "Jeremy—"

"I heard. Hang on."

55

"MIRANDA?" DRAKE MANAGED TO ASK WITHOUT SHOUTING. The comm tech had been unable to raise the plane after the captain's final call that they were going down.

"Hang on, sir." It was Jeremy Trahn. "I have to conference her in. Here you go."

"Miranda?"

"This is me, not a recording of me."

"Thank goodness. How are you and your team?"

"I'm not entirely sure. We have a dead US Marshal. And Andi says that Mike has broken his arm."

"I'm glad it wasn't me this time," Jeremy said. "Tell Mike I'll sign his cast." Miranda recalled that Mike had drawn pictures on Jeremy's cast that didn't look lurid but made Jeremy blush every time he'd been asked about them.

"Okay." And now Miranda understood. Mike had drawn pictures of Jeremy's interactions with Taz, long before they'd become a couple. If she had a cast, what pictures of Andi would be—

She shook her head to clear it.

"The captain would like to speak to someone."

"Put him on."

Drake only had to wait a few seconds before a voice said, "Captain Antony Capra here, who am I speaking to?"

"You have a full house, Captain: President, VP, Director of the NRO, and this is General Drake Nason."

There was a long pause. "Um, I was more hoping for my flight controller at the 109th Airwing."

"We've been in touch with him. He has a bird at McMurdo ready to head your way, but you landed in the leading edge of a storm that's building out of the pole and sweeping your way. It looks like it's going to get worse before it gets better."

"Roger that, sir. We'll hunker in place then. Plane is mostly intact and we stock plenty of supplies. We're safe enough for now."

"Can you tell us what happened?"

"If you've been monitoring, you probably know as much as I do. Vostok. Then a Willow missile—had to be to reach out and touch me that far away. Russians certainly didn't like us poking around their base. Got my girl down, thirty or so kilometers away from the station, but we're going to need a new left wing, a pair of engines, and a couple thousand pounds of fuel before we'll be limping home."

"I'll pass that along."

"Thank you, sir. I'd better see to my plane."

"Do that. Well done, Captain. Let me speak to Miranda again."

"Sir." And again the phone changed hands.

"What did you find at Vostok?"

"Were there any other nukes?" Jeremy asked.

56

"A FIZZLE?" MIRANDA ASKED.

The others had left the cockpit, with the one engine running. She supposed they had decided it was safe. Wang Daiyu had come forward, but now stood in the cockpit doorway as frozen as an ice statue.

Miranda was getting the hang of metaphors. She hadn't had to think about that one at all. She raised her free hand and patted herself on the back exactly as Tante Daniels had trained her to do as a child.

"There were two fizzles in that crevasse at the Whoop Whoop Skiway by my calculations," Jeremy replied. "That's assuming it was one of their standard variable-yield warheads similar to our W80. I'll assume that they were not armed to explode or maybe that the detonation of the four Kalibr missiles damaged them so that they couldn't fire. Either way, the ignition of the two collapsing charges intended to trigger the warheads would balance out the math. The prevailing wind was away from you, so you should be clean of radioactivity. And the worst of it is

probably buried under a hundred meters of ice. We'll need
to tell the Australians to monitor the area."

"Wait. A fizzle?" Daiyu's question echoed several from
the Situation Room.

"Yes," Miranda explained to Daiyu and the phone at the
same time, which was a disconcerting splitting of attention.
"It's when a nuclear weapon fails to achieve designed yield.
In this case, a complete failure except for the charges
intended to collapse the warhead into a critical mass. We
measured the effects of the additional explosives, but no
nuclear fission or fusion occurred or we would not have
survived."

Daiyu sat down in the vacant engineer's seat.

Miranda switched over to speakerphone, then wasn't
sure if she should have.

"Um, Roy?" She had to call his name louder a second
time to reach over the babble in the Situation Room. There
was a round of shushing.

"Yes, Miranda?"

"You should know that I have Wang Daiyu here on the
phone with me."

"Ms. Wang," Roy said politely.

Daiyu moved her jaw, but nothing came out.

"I think she says hello, Roy."

Daiyu nodded, then found her voice. "Hello, Mr.
President."

A voice at the other end announced a call for the
President. "A General Murov, calling from the Russian
Federation."

"Okay, nobody speak unless I specifically ask you to,"
Roy sounded stern.

Recalling her experience with Barty from the ATSB,

Miranda placed a hand over her mouth in advance.

"Put him through."

57

"THIS IS PRESIDENT ROY COLE OF THE UNITED STATES OF America."

Turgenev was definitely going to keep his mouth shut, the man sounded pissed as hell.

They were an hour from any possible satellite contact with Vostok Station. However, Turgenev recalled a note he'd found while ransacking Romanoff's files. It had been enough for Murov to initiate this call.

"President Cole. This is Army General Mikhail Murov of the Russian Federation. There has been a terrible mistake and I wish to avert any escalation."

"You mean the act of war of downing one of our research support aircraft in Antarctica with a surface-to-air missile?"

"Yes. Exactly that. Before his death, a Colonel Nikolas Romanoff left orders with the station master at Vostok to protect one of our historic buildings from any inspection by whatever means necessary. It seems that the station master took those instructions too literally after the visit of your inspection team."

"Anything else?"

Murov studied the wall over Turgenev's shoulder. There was nothing there. The portrait of the Russian President was on the other wall so that whoever sat at the desk must constantly face his judgement.

"My deep apologies. And, if ever the sanctions between our countries are lifted, we will be glad to recompense you for any material losses."

There was a long silence that seemed to stretch on forever before the American President finally spoke again.

"You will be receiving news shortly. You will take *no action* based on that news. If you do, your attack on our aircraft will be treated as an act of war. We will fix our own damn plane." And he cut the connection.

The silence in the office was complete for several minutes before Murov looked at him.

"Interpretations, Turgenev?"

"Their plane survived," he spoke slowly and carefully, giving himself time to form each thought. "Which probably means their people survived, or at least a few of them. Whatever they learned at Vostok was not compartmentalized with the firing of the missile by the station master. We know where they came down but I don't think we dare do anything about them."

"Regrettably..."

Turgenev twitched but no more than that. He was tired of being afraid for his life every time the general spoke. He'd done well, hadn't he?

Murov eased back in his chair and rubbed at his eyes, "Your assessment matches mine. Tomorrow, I'll put through the paperwork for your promotion to colonel. As of now, your command will include all Antarctic operations. For tonight, your orders are to do no action—exactly as the American President has stated—no matter what happens. Tomorrow, we will find a way to explain it to the world that it was done by our choice."

"Understood, sir."

Murov pushed out of the chair he had occupied across Romanoffs...no...across *his* own desk for the last few hours. He looked far more exhausted than could be explained by it being four in the morning. With his back turned, Murov stopped and spoke.

"We made a calculation that failed. Now we must pay the price."

Then he left the office.

Had he been talking to Turgenev or the President's portrait?

58

"You heard, General Zuocheng?" Roy spoke to the open conference call.

"I heard. General Murov must know about the Kalibr missiles and nuclear warheads, yet he didn't say a word about them."

Drake contemplated what he would have done in the same situation. *Yes, I sent cruise missiles with optional nuclear warheads to Antarctica against international treaty.* Maybe he would have kept his mouth shut as well, hoping no one figured it out. They had all been destroyed and buried deep in an icy crevasse after all.

That hadn't stopped Miranda and Jeremy though. Between them they'd unraveled the math of the explosion.

Roy was watching him.

Drake shook his head to clear it.

The Chinese Operation Ice Thunder was the question Roy was asking. The President's final instruction to Murov to *not act* said what the President's decision was, pending his own agreement.

If it was allowed to go ahead as Zuocheng had outlined, it *was* of interest to both China and the US. Furthermore, it indeed was *not* in common. Ice Thunder would create a seismic shift in the balance of power across much of Antarctica.

It might create a future problem, perhaps far enough into the future that it would fall under Sarah Feldman's presidency should she win the upcoming election.

However, it dealt with the immediate problem, while keeping America's hands clean.

He nodded.

Roy looked to Sarah. Her uncomfortable shrug and sigh before she too nodded said that she'd made the same assessment he had.

"General Zuocheng," Roy spoke toward the conference phone. "Operation Ice Thunder is in your hands. The United States will not oppose the action as long as it is kept within the bounds you described."

"Good, I'm glad that's agreed. Especially as it is already underway."

"Whatever they do," Wang spoke up through Miranda's phone, "don't let them fire at Vostok's Drill Building A. That's the one to the south."

"Excellent advice, Colonel Wang," Zuocheng agreed. "Exceptionally well done all around. I look forward to your return to Beijing."

"General, Cole here. I'm going to add one stipulation to our agreement. Whatever weapons you locate at the Russian stations *will be removed* from Antarctica."

"Of course. Goodbye, Mr. President."

And he was gone.

"What's Operation Ice Thunder?" Miranda asked on the other line.

Daiyu's voice answered, "It is incredibly bad news for the Russians."

59

THE FOUR XI'AN Y-20 HEAVY LIFTER CARGO JETS OF Operation Ice Thunder had departed Fiery Cross Reef in the South China Sea last night.

They had flown over ten thousand miles in flights of two, ninety minutes apart. For this mission, they were pushing their limits by not stopping for fuel at their normal halfway point in Perth, Australia. The lead aircraft of each flight bore cargos that could *not* be inspected.

One of each pair of the Y-20s was configured for midair refueling. High over the Antarctic circle, full loads of fuel had been transferred to the mission jets. The refuelers were now heading for Australia. There they would once again load to capacity, then position themselves to meet the two cargo lifters as they returned north from their Antarctic missions.

At Progress Station, the Russian icebreaker and the cargo ship it had accompanied had finished their annual chore. They were already ten kilometers away from the station, working north through the broken ice. There were quiet celebrations, which would soon become rather rowdy as illicit vodka was unearthed from hiding places and served round. This didn't matter, as their annual mission was accomplished and the worst injury was a broken nose suffered by a cargo handler after he ran it into the fist of a machinist at the end of a heated chess match.

When one of the Xi'an Y-20s reached the Antarctic shoreline, it lowered the massive rear ramp. At an altitude of a bare three hundred meters above the broken sea ice, it approached from over Zhongshan Station. The climbing roar of the engines echoed off the exposed hard rock hills as it headed for Progress Station.

The sound told Station Manager Min that this was the moment they'd been waiting for.

He'd positioned ten sharpshooters, dressed in white with white rifles among the snows surrounding the Progress Skiway. He had set himself at the highest point as spotter.

As the Y-20 passed over Progress Station, thirty figures tumbled out of the rear of the big jet. Their parachutes snapped open, and they all zeroed in on the station itself.

"The skiway, now!" Min ordered over the radio.

His sharpshooters met no resistance at the skiway. This was hardly surprising as the Russians had commandeered his Snow Eagle 601 and flown it toward Vostok. He'd watched as fifteen Russians had piled aboard bearing various weapons.

He'd wanted to shoot them, but Wang Daiyu had warned him not to act prematurely. Seeing thirty commandos parachuting out of China's largest plane was signal enough.

Min had been pleased to see that Viktor Petrov had departed with the Snow Eagle. According to Min's contact inside the station, this exodus had removed all of the military personnel from the station, leaving behind only mechanics, cooks, and scientists.

He watched the events at both the Progress Skiway and Progress Station from his high vantage. No military remained to raise a resistance. The surprise had been complete.

In a matter of minutes, the sixty-two Russians who had remained at Progress Station were fully overwhelmed.

Hu Min had seen how the parachute troops moved. He would easily win a bet that they were operators from the Falcon Commando Unit. Wang Daiyu had been from the Central Military Commission. And Falcon reported directly to the CMC, not to any other command authority.

Progress Station, which the Russians had founded thirty years ago and rebuilt less than ten years ago, was now China's.

60

VIKTOR PETROV WAS THE FIRST ONE OUT OF THE SNOW EAGLE 601 when it landed at Vostok. He didn't want to be, despite General Murov's order, but by being last aboard, he'd been closest to the door when they arrived.

The cold here was obscene. It didn't penetrate like the winter cold at Progress. At Vostok, at the peak of a summer's day, it stabbed like knives.

He'd never been to Vostok before. Finally, all of the new modules currently lined up along the shore at Progress made perfect sense.

A few haggard men stepped out of shacks that no self-respecting Muscovite would inhabit. Not even those living in the Shanghai slums of Garden Valley would call these livable.

"Viktor? What are you doing here?"

He squinted at the man and decided that if Viktor knew him, it would be Oleg Sidirov, his fellow station manager. When Oleg had passed through Progress at the start of the season two months ago, he'd been cleanshaven and less...haggard.

"I was ordered here for your protection, Ollie."

"My protection or what is in Drill Building A?" Ollie waved at the farther tower.

"I know nothing about that."

"What a strange day." Ollie blinked toward the sun.

People were filtering out of the hut until twenty people stood on the ice in addition to the fourteen he'd brought with him.

Ollie blinked again. And again.

To the south, a storm was definitely building and heading their way. He was an old enough hand to see that it would be a bad one.

But Ollie was facing northeast toward the lightly hazed sun; the last they'd see of it for a few days at least.

All Viktor saw was the yellow globe, surrounded by a great halo of refracted sunlight off airborne ice crystals. All of the light reflecting off the never-ending snow-and-ice field that stretched uninterrupted all of the way back to Progress Station.

Except the shape of the sun wasn't right.

It had...wings?

Black wings?

It resolved into a massive jet flying directly out of the sun. As it passed close overhead, everyone ducked as if the engines' roar could batter them to the snow.

People began spilling off of the jet's stern ramp.

A parachute opened above each in turn.

They opened so low that they swung once forward, once back, and landed on the ground.

Moments before there had been two groups of Russians

standing on the ice, all wondering how they'd come to be here.

They were mostly menial workers. The two trained military enforcers who raised their weapons dropped to the ground with red spreading rapidly across their chests.

Now they were one group of Russians, staring down the rifle barrels of thirty paratroopers in head-to-toe white gear. Each bore on his chest a small emblem of the Chinese flag.

Petrov did not raise his own weapon.

61

COLONEL ARTEMY TURGENEV SAT IN HIS SECOND-FLOOR OFFICE in the Lubyanka Building.

As each new report came in, he read it carefully, then set it neatly onto the stack. There was no need to call General Murov. He would have foreseen this possible scenario.

Turgenev hadn't.

But he did now.

He had expected the hammer to fall from the Americans. *You shot down our plane, we'll destroy one of your skiways.* A face-saving proportional response.

But Murov's departing comment now made more sense: *We made a calculation that failed. Now we must pay the price.*

Each new report said that his newfound role as Commander of all Russian efforts in Antarctica was fast becoming meaningless.

Progress Station: Gone. It would now be administered from China's far more modern Zhongshan Station. They would also have far better access to the sea.

The Progress Skiway: China made a press release

announcing the recent acquisition of the skiway in a *deal* with the Russian Federation. It would be renamed Zhongshan Skiway.

Turgenev briefly smiled at that one. China had recently announced plans to build their own skiway at the next nearest site, high on the ice plateau. Now they didn't need to.

Vostok Station: No direct news, of course. But another Chinese announcement that Vostok Station as well as all of the recently delivered modules for a new station had been acquired in a related *deal* with the Russian Federation.

Yesterday—was it only yesterday that he had congratulated Viktor Petrov on the successful unloading of the new station? Finally delivered to Antarctica after nearly a decade of delays. Now all the Chinese had to do was drag it across the ice, along a traverse scouted by the Russian Federation, and assemble the new buildings. A brand-new station at minimal cost.

Personnel: Of the seventy-four personnel at Progress and twenty-three at Vostok, sixty-eight had defected to China. Turgenev knew that those who returned would be quietly labeled as traitors and would never be heard from again. They knew things about how the stations had been lost that could never be made public.

Perhaps, as the remaining few loyalists considered this new reality, the defection rate would rise higher. The math wasn't hard. The cost-benefit of leaving behind Russia, and any family as well, would be survival.

Mirny Station: Eight hundred kilometers to the east of Zhongshan along the coast and the former major supply route to Vostok Station. Mostly gutted by fire in 2020, Turgenev knew he'd never be able to argue for the funds to rebuild it now. It would remain a tiny hardship outpost or be closed.

Three stations and over a third of Russia's most experienced Antarctic hands, gone—in a thin stack of reports.

Unrecoverable.

Because if Russia argued, the headlines would turn them into world pariahs for deploying nuclear weapons to Antarctica. Worse pariahs than the twice-damned *military operation* in the former Soviet Bloc had already made them.

Colonel Turgenev tapped the report into a neat pile as he considered them. What few stations were left in his power *were* his now. Last week Kurchenko had been removed. And with Romanoff's demise, he himself had risen fast and was in General Murov's favor. While nothing had gone well in Antarctica , it hadn't been his doing and Murov knew that.

He considered his fling with Aloysha. She had been exceptional in bed, but far too destructive. She acted as if she hated the world and was taking personal revenge on it one officer at a time.

Which might be an idea.

The Arctic remained open to Russia, more so every day with the melting of the northern ice. Perhaps he should introduce Aloysha to the general who headed the combined polar programs. Yes, that could be useful.

In the meantime?

There was a single portrait on Nikolas Romanoff's desk that Turgenev hadn't removed yet. Inessa Romanoff. They had met socially several times. She was a lovely woman of quality, one highly respected by Romanoff's superiors. The two of them had liked each other far more than she had appeared to like her now-deceased husband. Yes, later today he would make a point of visiting personally to offer his condolences.

After his work here was done.

Which wouldn't take long.

Turgenev began drafting a release for General Murov's approval.

The Russian Federation cites sanctions by the West, and the global recession that has been forced upon the Russian Federation's wonderfully robust economy, in its decision to close one of its stations in East Antarctica and to cede two others to the People's Republic of China as a gesture of goodwill between our countries.

Vostok, one of the earliest permanent stations on the continent, was founded in 1957 at the geomagnetic South Pole through the superiority of Soviet engineering. Placed there for the peaceful study of...

When he was finished, he backdated it three months.

62

IT HAD TAKEN UNDER AN HOUR TO SECURE THE SKIBIRD against the approaching storm. They'd have to bivouac out here in the middle of nowhere, but they were secure.

"Not too shabby, Stretch." Cap thumped her on the shoulder in what he hoped was a merely friendly fashion. They were standing aft of the cockpit and surveying the cargo bay.

Marshal Freddie Vaughan's corpse had been bagged and stowed out of sight. The others were organizing a camp in the middle of the cargo bay: pads, sleeping bags, camp stove, and supplies. Most of them were clutching thermal mugs of coffee and hot chocolate that Footie had cooked up.

"Was that actual praise, Cap?"

"Shit, woman. It would have taken me six hours, but I'm only a pilot, not a superstar flight engineer." In that time, she'd determined that the plane was safe as a shelter site. *And* managed to secure a parachute to block the wind and snow entering through the long gash in the left side of the fuselage. *And* unloaded enough supplies to make a safety camp a hundred meters away through the blinding blizzard, in case the plane was less safe than their assessment rated it.

The plane was damned cold. But when the engine died, they'd be looking at frigid. That would be the time to move into the sleeping bags.

"You're the one who landed us in one piece, Cap."

"Nah! That was Jackie. I was too busy not craping my shorts. That Miranda Chase chimed in at a crucial point too. Full flaps after the left wing broke, so we got them giving lift on the right wing only."

Stretch was nodding, "Wish I'd thought of that. A damn slick move. I would have bet on us going over."

"No way anyone's at your level, Stretch."

"Miranda's the one who found the three fuel bleeders from the busted wing faster than I could blink. I might have found one of them, but she took one look at the damage pattern and had me sealing them as fast as I could move. Without her, this plane probably would have been a roman candle and we'd have been hunkered hard on the ice worse that any training test at Raven Camp."

That was where Cap had first gotten to know her. Three days at the National Guard's Kool Skool, freezing their asses off in Greenland while they'd practiced with tents in high winds, carving dugouts into the ice, and having a hell of a good time.

"I'm proud of this team, Stretch. We done good. Better if we get out of this with no more losses. You done your husband or wife proud."

"My what?" Then she pulled off her left glove and stared at her ring. "Sorry, I forget at times. This isn't real, Cap. It's wolfsbane. Meant to poison any bad wolf's games."

She looked up and studied his face for a moment.

"You don't strike me as a bad wolf, Cap. Maybe you should call me Ginny."

He looked her square in the eye. Wasn't the least tempted to slither his gaze aside.

"Nah, couldn't do that, Stretch. Wouldn't mind looking into those dark browns of yours for a good while, though."

Her smile said maybe she'd like that too.

63

No one met Colonel Wang Daiyu at the airport, nor had she expected anyone. A person did not announce that they had worked with Americans in a place that had turned into a victory for China against their supposed allies the Russians.

She had read the quiet news releases about the changes in Antarctica on her flight home: McMurdo to New Zealand, then Hong Kong, and finally to Beijing. The general had sent the amusing Russian press release to her email—she had seen worse attempts to save face.

The taxi ride to her apartment took forever. The city sulked gray under the freezing rain, but she was past caring about any weather that wasn't trying to kill her.

Five days. Five long days they'd waited through the storm as the American Skibird shook and rattled. Once the engine had died, the inside had become as cold as the outside, hovering near minus thirty. They had set up two tents on the cargo deck to trap what body heat they could, which had helped but not enough.

Other than mandatory calisthenics, they rarely left their sleeping bags until the storm began to abate. Then they had to go outside to scout and mark a safe skiway for the rescue plane.

After three days of travel, she reached her apartment wanting nothing more than a shower and a warm bed.

She dropped her gear by the entry and could only stare stupidly at the man reading a book in one of the armchairs. The gray light from the open windows made him shine under the electric light.

"General?"

"Ah, Daiyu. You have excellent taste, I could gladly spend many hours with your collection of books."

It was a small collection, but they were her favorite novels. The room swam briefly and she placed a hand on the wall to keep herself from falling into it.

"Oh, my dear Daiyu, you must be exhausted. Come sit. I have made you some tea."

Her porcelain service had been set out, including the cherry blossom teapot she'd gifted herself while attending Dalian's annual Cherry Blossom Festival shortly after Zhang Ru's death. It was freshly heated enough that steam still swirled out of the spout.

She feared that she more plummeted than sat gracefully across from General Liú, but she had little control over her body.

Wasting no time on ritual, he simply poured her a cup of tea and set a plate of cookies, rice cakes, and a few other teatime treats near at hand before returning to his chair.

Daiyu sipped at the warmth and felt it seep into her bones, finally purging the last of the Antarctic chill.

"You have once again exceeded expectations, Wang Daiyu. And under most trying circumstances."

"Thank you, sir."

Her exhaustion was too great to worry, all she did was wait and sip her tea as the silence settled comfortably around them.

"I wanted to see for myself that you had returned safely and unscathed."

"I did, sir. The Americans were very well trained in how to manage living in cold environments and made sure that no one suffered frostbite or hypothermia. They had no medic, yet were constantly on the lookout for signs of altitude sickness as well."

"Altitude sickness?"

"We had traveled from sea level to thirty-five hundred meters in elevation in mere hours, higher than any major city in the world except for La Paz, Bolivia." She smiled at the memory.

The general tipped his teacup ever so slightly in question.

"Miranda Chase, as you had told me, is a surprising woman. The elevation of every major airport is but one of a thousand pieces she carries in her mind. The team that surrounds her is of equal caliber, if not a similar capability."

Actually, after five days trapped on the Skibird, they had been a shambles. Because they couldn't set his broken arm properly, Mike Munroe had been heavily dosed with painkillers the entire time. Holly Harper hadn't moved from his side for a moment she didn't have to. And whatever was happening between Wu Andi and Miranda Chase had driven them both into deep silences.

Daiyu had tried many times to breach those walls, as

their mutual pain had been palpable, but she had failed in that effort.

She considered telling these details to the general, but felt that it was neither her business nor his and therefore kept those thoughts to herself.

"What is it you would like to do next, Daiyu?" the general asked as he refilled their teacups and selected a dried plum.

"Other than a shower and sleep in a bed rather than on the hard deck of a freezing airplane? I have given it little thought." Actually, she'd given it a great deal of thought but hadn't expected to be asked for an actual opinion.

"Indulge me."

She gazed about her apartment. Even by Beijing's standards, her apartment was a modest one. The furnishings were sufficient to her needs and little more. The only luxury was the view; she'd selected a high enough floor to have a clear view over a small park—at least on less rainy days.

Home life was not what she wanted. If it had been, she could have stayed in the palatial apartment overlooking Hong Kong that had become hers after Zhang Ru's demise.

"I understand, General Liú, that this was a unique opportunity in Antarctica. Perhaps the extent was unanticipated, but I felt as if I was the right person in the correct place at the proper time. I liked that feeling very much."

General Liú smiled slightly as he bit the end off the plum.

"I would like to continue to be of service should a similar opportunity arrive."

"I was rather hoping you would say that. You have demonstrated multiple qualities that rarely are gathered into a single individual: loyalty, intelligence, and great tenacity mixed with a certain ruthlessness when necessary. I need eyes in many places."

"I would be honored to serve, General Liú." And she would if it took her on such adventures.

Again his slight smile.

"How's your Russian?"

"Fully fluent, sir."

"And your feeling about the Russians?"

"Much as you might surmise, sir." He would be familiar with her file and her family's history.

His nod closed the topic. He relaxed, settling back in his chair for the first time.

"So, tell me of Antarctica. I have never had occasion to travel there. I would appreciate a first-hand view."

The rest of the afternoon passed in very pleasant conversation.

64

"DAMN YOU, MIKE."

"What for this time, Holly?"

"You aren't supposed to be so comfortable to lie against. Even that cast on your arm isn't putting me off." Instead, she was snuggled deep under the quilt on the sofa, safe back in Miranda's second-story sitting room.

The view out the window was such a relief. The snow had melted while they were gone, and all there was to see under the afternoon sky was conifer green and Puget Sound's darkest blue water. For a change, the running whitecaps up the channel weren't bothering her one bit.

"It looks warm and cozy out there, doesn't it?"

Holly nodded. "Beats our Christmas."

"I don't know. That story is a winner in any one-up-your-horrible-holiday competition. Marooned a thousand kilometers from anywhere—"

"Other than Vostok Station."

"—with nothing to do but lie in each other's arms."

"In the bitter cold with you blithering away on painkillers. I'll pass."

Mike grinned. "Want to go for a walk? Looks nice and brisk."

She didn't even waste the energy to stick her tongue out at him, just pulled the quilt up tighter.

The wind was slashing through the trees, waving the towering Doug firs back and forth. The bigger gusts barely made the house shudder.

She'd always wondered at how powerful the storms had always seemed when they struck here—until she'd spent five days riding out an Antarctic whiteout blizzard inside a steel can at eleven thousand feet and forty below. It had built to over eighty miles an hour, gusting to one-ten. Because the Skibird had been parked facing south and it sat up on skis, the snow had mostly ripped by instead of drifting against the plane. If not for that, they'd probably have been buried.

Then, once the storm had begun to abate but been far from giving up, they'd had to go outside to survey a safe landing area for their rescue plane. Holly was convinced after that that she'd never be warm again.

Yet her she was, in Mike's arms. Happy as—she tried to cut off the thought, but couldn't find much energy to put in it.

Happy as... "A couple?" She swallowed hard but the words were already out. "Sorry, I meant that question for myself. It kinda slipped out to go walkabout on its own."

Mike placed his mouth close by her ear and whispered, "Scare the daylights out of you?"

Holly could only nod.

"Welcome to the club. Been giving me twitches since

about the first time I ever saw you. Coupling isn't either of our styles...but I'm willing to try it on if you are."

She shrugged a maybe, or intended to, but instead nodded her agreement. "After all, we've only been shacking up together for two and a half years. Good practice that."

"Two years, seven months, eight—" The air whooshed out of Mike's lungs as surely as if she'd elbowed him in the gut.

But she hadn't this time.

"I can't believe I know that."

"Me either!" Holly gave it her best eye-roll tone but couldn't help feeling charmed. She snuggled down deeper under the quilt, more than happy to lie against Mike and wait for the others to arrive.

65

"MIRANDA!" JEREMY SHOUTED AT HER ABOVE THE SOUND OF the helicopter's beating rotor the moment he jumped out of the helicopter.

Andi had flown down to Sea-Tac Airport to fetch Jeremy and Taz for New Years.

Miranda, far too nervous to go with her, had stayed on her island. Yet peace had eluded her as she completed the neglected island chores. Yet again, more ugly facts were revealed. Having Andi by her side meant that she hadn't had to fly down to Sea-Tac herself.

"You wouldn't believe what I found. I wanted to tell you in person." Jeremy gave her a big hug that she was in no state to attempt returning. "Let's all get inside out of the cold so I can tell the others. You won't believe it."

It didn't seem that cold. It was several degrees above freezing and the wind here on the tree-lined runway carried a damp freshness rather than Antarctica's frigid shards.

With the ease of long practice, she and Andi soon had the helo tucked away in its corner of the island's hangar.

Miranda drove them all down to the house in her golf cart. Andi sat in back rather than beside her.

Taz had ended up in front, looking at Miranda with questions that she couldn't guess at. She also suspected that if she could, she wouldn't want to answer them.

Andi had probably answered all of the basic questions about Antarctica on the flight back up from SeaTac. It made the half-mile drive to the house pass very quietly.

Miranda normally cherished the island's silence but today everything was jarring. At one spot, the mud from the melted snow filled the track and made the golf cart skitter aside. Past that, she missed ramming the garden fence by mere inches. Then a Steller's jay had chittered at her angrily from the top of the garage for no reason Miranda could understand. She'd refilled the bird feeders as soon as they'd returned this morning.

Nothing was right.

She was the last in the house. She could hear the others upstairs, making noises over Mike's cast. Joining them was... the only option she could think of. Even the kitchen was clean, she'd set it to rights after their brunch while Andi was flying to the airport. Mike, with his broken arm in a cast, hadn't been able to help. It had saved her the usual need to reorganize everything properly after he left.

Holly and Mike were curled up on one sofa. Taz was already in the oversized armchair that she and Jeremy usually shared when they were here.

Andi was sitting in an armchair that only guests used, yet their couch was empty. Which hurt worse than—

The moment he spotted her, Jeremy pulled out a piece of paper and began waving it about.

"What is it?"

"The spectroscopic analysis of those samples you recovered from inside the Ilyushin-76's fuel tank. I've been back and forth with McMurdo ever since you handed them over to the lab there. You'll never guess what they were."

Miranda's legs wouldn't support her any longer. But neither did she want to sit on *their* couch without Andi. She perched on the edge of a footstool, which put her back to Andi. She hadn't meant to do that and turned to apologize, but Andi was looking down. Miranda saw a tear on her cheek.

Miranda looked away when Jeremy flapped the paper at her again. She tried to speak but could find anything to say.

"It's not a new hypersonic weapon," Jeremy launched in. "China didn't shoot down the Ilyushin-76 to start an international incident so that they could confiscate the Russian stations. The US didn't shoot them down as part of some sanction effort to further force Russia back into a corner."

Miranda didn't care who did it anymore. All she could do was cross her arms over her chest and try to hang on. She didn't want to have a meltdown in front of her friends—or ever again. But she'd been holding on so hard for so long that it was all that was left of her, that iron-clad grip on her panic that kept threatening to explode like a Kalibr missile inside her chest.

"It was none of that." Jeremy unfolded the sheet and began reading the chemical makeup.

He was two-thirds down the list before her thoughts connected the pieces. "But that makes no sense. No one would mix iron ferrite or such a high percentage of carbon into a weapon. It struck as if fired from an outer space rail gun. Immense kinetic energy as if it had fallen all the way from..."

"Yeah! Yeah! You get it now, don't you?" Jeremy was jumping about. "As if it fell all the way from the Kuiper Belt. It was a high-metal meteor. All of what you went through was because, by pure chance, a meteor hit a Russian cargo jet filled with illegal weapons. It's also only the second time in recorded history—after the recent discovery of that 1888 Turkish record—that a meteor has killed anyone. Without this chance strike, we'd never have known what the Russians were up to until it was far too late. Isn't that amazing?"

Miranda had to admit it was.

It was the *only* thing that was.

66

"Out, out. Everyone out."

Miranda looked up. Talk had circulated all around her as she'd sat on her footstool. Talk about the meteor, the events on The Ice, and the incredible piloting job by the doomed Russian pilot that had been revealed by the flight recorder she'd turned over to the ATSB.

She could only sit and stare at the chapping on her fingers from the dry-cold of the high Antarctic plateau.

Taz was shooing Jeremy out of the room. She soon had Mike and Holly out from under their quilt and on the move as well.

Miranda didn't know where they were all going, but she tried to stand. Her legs didn't cooperate.

Taz rested a hand on her shoulder. "Not you. Or you," she looked over Miranda's shoulder toward the armchair where Andi must still be sitting.

At the archway to the sitting area, Taz turned and spoke.

"You two. It's now your turn to talk." Then she was gone downstairs with the others.

Miranda didn't know what to say. She'd never been good at confrontation, it usually made her physically ill. Or it drove her into an autistic episode. She hadn't had one of those since before she'd started dating Andi but she could feel its slippery slope whirling about her like an Antarctic storm.

For a moment she wished she was back in that roaring cocoon of the Antarctic storm. The flight crew had kept them working hard while the fuel lasted for the Skibird's one remaining engine to generate heat.

She and flight engineer Stretch had gone out in the gathering storm, carefully roped to the plane so that they couldn't lose their way, and made an inventory of the external damage. The wingbox itself looked to be intact, which meant that a new wing could be readily mounted to recover the plane. Both engines on that side would need a complete rebuild. Other than long tears in the hull metal, the structural ribs of the Skibird tested sound. With a quick patch over the gash, once the broken left wing was replaced, it would be functionally flyable.

Only a few wrecks in Antarctica had been outright abandoned on the ice, at least by the Americans. The tough Skibird LC-130H that had saved their lives wouldn't be one of them.

Then, with the internal heat gone, everyone had moved into their sleeping bags as much as possible. Other than meals and daily calisthenics organized by the crew, she'd rarely left her own. She certainly hadn't joined in the social hours despite several attempts to engage her.

For five long days, they'd been trapped as the storm roared over the plane, blasting it with blown ice crystals. Their impacts were so loud upon the hull that speech was often impossible anyway. That had been fine with her. Christmas had passed unremarked as—

The armchair creaked as Andi stood. The sound of her footsteps shuffled closer.

"Why are you shutting me out?" Andi's voice cracked like old glass underfoot. No, like the shattered ice of the blown-up crevasse.

Miranda decided that congratulating herself on the metaphor would be inappropriate. "I—" But she didn't have any words.

"Aren't we good together?"

Miranda nodded, but couldn't look up. She could see the tips of Andi's house slippers. Not ones that Miranda kept in the basket by the door for guests, but silly ones that looked like Andi's mother's Shih Tzu dogs. They were shifting about more actively than a real dog eager to go for a walk.

She didn't sit.

Miranda didn't look up.

"Did I do something wrong?"

Miranda shook her head.

"Is this one of those things you don't know how to put into words?"

Andi knew her so well. That too was useful. *Useful.* At least as awful a word as *convenient* or *efficient* as a relationship basis. Usually the only words she knew were of no help.

But this time was different.

Miranda *hated* these three words.

They'd been chewing away inside her for this entire investigation until she felt as hollowed out as the empty Skibird they'd left half-buried on the ice. A Basler BT-67 had fetched them to McMurdo and flights home.

The Skibird remained alone, high on the Antarctic ice, with a radio beacon marking its location, awaiting repairs.

Miranda imagined herself alone, with a radio beacon to help Andi find her. But there were no repairs waiting for her.

"I—" She knew it was up to her to say those three awful words she already knew, but each one hurt as she extracted them. "—don't want you to be in a relationship with me because it's *efficient* for me." That was one. Somehow she'd manage the other two, though it felt as if they'd kill her more surely than the Russian missile.

"Efficient?" Andi sat on the couch. Only a few feet separated their knees, but Miranda kept her focus on the Shih Tzu slippers, which continued to twitch nervously.

"It's *efficient* to have you help me with what people are feeling. It's *convenient* when you fly the helicopter. You're *useful* in making it so that I don't have to explain myself. Or to keep me safe in dangerous situations. You shouldn't be with me because you're *efficient, convenient,* and *useful.* That's not fair to you. You should be more than a body extension who attempts to compensate for my autism."

"That's what all of this has been about?"

Miranda began to nod but Andi cut her off, which tipped her closer to that dangerous edge of a meltdown, a cliff she never wanted to fall off again.

"Miranda, that's what you're *thinking.* What are you *feeling?*"

"Like I would know." Everything inside was a complete jumble, worse than the remains of the Ilyushin-76 after it had blown it up.

Maybe she *should* simply crawl into the crevasse of her autism and stay there. It had always worked before Andi had come into her life.

It could work again, couldn't it?

During the long silence, the only sounds were a gust of wind against the house and the voices of the others downstairs. It sounded as if they were starting on the laggard Christmas decorations. They'd decided to have Christmas and New Years on the same night. If the house had an attic, she might consider going there to hide until everyone was gone.

Andi reached out and rested a hand on her knee.

She liked the way that felt. Kind. Comforting.

"At the risk of being efficient, can I try to help you with that?" Andi's voice sounded more cracked than fractured ice.

Miranda closed her eyes and felt even more awful, which quantitatively shouldn't be possible. But she nodded because she didn't know what else to do. *Andi is always kind.* She repeated that truth to herself several times.

"First, I'm going to point out that it wouldn't be hurting you at all if you weren't thinking about how I feel—how *another person* feels. You know that's a huge step forward for you, right?"

It was. "But that doesn't make it any better."

"Okay. Huh. Let's try this. Maybe you wouldn't be so upset by the thought that I was merely being useful to you if you didn't care so much about me."

Miranda blinked at the Shih Tzu slippers in surprise. They were no longer shuffling about. They had come to rest.

"I *do* care about you. That's why it's so awful that I'm only keeping you beside me because it's so eff—"

"No, Miranda! It doesn't work like that. It's because you care so much about me that the idea itself is upsetting you. Listen to your own words."

"I do." And then she *did* hear what she'd said and looked

up at Andi in surprise. "I *do* care." Three *new* words! "About you. Very much."

Andi was now both smiling and crying at the same time.

Miranda didn't recall that from any of her reference emojis.

"You correctly projected an emotion of another person but you got it all snarled up in that logical part of your head. I, too, care about you, very much, Miranda. As you are. The way we are together."

"I—I *do* feel like that." And when Andi wrapped her arms around her, she liked that feeling as well and returned the gesture.

After they broke apart, Andi helped her to her feet with joined hands. She led them out of the room and past the head of the stairs. She could hear Bing Crosby crooning out a "White Christmas" and Holly complaining bitterly about musicals. All so normal that it made her feel...giddy?

"Shouldn't we join the others?"

"Later," Andi led her along the upstairs hall.

She needed to make an entry in her notebook that logic and emotion were significantly more closely related than she'd previously considered. She needed to pay attention to the emotion *behind* the logic.

Perhaps later.

For now, her footsteps followed two fluffy Shih Tzu slippers as they led her toward the bedroom they'd shared since Andi had first come to the island, not as an efficient teammate but as her partner.

AFTERWORD

On June 23rd, 1961, the Antarctic Treaty came into force. It had twelve signatories, those with active stations on the continent for the International Geophysical Year of 1957-1958. That treaty, along with subsequent conservation treaties, have since been compiled into the Antarctic Treaty System (ATS), which controls all resources from sixty degrees south to the South Pole. These have been ratified by fifty-four parties, including China, Russia, and the US.

The ATS clearly defines what is and isn't allowed. Scientific research and international cooperation—yes. Mining, environmentally damaging activities, and militarization—expressly forbidden.

On June 5th, 2022, President Vladimir Putin stated his willingness to walk away from the ATS. It is believed that, rather than continue the sixty years of consensus cooperation with other countries, explicitly *including* the West, Russia may seek a new deal. Perhaps with China, the Russian leader is considering open exploitation of mineral and wildlife resources in the Southern Ocean and on the continent. More than one commentator believes he is willing to back that up with military power.

Once again, the news has caught up with my story before I could finish it. I can only hope that this scenario doesn't come to fruition before this is published—or ever.

M. L. "Matt" Buchman
North Shore, Massachusetts
24 August 2022

———

If you enjoyed this story
please consider leaving a review.
They really help.

Keep reading for an exciting excerpt from:
Miranda Chase #12 Nightwatch
(Coming winter 2023)

NIGHTWATCH (EXCERPT)

IF YOU ENJOYED THAT, YOU'LL LOVE THIS
TALE!

**Coming
Early 2023**

NIGHTWATCH (EXCERPT)

Sea Level
77°10'50" N / 67°42' 23" E
Arctic Ocean
20 km north of Severny Island, Russia

CAPTAIN YŬ LING NEVER SAW THE MISSILES THAT STRUCK HIS ship, though they hit in broad daylight at 0300 hours local time.

Ling had woken at 0200 to observe this particular section of his first voyage through the Arctic Ocean. It was summer here and they were far north of the Arctic Circle. The twenty-four-hour daylight meant he was sleeping little anyway. It was the first time that such a large container ship was taking the Northeast Passage from Shanghai over Russia to Europe, and it was her maiden voyage. All of his previous journeys had taken the longer southern route past Southeast Asia, India, and up through the Suez Canal.

He much preferred the peace of the high Arctic. Here they traveled alone except for the occasional Russian cargo freighter.

From the bridge wing of the *Lucky Passage,* he could see the far white horizon of the pack ice to starboard as little more than a thin white stripe between the dark blue of the ocean and the light blue of the sky.

It was what his wife's photographs always looked like when they vacationed by the sea. They must have a thousand pictures of a stripe of sand, a stretch of ocean, and sky of blue. She could never explain in a way he could understand why they were each different, but the thought of her taking such photos made him smile in this barren place. She certainly still looked fine in her sleek black one-piece. Though she rarely went in the water now that she was older.

Ling took a photo with his phone to send to her the next time he was in port.

He leaned out to look down the twenty-story cliff that was the side of his container ship. Waves less than a meter high and no free ice at all—they'd left that behind in the Vitlovsky Strait. Clear water all about.

He shrugged on a parka as he crossed the seventy-five meters through the warmth of the main bridge and out to the far end of the port-side bridge wing. The sea there ran much the same, but the view of the horizon held more interest. Twenty kilometers due south, Severny Island shone brilliantly white. It boasted the largest glacier in all of Europe. In fact, as the northernmost extension of the Ural Mountains, in passing this island, they transited from Asia to Europe as he watched.

Like his father had told him on his first sailboat, *Put your nose into the wind, Ling.* He split the wind with his nose, turning his head until the breeze landed evenly on both his cheeks. Now he was facing exactly into the apparent wind— ten degrees port of straight ahead. Knowing that the ship was making twenty-three knots told him they were facing only the lightest of winds from the southeast, a fact confirmed by the ripples upon the sea far below.

Despite the cold, a few degrees below freezing, he stayed out on the bridge wing to watch the world and his ship. The air here tasted as if he was the first person to ever breathe it: crisp upon the tongue, fresh and cleansing in the nose and lungs. Maybe those photos were how his wife found inner peace. For him, it was these quiet moments with only the low thrum of the ship's engines and the cry of curious gulls to keep him company.

At 0230, an eager *zhong wei* brought him a thermal mug filled with tea, which was much appreciated despite the brief disturbance. The lieutenant (junior grade), reading his mood with a delicacy that boded well for the girl's future in the merchant service—as voyages were long and few crew were required—retreated and left him to his thoughts.

They were sailing along at twenty-three knots. It was so arcane that shipping continued to use such terms but that was how his first captain had trained him. In turn, he made sure that his own crew was equally comfortable with knots and the far more logical forty-two kilometers per hour they were traveling.

Again he studied the ship. Designed to the very limits of the Suez Canal's abilities, it was precisely a tenth of a meter under the four-hundred-meter limit in length and the same under the maximum beam width. The *Lucky Passage* carried twenty-thousand TEU of containers. Yet another arcane measure—twenty-foot-equivalent-units. The power of the

Americans to keep the world locked into the outdated English units system rankled.

The *Lucky Passage* carried twenty-thousand TEU, as ten thousand forty-foot-long containers. And they had to be forty feet or they wouldn't fit the cranes, trains, or trucks of the Western world.

He sighed. It couldn't last. One decade, perhaps two, and then China could dictate the international standards of measurement.

Focus on the positive, Ling.

And he did. The midnight sun was warm though it shone low from the north at this early hour. His ship—with the strengthened hull to brush through the occasional patches of new ice—had cruised the Northeast passage above Russia's frozen wastelands without slowing once. North from Shanghai, past the Koreas, Japan, and along the Arctic length of Russia. Only Murmansk and the Scandinavian countries to go before he turned south once more. They had cut twenty-four percent off the trip distance from Shanghai to Rotterdam.

With a route twenty-five hundred kilometers shorter, they'd saved time, payroll, and twelve-hundred tons of fuel. They'd avoided pirates operating in the Malacca Strait of Malaysia—the entry to the Red Sea past Iraqi and Arabian squabbles—and past the Somalis. And they had avoided the six-hundred-thousand-dollar transit charge to pass through the Suez Canal.

Goods delivered from China to the greed of Europe faster and cheaper than ever before.

He patted the railing he leaned upon to thank the *Lucky Passage* and to let his ship know they were through the worst of it. From here, the sea was reported clear all of the way to Rotterdam.

They were hoping for a record speed run. All twenty thousand TEU would be coming off in the single port of Rotterdam, rather than five thousand here and five thousand there. Then they'd take on nineteen thousand of empties and one thousand more of luxury items before retracing the same route.

He checked his watch, 0255. Another hour closer to his destination. When they were done, it could be the fastest round-trip ever recorded.

There were rumors he might make senior captain if he succeeded in breaking the record. His wife would very much like the status and pay of that. He'd have to find a new beach for her to photograph as a celebration.

———

THE UPGRADED CASC RAINBOW CH-5 HAD BEEN BUILT IN THE Anhui Province of Eastern China. The HALE UAV—high altitude long endurance unmanned aerial vehicle—had been aloft for thirty-two hours to reach the Arctic Ocean and to loiter twelve kilometers high, watching for signs of cargo ships passing below.

It only had enough fuel for three more hours of loitering time before it would have to dump a half-million dollars of unused missiles into the ocean to save weight and make the trip home. But a lot of hard work, and more than a little luck, had placed it in the sky above the newest jewel of the Chinese cargo fleet.

It spotted the *Lucky Passage* at thirty kilometers, when it was no bigger than a bright button on the distant sea.

Satcom messages flashed back and forth with the command-and-control center but little verification was needed. It was exactly what they'd been searching for.

The AR-1 missiles were only rated to a maximum of eight kilometers.

The Rainbow UAV circled down until it flew ten meters above the ocean's surface, seven kilometers off the stern of the ship.

————

SECOND LIEUTENANT SŪN JIA STOOD AS ASSISTANT OFFICER OF the watch on the bridge of the *Lucky Passage*. She wished she could have found the nerve to stand by the captain and enjoy the passage in silence, but she hadn't. Though the captain had never shown anything but kindness, she still had trouble speaking in his presence.

She should have asked the captain a question, she had a thousand of them but...she hadn't.

So, she had retreated to the bridge and watched Lieutenant Chen standing his watch. She was supposed to observe and learn, but Chen was lazy. A farmer's son from Henan province, he was content to set the autopilot and perform only the required checks—at least he was diligent about those. She had already learned more than Chen would ever know. Not that she could ever admit that aloud.

He had made a pass at her, but even that had been more perfunctory than enthusiastic.

On the radar scope, there was a faint blip astern.

Crews of non-military ships rarely paid attention to what lay aft of them. Lieutenant Chen most certainly did not.

Sūn Jia noted the new signal off the stern. It was neither

big nor bright, definitely not a ship. Barely even a boat. But she remembered the stories her first captain had told her about Somali pirates taking huge ships with little more than a day-fishing boat.

"Excuse me, Lieutenant Chen. But what do you think this is?" she pointed at the screen.

He glanced down and shrugged. "Did we drop a container overboard?" Highly unlikely in this calm sea. The radar atop the bridge was high enough that their visible horizon was over twenty-five kilometers—the object was only seven astern.

"It moves quickly."

"Maybe it's a whale," his tone warned her that this conversation was over. Daughters of her generation were still the unwanted children of the one-child policy. Her father had despised her for not being a son. Most of her generation, and the several before, never thought a woman could have value. It had always been a struggle to make herself heard.

Chen was not worth the effort.

The only other crew member awake was the captain out on the port bridge wing.

She moved to the end of the starboard bridge wing and looked aft.

————

AT 0259:40, THE CASC RAINBOW CH-5 FIRED ALL SIX OF ITS AR-1 missiles. Each measured a meter-and-a-half long and carried ten kilos of high explosive.

Within the first second, they reached Mach 1.

It was 0259:41. There were now nineteen seconds left before the missiles struck their target.

The UAV turned away to the south—briefly reflecting sunlight off its belly and toward the ship—then climbed rapidly. Within moments, it was above the area observed by the surface-scanning radar. The low-resolution weather radar would not show the UAV on Lieutenant Chen's screen, even if he cared to look down—it would be twenty-seven more minutes before it was time to check the weather again, so he didn't.

Besides, he was too busy admonishing himself. Next time he talked to Sūn Jia, he could not turn into the babbling idiot he always became around women. *Maybe it's a whale?* She certainly hadn't laughed as he'd intended. What had he been thinking?

———

Second Lieutenant Sūn Jia saw a bright flash far astern at precisely 0259:43. The sun catching an iceberg? She didn't think so as there were no other icebergs about. But she couldn't be sure.

For ten long seconds, she continued to lean out to watch astern, but saw nothing more.

She hurried once more into the bridge, wondering if she should disturb the captain from his contemplations.

As she crossed behind Lieutenant Chen she thought she saw—for the briefest instant—a flash on the surface radar. A piece of ice bobbing up astern?

Very close astern.

But then it was gone.

———

THE SIX AR-1 MISSILES PERFORMED EXACTLY AS PROGRAMMED.

They'd flown at sea-skimming levels half the height of the UAV's passage, a mere five meters above the low Arctic Ocean waves.

At 0300:00—a hundred meters and a third of a second before reaching the ship—they angled down and plunged into the waves. Fired in a spread to assure a hit, the left-most missile and the three on the right missed the ship. Their detonations weren't observed by anyone and the fountains of water they threw aloft were erased within seconds by the stern wake as the ship continued forward.

The two remaining missiles struck the Number Two blade on the three-story tall propellor.

The damage to the blade was not initially apparent on the bridge—the hundred-and-twenty-ton propeller continued to turn at eighty-percent revolutions moving the ship ahead at the twenty-three-knot design speed. There was no shock transmitted up the length of the ship to the command bridge.

Even the watch officer in the engine room felt nothing to cause him alarm despite seventeen years' experience in the merchant navy.

One missile had struck in the middle of the vast copper-aluminum-iron alloy blade. It created a few micro-fractures but nothing that would be significant in the next hundred thousand kilometers of normal usage—if that was the only damage.

The other missile had almost missed the blade entirely. If it had, it would have struck the outer hull plate at the ship's stern and caused equally little damage. However, it caught the leading edge of the Number Two blade and knocked off a piece little bigger than Lieutenant Sūn Jia's cap —an insignificant area on such a large blade.

Yet with each turn of the blade, the fractured surface cavitated more and more. Instead of smoothly slicing into the water, the blunt surface of the break impacted the water creating a high pressure zone. As the water escaped past the broken edges, the sudden drop in pressure caused the water to explosively vaporize. Each molecule that did, carved another molecule out of the alloy.

Fifty kilometers later, long after the UAV had flown high and turned for home in what the controllers assessed as a failure, the cavitation had scored a deep groove in either side of the propellor blade. Still, it would have been of little long-term consequence if it hadn't intersected the microfractures created by the first strike.

Most of a propellor's weight lay in the hub and the thick base of the blades.

But when the Number Two blade failed, it lost six thousand kilograms that broke off one side of the propellor. The blade itself plunged down into the depths. But the uneven loading set off immediate alarms on the bridge and in the engine room.

Second Lieutenant Sūn Jia had ended her watch, as had Chen. They'd each fallen asleep quickly in their separate bunks and didn't wake to hear the distant alarms on the bridge. And neither had been long enough at sea to be woken by the sudden silence of the stopped propellors.

———

As soon as Captain Yú Ling heard the reports from the bridge officer and the engine room officer, he knew what had happened. The pictures from the UUV—underwater unmanned vehicle—that they lowered into the water held no surprises.

They'd thrown a propellor blade.

Three hours of careful testing and they were able to proceed forward at eleven kilometers per hour, a quarter of their normal speed.

With the blade was also lost any chance of a record-breaking run.

But *how* had they lost a blade?

Was it poor manufacture? That would be vehemently denied by the shipyard, of course. And they had the security of servicing long-term large military contracts as proof of their skills. They were safe with the political heft to brush him off as his ship might overrun an errant snowball.

Had they struck something out in the middle of the Arctic Ocean? Unless it was a whale, he knew they hadn't. He'd been watching the open sea ahead at the time it happened. There had been no ice, no Arctic hazard. Not that he would be believed.

The blame would land squarely on his shoulders.

Instead of being four days from Rotterdam, they were now fifteen days. When they finally limped into port, they would have to wait weeks, perhaps months for a repair.

He searched for any bright light. He had to stand at the rail for a long time with the wind light on his cheeks before he found it.

Well, he and the crew would have plenty of time to get to know each other much better.

———

"This is beyond amazing, Jeremy."

"Um, yeah." He didn't see why Taz was so excited, but he'd long since learned that it was always safer to agree with her—especially lately. Since she'd become pregnant she was even less predictable than usual. Though neither of them had figured out what was happening until two weeks ago.

The whole becoming a father in seven months was making his head hurt. They weren't even married yet. Though he'd proposed right away, and had already bought the ring so she knew he wasn't feeling forced into it. It was kind of cool actually. For weeks he'd been trying to figure out how to arrange the right moment and now he didn't have to —the moment had found them.

He'd never seen her cry before, but she insisted that was merely hormones.

But Taz! Hard-driven, take-on-the-world Taz had turned into a maternal lunatic: she was already picking out boy versus girl room colors—soothing if a boy, otherwise vibrant and inspiring, whatever that meant.

"I mean just look around you!"

He did...again. They'd been sent by the National Transportation Safety Board to inspect a crash, and here it was. An Embraer 175 passenger jet configured for seventy-eight passengers seated two-and-two across a narrow aisle had gone down. For reasons they were here to determine, the jet had catastrophically lost power an hour into an hour-and-twenty-minute direct flight from Boston to Montreal.

The pilots had managed to land the plane relatively intact on a lake. The plane hadn't caught and tumbled—it was as picture perfect as the landing of the Airbus jet on the Hudson. Better even. Instead of leaving it in the water, they'd managed to glide it along the surface and park it on the only sand beach along the whole shore.

The passengers, except for the few idiots who'd refused to put on their seatbelts, had stepped off the plane onto dry sand. The idiots were removed on stretchers.

"The pilots did a good job."

"A good job? *A good job?* Jeremy, wake up, you're standing on the shore of Lac Brome in Knowlton, Quebec."

"Uh-huh," seemed like a safe response.

It wasn't, Taz rolled her eyes. "That does it, I'm taking away your aircraft structural manuals until you read a couple of real books."

"*Real* books?" Again he went for an even tone. Again it didn't help.

"My favorite murder mysteries are all set right here!"

"I don't think anyone was murdered here other than a few sand castles." The Embraer was a hundred feet long with a wingspan of eighty-five. It took up about half of the beach.

Taz laughed and then wrapped him in a hug. He rested his chin on top of her head and held her close. Whatever he didn't understand, at least he had Taz in his arms.

Coming Winter 2023
And please don't forget that review for Skibird

MIRANDA CHASE SO FAR

AVAILABLE IN EBOOK, PRINT, AND AUDIO

ABOUT THE AUTHOR

USA Today and Amazon #1 Bestseller M. L. "Matt" Buchman has 70+ action-adventure thriller and military romance novels, 100 short stories, and lotsa audiobooks. PW says: "Tom Clancy fans open to a strong female lead will clamor for more." Booklist declared: "3X Top 10 of the Year." A project manager with a geophysics degree, he's designed and built houses, flown and jumped out of planes, solo-sailed a 50' sailboat, and bicycled solo around the world...and he quilts. More at: www.mlbuchman.com.

Other works by M. L. Buchman: *(* - also in audio)*

Action-Adventure Thrillers

Dead Chef
One Chef!
Two Chef!

Miranda Chase
Drone*
Thunderbolt*
Condor*
Ghostrider*
Raider*
Chinook*
Havoc*
White Top*
Start the Chase*
Lightning*

Science Fiction / Fantasy

Deities Anonymous
Cookbook from Hell: Reheated
Saviors 101

Contemporary Romance

Eagle Cove
Return to Eagle Cove
Recipe for Eagle Cove
Longing for Eagle Cove
Keepsake for Eagle Cove

Love Abroad
Heart of the Cotswolds: England
Path of Love: Cinque Terre, Italy

Where Dreams
Where Dreams are Born
Where Dreams Reside
Where Dreams Are of Christmas*
Where Dreams Unfold
Where Dreams Are Written
Where Dreams Continue

Non-Fiction

Strategies for Success
Managing Your Inner Artist/Writer
Estate Planning for Authors*
Character Voice
Narrate and Record Your Own
Audiobook*

Short Story Series by M. L. Buchman:

Action-Adventure Thrillers

Dead Chef

Miranda Chase Origin Stories

Romantic Suspense

Antarctic Ice Fliers

US Coast Guard

Contemporary Romance

Eagle Cove

Other

Deities Anonymous (fantasy)

Single Titles

The Emily Beale Universe
(military romantic suspense)

The Night Stalkers
MAIN FLIGHT
The Night Is Mine
I Own the Dawn
Wait Until Dark
Take Over at Midnight
Light Up the Night
Bring On the Dusk
By Break of Day
Target of the Heart
Target Lock on Love
Target of Mine
Target of One's Own
NIGHT STALKERS HOLIDAYS
Daniel's Christmas
Frank's Independence Day
Peter's Christmas
Christmas at Steel Beach
Zachary's Christmas
Roy's Independence Day
Damien's Christmas
Christmas at Peleliu Cove

Henderson's Ranch
Nathan's Big Sky
Big Sky, Loyal Heart
Big Sky Dog Whisperer
Tales of Henderson's Ranch

Shadow Force: Psi
At the Slightest Sound
At the Quietest Word
At the Merest Glance
At the Clearest Sensation

White House Protection Force
Off the Leash
On Your Mark
In the Weeds

Firehawks
Pure Heat
Full Blaze
Hot Point
Flash of Fire
Wild Fire
SMOKEJUMPERS
Wildfire at Dawn
Wildfire at Larch Creek
Wildfire on the Skagit

Delta Force
Target Engaged
Heart Strike
Wild Justice
Midnight Trust

Emily Beale Universe Short Story Series
The Night Stalkers
The Night Stalkers Stories
The Night Stalkers CSAR
The Night Stalkers Wedding Stories
The Future Night Stalkers

Delta Force
Th Delta Force Shooters
The Delta Force Warriors

Firehawks
The Firehawks Lookouts
The Firehawks Hotshots
The Firebirds

White House Protection Force
Stories

Future Night Stalkers
Stories (Science Fiction)